Although this wasn't  mattered more than any oth

He kissed her again. teeth and then into the juicy cavern ~~ ~~~ ~~ did not refuse him as he suckled her tender lips. She responded to his kiss, pulling him near, offering more of her mouth. She moaned quietly and ever so slightly eased her body closer to his as her hands worked their way up his back.

Pausing briefly in the most delicious kiss he'd ever had, he whispered, "My name is Hugh Cullane." He brushed his lips against hers again. "What should I call ye, my beautiful princess?" Softly he licked her lips with his tongue.

"Call me whatever ye wish," she said, locking her fingers into his hair and snapping his head and shoulders away from her with unexpected strength. She swung her right fist squarely into his jaw, and after a quick jerk of her knee into his groin, he fell to the ground, coughing and gagging. With one last powerful kick to the ribs, she ran madly away around the hill.

As he struggled to take a full breath, a sharp jab of pain bit through his side. Letting his head drop to the ground, he rolled over onto his back.

"Oh, my Lord!" he said aloud between coughs. "I do believe I have offended the lady."

Praise for Susan Leigh Furlong and...

STEADFAST WILL I BE

"Susan Leigh Furlong's well-crafted tale will sweep lovers of historical romance into sixteenth-century Scotland."

> ~Nina Barrett, author of Return of the Dixie Deb,
> A Man to Waste Time On,
> and Renegade Heart
> (The Wild Rose Press)

~*~

"Set during the reign of James the V, STEADFAST WILL I BE focuses not on the intrigues of court but on the everyday happenings Scottish lairds and their subjects faced. The well-developed character arcs are intense and provide a satisfying happily ever after. A certain hit for those who love highland historical romances!"

> ~Juliette Hyland, author

~*~

BY PROMISE MADE

"Susan Leigh Furlong breathes life into a troubled time in Scotland's history during the reign of the infant Queen Mary. She weaves a tale full of action and intrigue, well rounded and memorable characters, as well as a tender love story."

> ~Marilee Hartland Lake, author

By Promise Made

by

Susan Leigh Furlong

By Promise Made

Cover Art by *Abigail Owen*

The Wild Rose Press, Inc.
PO Box 708
Adams Basin, NY 14410-0708
Visit us at www.thewildrosepress.com

Publishing History
First Tea Rose Edition, 2020
Trade Paperback ISBN 978-1-5092-3228-4
Digital ISBN 978-1-5092-3229-1

Published in the United States of America

Dedication

I lose myself in the stories,
and I dedicate this book to all my family and friends
who, whether they know it or not,
are somewhere in what I write.
Thank you!

By promise made with faithful assurance,
Ever you to serve without variance.
> ~*a fifteenth-century poem from*
> *the Findern Manuscript*

Chapter One

Musselburgh, east of Edinburgh on the Firth of Forth, 1547

Death circled him like a vulture.

Hugh Cullane, on his knees in chains and surrounded by her guards, gaped at the queen's guardian in disbelief.

How could this be happening to him? All he wanted was to get back to his family home at Makgullane in the southern Highlands. All he had intended was to stop here at Fawside Castle, deliver his message from the duke, and head for home. He'd already wasted five years of his life, gambling and carousing in London. It was time to go home.

"Why?" he beseeched her.

"Ye will be beheaded in the morning," she repeated calmly as if she were ordering porridge for her morning meal, "because the Duke of Somerset abuses his power as regent for the young English king Edward, and because he thinks our babe, Queen Mary, has no one to protect her. He will soon find out how wrong he is."

Hugh's breath came in quick gasps. "I was sent from London to offer a proposal of marriage between Queen Mary of Scotland and King Edward VI of England. Surely ye can see the advantage of joining the two countries peacefully."

She spit out the words. "Peacefully? Ha! Somerset thinks he can marry off four-year-old Mary to a nine-year-old child they call king. 'Tis obscene! He doesna want a marriage. He wants Scotland to fall at his feet. He's a loon! Yer head will send a message that his ruthlessness will be returned with equal ruthlessness."

"But I didna come to conquer Scotland," he implored her. "Can ye no' hear my brogue? I am a Scot, same as ye."

"After all these years of invasion by old King Henry, why would Somerset send only a single messenger? And a Scot to boot? Do ye think me an *amadan*?"

"Nay, mistress!" He was the *amadan* for leaving Makgullane and the adopted father he loved.

The woman continued to rant at him. "Our land has been ravaged by war over a tiny babe, and still, even after Henry's death, ye want to slaughter us. The Duke of Somerset is a brutal man who will get the same in kind. Yer head in a jar will show him exactly that!"

"Please, mistress, I merely came as ordered on the demand of wee King Edward. I had no choice but to come."

"Then ye will have no choice but to die. Take him away."

As the soldiers dragged Hugh out of the courtyard, his heart sank. He cared nothing about the politics that called for a royal marriage. All his life he had made his way in this world by his wits, and what kings and queens did, over whatever piece of land they claimed to rule, mattered little to him. The boy king of England could marry the baby queen of Scotland, and he'd wish them every happiness. All he wanted to do was deliver

2

a message and return home.

His orders from the Duke of Somerset on the behest of young King Edward were to deliver the marriage proposal to Queen Mary of Scotland's guardians. Somerset had information that the queen, who was often moved for her own protection, now lived at Fawside Castle in Musselburgh, and so here he was.

Hugh had been told this would be a simple task. He was to ride north from London to Musselburgh, deliver the message, and send word back with the answer. After that, he was free to go wherever he wanted. Somerset promised him the protection of the English navy and army that were installed in and around nearby Edinburgh, so what could be easier and safer? Or so he thought.

Of all the troubles he'd faced in his twenty-five years, first as an orphan living on the streets, and then as a devil-may-care rogue living off the next throw of the dice in London, none of them had been this life-threatening. When had he lost control of his life?

He remembered when it happened six weeks ago. He'd lost a wager at dice, had seen a man die, and then had been accused of his murder. Walton's death was an accident. Not his fault. Aye, he had begun the argument, and, aye, he had chased Walton into the woods, but he didn't kill him! An owl did!

****

"The jury has reached a verdict. How say you, each one in turn?"

Each juror stood and called out the same dreaded word, driving it into Hugh's heart like nails on the cross. "Guilty, guilty, guilty…"

Hugh latched his hand onto Garret's shoulder to

3

steady himself, praying the words would be different.

But over and over, came the same single word, "Guilty, guilty, guilty," until the twelfth man stood, pointed at Hugh, and shouted, "Guilty!"

The steward declared, "So say you all. Hugh Cullane of Makgullane, you have been found guilty by a jury of your peers, all free landholding men, for the death of Walton Blackwood. His cousin, Rutherford Blackwood, as the principal accuser, will secure a hangman or perform the office himself by tomorrow morning at first light when the guilty party shall be hanged by the neck until dead. This royal court is closed."

****

A royal pardon offered him his freedom from the hangman in exchange for what seemed like the uncomplicated task of delivering the betrothal message. Grateful for a trip back to his native Scotland, he now found himself about to be executed by this woman, Katherine Payne, for carrying a message! How could he be facing death again?

After the guards shoved him into the dank prison cell in the vaulted basement beneath the castle, Hugh slumped against the cell door. He closed his eyes, remembering the life he had tossed aside five years ago.

An orphan on his own for as long as he could remember, at ten years old he had ended up living with a band of thieves and beggars led by a man with a red stain on his face who terrorized the southern Highlands. That's when he met Robin Cullane of Makgullane, the first man who ever showed him any kindness. Robin and Robin's father, Bretane, Laird of Makgullane, adopted him, offering him a life free from the chaos he'd always known, and Hugh was deeply grateful.

Life with Robin was one of order and consistency and most of all love, something Hugh had never experienced, and the adjustment wasn't always easy. Keenan, the man with the red-stained face, had led his band of thieves with violence and terror, and Hugh often challenged the gentler way his foster father enforced the rules. He remembered the long talks he'd had with Robin about the way a man needed to behave, about how to treat other people with consideration and respect, and most often about being truthful in all his dealings. These lessons were hard for a lad who had survived by doing the opposite, but despite it all Hugh thrived and was happy.

Until he turned twenty and the peaceful and satisfying life at Makgullane became dull and mind-numbing. On the day he couldn't bear to open his eyes to yet another morning where everything would be the same as yesterday, he left.

His da and mum, Robin and Suannoch, said they understood his need for freedom to make his own choices and live his own adventures. They only hoped he wouldn't settle for the aimless drifting that had been his early life. Unfortunately, he had done exactly that.

As Hugh said his goodbyes, Robin handed him a newly forged dagger with the Makgullane crest on it.

"For the past ten years, we have both lived by promise made, me as yer father, and ye as my son. This dagger is a sign of that promise."

Suannoch's fierce, but wordless hug told him the same thing, and it would break their hearts if they discovered the truth about the life he'd chosen. If they knew how his life of gambling and free living had

5

brought him to this terrible end—and sentenced him to death, not once but twice—his own heart would break with their tears. They had offered him far more than he deserved, and now he would lose his head before he could return to Makgullane and repay all he'd been given.

Hugh scraped his hand along the rough wall of the cell, drawing small drops of blood on the pads of his fingers, remembering how this morning he had high hopes for earning his pardon and for being able, at long last, to return home to Makgullane and a life that counted for something.

According to his map, he had been only one day's ride from his destination of Fawside Castle where he'd been told the baby, Mary, resided. The only thing left for him to do had been to arrive, introduce himself as a messenger from King Edward, and greet the queen's guardian, who would, of course, be overjoyed to see the queen blessed by this marriage to unite two countries and end many years of war.

Today had begun delightfully as the first rainless day in over a week, and he intended to enjoy it. No more regret. Just for today he would think of this trip as a glorious adventure. No more worries about a noose choking him. Just for today he would enjoy being alive.

He camped in the first large stand of timber he'd seen in a long while. Tall oaks and birch trees created a friendly canopy for his tent, and he enjoyed the familiar sounds of the birds and woodland animals. Thanks to a clear, fresh stream burbling nearby, this place and this day seemed flawless.

Unsaddling his horse, he slid the dwindling bundles of supplies off the two pack mares. Next, he soaked all his clothes in the stream and jumped into the water himself. After nearly a month on the road, his clothes itched so badly and he smelled so rank that even he couldn't stand to be near himself.

With the soap stashed in his rucksack, he worked up a lather and rubbed it all over his chest and stomach, following the path of manly hair down to his long, sturdy legs. He paid special attention between his legs just in case he met a woman who might be grateful to see a strapping, fine-looking man. To complete his bathing routine, he washed his curly brown hair with those auburn streaks that so many lasses fancied, and then shaved the red-tinged whiskers off his face so they wouldn't scratch a woman's soft cheeks.

After hanging his shirt, breeches, and hose over tree limbs and bushes to dry, he stretched out on his blanket. The sun felt warm against his bare skin, almost strange after the nearly constant rain and drizzle since he left London.

Two pleasurable hours later, Hugh slipped on a still-damp pair of brown, drawstring breeches and a shirt and went looking for dinner. Fresh rabbit sounded good. After finding a grassy mound covered with rabbit tracks, he set up his snare and climbed into an overhanging oak to wait. Nestled against the trunk with the sun warm and the breeze cool, he fell asleep.

In the middle of a dream about his mother's frumenty pudding, the sound of twigs snapping awakened him. He shot a glance down. His trap remained undisturbed. More swishing of thin branches caught his attention, and he sat up straight as the creature making the noise approached.

A woman dressed in a kirtle of faded blue linen

7

without any embroidery or decoration walked through the trees toward him. She wore no cloak and no headpiece or jewelry, not that she needed anything to adorn her enticing figure. He decided she had to be a lower sort, possibly a tavern girl or peasant's daughter, and the sight of her made his neck, and other regions of his body, suddenly warm.

The finer points of her face made her without a doubt the most enchanting thing he'd seen in a month. Her eyes, large and round, reflected the sunlight off their striking rich blue color every time she blinked. Her eyebrows and lashes were thick and dark just like her chestnut hair, which she wore in a grand braid down her back. From her rose-colored lips to her regal jaw line to her high cheekbones, everything about her declared her to be perfectly formed.

She muttered to herself. "I'll no' allow it. 'Tis no' right. No matter what."

Hugh's lips turned up in a cocky smile. A lover's spat. There was no better time to kiss a beautiful woman than when she was angry. Her anger might make her kisses hesitant at first, but when she gave in, as she always did, they became fierce and strong.

Many a girl found him handsome enough with his broad shoulders and his warm hazel eyes to offer him her kisses. He enjoyed every one of them, often enjoying a great deal more from willing lasses. Still, stolen kisses were the ones he liked the best. Pursuing a girl who paid him no mind excited the hunter in him, and when she finally gave in, as she always did, her lips proved the sweetest of all. He wanted to complete his perfect day with the sweetness of this girl.

He felt invincible, intoxicated by the presence of a

beautiful woman under his tree, so when his curiosity and her allure got the better of him, he latched onto the branch, swung down, and landed on his feet in front of her.

"Hello, mistress," he said with an exaggerated bow.

"Who are ye?" she asked in a startled gasp, her mouth forming a perfect circle of rosy lips.

"Ye may call me Master of the Forest. I have come to court ye and make ye my own." Flashing his renowned grin, he swept his arm across his chest and bowed again. The mere look of her sent long-denied vibrations of desire through him.

Her mouth opened with a mixture of surprise and curiosity. "I'm afraid that canna be," she said. "I must be going."

"Oh, my fine lady, dinna go on my account. Please, stay on my account."

Her breath quickened, drawing his eyes to her breasts that now heaved against the form-fitting cut of her bodice. He could almost feel the warmth of those breasts in his hand.

"Mistress, ye're the most divine-looking woman I've seen in a verra long time. Please, dinna leave me. It would break my heart." No lass had ever wanted to break his heart since he was fifteen when the dairy maid showed him the pleasures between a man and a woman.

Smiling beguilingly, he took a step toward her. Her eyes flickered enchantingly like bright stars on a cloudless night.

"I have come to give ye something," he said. He took another step closer, trapping her luscious body against the tree, and just as he thought, the soft places on her didn't melt away. His hands moved to caress her rounded hips, and his palms tingled as they lightly and slowly stroked her.

All at once her eyebrows went up in alarm, and he realized that, instead of her being aroused as he had hoped, he frightened her. Some might call him a scoundrel, and many did, but he had ethics, especially when it came to women. He never took anything from a lass that wasn't willingly given. He moved his hips away from hers so his growing desire wouldn't be as evident and decided to settle for a kiss. No woman had ever refused him a simple kiss.

"Believe me, mistress, I mean ye no harm," he said. "I am a man of my word, and if ye will honor me with one kiss, I would be truly grateful. I'm no' greedy." He had said these words often enough before, and he had always received that kiss. Holding her with a relaxed, steady gaze, he said, "One kiss from the sweetness of yer lips is all I ask, nothing more."

He lowered his lips until he felt her body heat on his face as he murmured in husky tones, "Just one kiss to remember for the rest of my life."

Locking eyes with her, he waited until she nodded ever so slightly. Then he kissed her, tenderly. She tasted like warm honey. A whimpering sigh left her throat that encouraged him to lean ever closer so his tongue could gently wet and separate her full lips. She opened her mouth a bit and kissed him back.

Lifting his head, he looked at her curiously. Something stirred inside his chest, something he'd never felt before, and he didn't quite understand it. All he knew for sure was that just one kiss from this beautiful woman would never be enough. He wanted to know everything about her. He wanted to hear her voice, to see her smile, and to find out all about her. Who she was and who she wanted to be.

He wanted this woman to know his secrets, to hear his wishes. That itch inside him, the one he could never quite scratch, the one that made him restless and careless, eased and softened. Although this wasn't his first kiss, it somehow mattered more than any other kiss he'd ever had.

He kissed her again. His tongue darted along her teeth and then into the juicy cavern of her mouth. She did not refuse him as he suckled her tender lips. She responded to his kiss, pulling him near, offering more of her mouth. She moaned quietly and ever so slightly eased her body closer to his as her hands worked their way up his back.

Pausing briefly in the most delicious kiss he'd ever had, he whispered, "My name is Hugh Cullane." He brushed his lips against hers again. "What should I call ye, my beautiful princess?" Softly he licked her lips with his tongue.

"Call me whatever ye wish," she said, locking her fingers into his hair and snapping his head and shoulders away from her with unexpected strength. She swung her right fist squarely into his jaw, and after a quick jerk of her knee into his groin, he fell to the ground, coughing and gagging. With one last powerful kick to the ribs, she ran madly away around the hill.

As he struggled to take a full breath, a sharp jab of pain bit through his side. Letting his head drop to the ground, he rolled over onto his back.

"Oh, my Lord!" he said aloud between coughs. "I do believe I have offended the lady." He stuck his finger in his mouth to see if she had loosened any teeth. She hadn't. As he watched the blue of her kirtle disappear into the trees, it occurred to him that he wanted her to come back. She had brought him to his knees, but, strangely, he didn't resent or regret that she had.

The first drops of rain fell on his face as his perfect day turned unbelievably sour. He had a sore jaw, an empty snare, and a bruised ego.

The sounds of charging footsteps belonging to four surly soldiers dressed in unfamiliar heraldry raced toward him. Hugh bolted to his feet.

"Take him!" snarled the tall, fair-haired man clearly in charge.

"Aye, Captain Rand!"

"I'm Hugh…" Hugh began.

"Quiet!" snapped Captain Rand as he jabbed his sword in the direction of Hugh's neck.

Two more guards roughly jerked his arms behind his back and heavy iron shackles snapped shut, binding his wrists together. Two more manacles connected by a short chain tightened around his ankles, and he fell once more to the ground.

Hugh quickly learned that the guards who had been derelict in allowing him to get close enough to molest their mistress, whoever she was, didn't care a whit about his mission from the English king. They had no intention of directing him to Fawside Castle to verify his identity. They only wanted to pound their fists and their feet into him at every opportunity. After dragging him out of the trees, two of them lifted him facedown over a saddle and gave him a short but uncomfortable ride up a hill to a four-story keep built on a high ridge overlooking East Lothian and the Firth of Forth that led to the sea.

"Where are we?" asked Hugh.

The soldier responded by grabbing him by his shackled arms and throwing him down. Hugh landed with a grunt in an awkward heap on the bailey cobblestones.

"If ye take me to Fawside," said Hugh, "I can prove who I am."

" 'Tis lucky for ye then," said a particularly churlish soldier, "because here ye are."

"This is Fawside?" Why hadn't he read the map more carefully?

The captain of the guard pulled on a bell cord outside the building's door, and a young girl about ten years old came running out.

"Tell Mistress Katherine we have returned with the prisoner," said the captain to the girl, who turned and disappeared into the castle.

"Ye will be sorry when she gets here," said Hugh, spitting the dirt out of his mouth.

A soldier dragged Hugh up to his knees. "Why is that, ye toad?"

"I told ye. I have come from King Edward and his regent, the Duke of Somerset. There are papers in my saddlebags at my camp. I'm to meet with Queen Mary's guardian with my offer of betrothal and send word back as to the answer."

At first the man responded with amazed silence and then with raucous laughter. "He says he's from the king, and we'll be sorry when our mistress finds out. He says the babe is going to marry!" The rest of the guard joined him in what appeared to be the funniest joke since the Vikings.

He thought, Whoever comes out here winna think this is so funny. She will be pleased to finally have the Scottish queen marry and peacefully join the two countries as one.

"Look what we found, Mistress Katherine," said one of the guards.

The beautiful woman from the forest stood in the doorway. She certainly didn't look like a lower sort lass now, wearing a yellow silk overdress that opened to her waist at the neckline and under the arms to expose a brilliant green, form-fitting chemise. A woven golden fret, clipped at the top of her head with a diamond-studded clasp, sheathed her plentiful nut-brown hair. What a magnificent beauty, made even more so by clothing that flattered her so well.

He had offended Mistress Katherine with his stolen kiss. He had taken unwanted liberties with a woman who had the authority to render a judgment against him, a judgment he wouldn't like. How quickly could he apologize?

"I'm Hugh Cullane," he said with all the dignity he could muster from his awkward position on the ground. "I'm on a mission of great importance."

"Importance? Ye?" Her throaty voice overflowed with hostility, and her eyes glowered with enough rage to incinerate him.

"Mistress Katherine," he began again, "I beg yer forgiveness. If I had kenned—"

"If ye had kenned what?" she interrupted. "If ye had kenned I was the mistress of the house, ye would have been a little faster to rape me?"

His eyes widened. "Nay, mistress!"

"Take him to the dungeon. He will be flogged tomorrow."

As the soldiers started to drag him away, Hugh called back to her, "I'm on royal business from the king of England. I'm the messenger of Queen Mary's betrothed. I have a message for her guardian."

"Stop!" she ordered.

Aha, the guards were wrong. All he had to do was mention that Mary would soon be part of the English royal family, and they would take him immediately to the young queen's guardian. His indiscretion would be forgotten.

"Let me see him," she said. The soldiers jerked Hugh around to face her.

Haughtily sticking out her chin, she said, "I am Queen Mary's guardian, and any request for a betrothal to that doity English king is rejected."

Hugh couldn't believe his ears or his eyes. The queen's guardian was a woman. A beautiful woman who made his heart race. A man might forgive his indiscretion in the woods, but a woman? Nay.

"I beg yer forgiveness, mistress," Hugh said with his eyes on the ground, hoping she'd see his embarrassment and his regret at his mistake.

She took a step closer and put her finger on his chin. "Upon a closer inspection, the look of ye is verra pleasing." She put her hands on her hips. "I think I will forgive ye. There will be no need to flog ye."

With a sigh of relief, Hugh smiled and two half circles in his cheeks surrounded his mouth. He had every confidence in his smile to win her over. "Thank ye, mistress. I'm truly sorry I offended ye."

His smile, however, vanished when her face

quickly twisted into a bitter grimace. "Now that I ken ye to be an unprincipled, self-serving lecher sent by the most unprincipled, self-serving lecher of all, the Duke of Somerset, ye should ken why ye will be beheaded in the morning."

Hugh's stomach bolted to his throat. "Mistress? Beheaded?"

She hissed out each word. "Queen Mary will ne'er marry the king or allow him to claim Scotland in his name. He can send messengers and armies alike, but Scotland will ne'er surrender."

Hugh caught in his breath. "If she dinna want to marry, I'll go back and tell him so."

"That would no' be enough to convince him. To be certain that Somerset understands once and for all, I'll send yer head back to him in a jar. Throw him in the dungeon."

Hugh roared in protest, driving his shoulder into one soldier's gut. Swinging his chains behind him like a mace, he cleared the rest of the guards away, but before he could take two steps, the captain hooked his foot under the chain between Hugh's ankles and, with a quick jerk, flung the prisoner to the ground.

Hugh landed facedown at the furious woman's feet. Raising his eyes to her, he pleaded, "Mistress Katherine, please hear me out before ye condemn me. I come to ye as an innocent."

"Innocent? Ha!" she snorted. "Ye're probably guilty of far more than we ken."

Hugh pulled himself up to his knees. " 'Tis true, mistress. I have spent most of my adult life seeking my own enjoyment instead of the betterment of others, but stealing a kiss is hardly a crime for beheading. I beg yer forgiveness."

"Have ye no' been listening to me? Ye will be beheaded in the morning," she repeated, "because the English think nothing of killing hundreds in a quest to conquer Scotland, and they want to use a tiny babe to do it."

"But I didna come to conquer Scotland," he implored her.

"The man who rules England in the boy king's place is a brutal man who will get the same in kind. Yer head in a jar will show him exactly that!"

"Please, mistress, I merely came as ordered on the demand of King Edward. I had no choice but to come."

"Then ye will have no choice but to die. Take him away."

Chapter Two

Later that afternoon

Katherine pulled the brush through her hair, sweeping it off her face back toward the nape of her neck. Reaching around, she plaited it into a single, thick braid that hung nearly to her hips. She'd braided her hair a thousand times before, but today the strands slipped relentlessly out of her grasp as her mind wandered to the prisoner in the dungeon. Never before had she ordered anyone's death.

As the queen's guardian, she had complete charge of every aspect of life here at Fawside, and while it was unusual for a woman to be in command over guards and soldiers, she had been highly trained for exactly that job. She demanded obedience, and it was given to her or the consequences were dire, but today guilt and regret filled her. Although she believed the prisoner's death to be the only way to protect the queen, she also knew that the severity of her decision came from the lingering terror of the attack on her and the baby three nights ago.

****

She couldn't see him, but she had felt his presence. The blackness of night covered most of the bedchamber she shared with the baby. Mary's crib, pushed between the wall and the head of Kit's bed, made it easy for Kit to get to the now four-year-old girl, but difficult for anyone else to get close enough to do her harm.

The only light came from a wide stream of moonlight through the window, showering the foot of her bed. He would have to pass through that beacon of light to get to Mary. When he did, she could see him, and even if only for a split second, she would slice his leg with the knife she kept under her pillow just as Captain Rand had taught her.

As she crouched against the pillows at the head of the bed, a sense of dread filled the pit of her stomach, but she ignored it. She wiped the sweat out of her eyes as the intruder's nearly silent footsteps edged toward her.

Step into the light, curse it! Step into the light!

As if on command, he did.

Springing forward, she plunged the knife into his thigh and, with a quick thrust upward, slit the skin open. He collapsed into a bloody heap on the finely woven tapestry rug on the floor.

"Guard! Guard!" she screamed, leaping from the bed and fumbling to light a lamp.

The body on the floor groaned.

She screamed again, "Guard! Help me! I need ye now!"

As the light from her lamp flooded the room, three soldiers burst through her door, swords drawn.

"Mistress Katherine!" said one of them when he caught sight of an arm hanging out beyond the edge of the bed. "Mistress, what happened?"

"What do ye think happened?" she screeched. "He's an assassin. How did this man get inside this room? Where were ye?"

Little Mary awoke with screaming of her own, and Kit rushed to pick her up and cuddle her in her arms. "Hush, wee one. 'Tis over. Shh, shh."

The guard's mouth went dry. "I…I dinna ken how he got in here, mistress. I…we…were on duty and awake. I swear we were awake."

"He's still alive," she shouted, bringing on new wailing from Mary. "Take him."

The guards quickly hauled the man to his feet as he cried out, hopping on his remaining good leg.

Captain Rand, a man in his late forties, strode through the archway. "Step aside, ye dolts. Let me see the man. Are ye hurt, mistress?"

"Nay, but the babe is trembling like a leaf," said Katherine. "He didna hurt me, and more importantly, he ne'er reached the child."

Rand tugged on the hooded mask covering the intruder's face. It slid off, revealing Simon, a new recruit to the guard.

"Simon? How could this happen?" said Katherine, rocking the baby whose whimpering increased with each outburst. " 'Tis all yer fault, Rand. As captain of the guard ye should have kenned."

"I take full responsibility," said Captain Rand, stiffening his shoulders to attention.

"How could ye let it be someone in yer own guard? What kind of a shandy berk are ye?"

"Katherine!" came the sharp voice of the frail, elderly woman hobbling into the room. "A lady must always behave like a lady, even when she is terrified. Come over here and help me to a chair."

The woman, Juliana Reed, once tall and regal, had been withered by age and disease to a wizened version of her former self. Although her snow-white hair remained thick and shiny, and her shadowy blue eyes sparkled, arthritic pain twisted her bones and stiffened her joints until every movement became arduous. As the long-time devoted nursemaid and then nanny for Mary's father, King James V, Juliana's painful rheumatism now forced her to find comfort in her bed, leaving the duties of caring for a royal child to Katherine. She remained in service to teach and advise, and Katherine appreciated her company and advice.

"Aye, Juliana," said Katherine, chastised and at the same time calmed by her mentor's presence. While still comforting the child in her arms, she guided the older woman to a padded high-backed chair and gently propped pillows around her.

"Rand," said Juliana once she sat safely in the chair, "after all these years of fighting to try to force Mary into a betrothal, why send an assassin now? With Henry dead, has Somerset given up on the idea of a marriage?"

"I dinna ken his motives. Mayhap 'tis no' Somerset who sent this man. Many people have their own interests in who she marries. I will find out all I can from this one."

The attempted assassination made Kit protest frantically. "I will ne'er allow the baby to wed at age four!" When Mary again complained loudly, Kit brought her voice down to a near whisper. "I dinna care who he is. Our precious babe willna be sold in some bloody attempt to conquer Scotland."

Everyone in the room acted to restore peace and calm. The assassin was hauled away, and little Mary cuddled back to sleep.

When all seemed aright, Juliana said, "Rand, will ye help me back to my room?"

"Aye, mistress," said Rand, taking her arm and acting as her cane as the pair limped back to Juliana's bedchamber next to Kit's.

****

Juliana climbed into her bed, and Rand gently pulled the quilts over her.

"I am sorry, mistress," he said. " 'Twill no' happen again. I swear. No new guards will be employed even if they carry the recommendation of the Lord himself."

"She will be scouring the countryside for a new place to take the queen."

"Aye, I ken. I will do whatever I can to help."

"Do ye think she kens the truth?" asked Juliana, curling up and sinking into the soft mattress.

"I dinna think so, but the longer we keep the secret from her and the others, the better."

Juliana stared at the canopy over her bed with her eyes half-closed. "I remember the first time I met her. She walked through the door of the nursery in Stirling Castle like the queen herself and announced to me, 'We're leaving for a safer place. 'Tis too dangerous here for the lass. Pack up what she will need.'

"My first thought was 'Who is this brash young woman without manners?' So I said, 'My name is Juliana.'

"She said, 'I ken.' Then she added, 'Forgive me. I am used to ordering the guard around.' We became fast friends after that. Ye taught her well, Rand."

"I trained her as best I could to make her strong. Her task required that she be able to handle any threat, of which there would be many, as we have seen."

"How did ye ken she was the one?"

"The lass I needed had to be one with no hope of a real future, an orphan with no family. I first met her as a child at the convent where the nuns raised her, and I saw she was quick-witted and determined, but I forgot about her until the church married her at age sixteen to a man three times her age. After she was widowed and left penniless, she truly had no hope. Just as King James requested: a woman with no ties to protect his daughter."

" 'Tis a lonely life being in royal service. Kit has given up everything to be Mary's guardian just as I gave up everything to be nursemaid to Mary's father. If only this rheumatism didn't trouble me so. Sometimes I feel so alone and useless."

Rand put his hand over Juliana's. "Ye are no' useless, and ye are no' alone."

Smiling, she said, "I have ye, and I am grateful. We will keep our promise."

"Aye, we will." Lifting her hand, he kissed it and left the room.

****

Three days after the false guard's attack, and after sentencing the messenger to death, Katherine paced back and forth across the narrow courtyard, trying to understand why her emotions were in such a jumble. She'd done the right thing. Although the prisoner was tall, handsome, and had ever-so-sweet kisses, his arrival from the south meant yet another security breach, and she had to eliminate that threat to her beloved charge. His death was the right thing to do.

When the dark-haired charmer kissed her in the forest, for an instant she'd felt like someone else. For that instant, she was no longer a guard and protector, no longer a woman trained to be as strong as any man, but someone who could melt into this man's arms and live for his kisses. The feeling lasted only a moment, but the memory remained. She wanted to experience that feeling again, to explore it, and see where it might take her, but she had sentenced the man to die, and for the safety of her queen, he *must* die. Her judgment had been ruthless, but she had to be ruthless, as ruthless as any man who wouldn't hesitate to kill his enemy.

Her royal service had begun with a difficult year of training under Captain Rand's demanding eye. She learned to wield a sword and dirk effectively and to shoot a crossbow. Rand fashioned a longbow to fit her size and taught her to load and fire a standing cannon, but her expertise would be in hand-to-hand combat against bigger and stronger men. Kit was to be Queen Mary's last defense.

Kit worked until she could run five miles without stopping while carrying a twenty-pound weight as practice for escaping with the baby strapped to her back. Later the weight increased to forty pounds, knowing the child would grow. Many members of the guard, and other men hired for the same purpose, made surprise attacks on her, and she dispatched all of them. One particularly persistent attacker lost his hand from Kit's knife.

The day she turned twenty-two, Kit came into complete charge of the infant queen. The babe was a little over a year old when Kit took over all the child's moves to various places of safety, the most recent being Fawside Castle. Captain Rand served only as Kit's advisor, not her commander, and although some of the men in the guard and on the staff resented taking orders from a woman, Rand had instilled in her the leadership skills she needed, and the men soon learned to respect and obey her.

Kit loved that little girl as if the babe had been born to her, knowing full well that she, as a woman in royal service, would never marry, never have children of her own, and never even know true love. She had willingly made that commitment to Mary for as long as she lived, but the stranger's kiss gave her an unsettling feeling of regret.

She had carried out her duty to dispatch all threats to the queen, but this time Somerset sent a seemingly harmless messenger, a Scot no less. Still something didn't feel quite right about such a ploy. Somerset's motives escaped her, but she'd figure it out sooner or later.

Unfortunately, it would have to be after the messenger was dead.

Chapter Three

Hugh's brief glimpse of Fawside from the courtyard gave him the impression of quite a remarkable castle for this area. Built in a rectangle of four stories, about eighty feet on a side, it had only one tall tower, not that it needed more. Its location high on the ridge gave clear sight lines to possible attackers from all sides as well as a long view of the river Esk to the west and the Firth of Forth to the north. The Pinkie Cleugh, Gaelic for a narrow valley, ran between the two waterways just below the castle.

Hugh might have enjoyed how stately the castle was if he hadn't been locked in a damp prison cell in the lowest level. Refusing to sit on the lice-laden blanket on the cot, Hugh stood against the rugged stone wall, shivering so deep his bones shook, and his head ached from the musty odor.

Resting back against the wall, he closed his eyes. "How can this be happening to me? I might be a rogue and a gambler. I might have wasted the last five years of my life, but I dinna deserve this."

He wished he could start the day over. Nay, he wished he could start the year over. Then he never would have gambled or gone to the tavern that fateful night. He wouldn't have lost his beloved dagger, a gift from his father, or chased Walton into the woods or watched him die. His life would have been exemplary, beyond criticism.

He looked around the dingy jail cell. This might be the last place he saw in his lifetime because, despite the heat in her kiss, Mistress Katherine was as coldhearted as the winter snow. It would take more than a pardon from the king to save him this time. It would take a miracle from the Lord Almighty.

His chin dropped to his chest. It wasn't so much the dying he regretted, but that his father and mother would never know what happened to him. Robin and Suannoch had rescued him from a murderous band of thieves and beggars and surrounded him with love, but his stubborn, restless nature led him away, led him to this. He couldn't bear the thought of spending eternity knowing that his da and his mum wept for a son who would never return.

He nervously jiggled the three wooden dice in the pouch around his belt. Removing them, he squatted down and tossed them on the floor. To his surprise, the pips came up one, two, and three. The odds against rolling that combination again were enormous, but could he do it? Had his luck changed? He shook the dice in his hands, said a little prayer, and tossed them on the floor.

The pips came up three, six, three. The single word "Nay!" screamed in his head. Bolting forward, he clutched the bars on the small window of his cell door, rattling them. As he did, the heavy iron door at the end of the hall scraped open against the stone floor.

His pulse pounded in his ears. *She promised no' to cut off my head until tomorrow.*

His knees went weak. *I still have a few more hours of life. 'Tis only a terrible dream. She's no' really going*

27

to execute me!

The face that appeared at the window wasn't a guard to take him to his death, but the Mistress Katherine herself. "Step back," she ordered.

He took a step back.

She moved closer to the door and glared at him through the bars. "Tell me why ye're here."

Even though her face showed her anger, her eyes were still blue enough to color the sky.

"Ye ordered me beheaded," he answered with a hint of his well-known sense of humor. "Most people dinna like being beheaded, but I'm no' most people. If ye let me out of here, I promise to wait patiently in the garden for the executioner."

Slapping her hand against the door, she said, "If ye intend to be sassy with me I'll leave, and yer sentence will be carried out in the next five minutes."

He dropped his head. Charm was not doing him much good with this woman.

"Tell me why ye're here."

What kind of a game is this? he thought, but he said in all seriousness, "What is it ye want to ken?"

"Ye're no' here because ye're a friend of King Edward or that Edward Seymour, the Duke of Somerset. Why did ye agree to come here?"

"I thought ye would be happy to get a proposal of marriage that wasna at the point of a sword."

"Any proposal from those Sassenachs is at the point of a sword. Ye're a Scot, so why did they send ye?"

He took a slow deep breath and puffed it out his nose. " 'Tis a long and distasteful story in which I dinna come out in a favorable light."

"It certainly could no' be worse than how I see ye now." She crossed her arms. "I'm listening."

He had a shameful story to tell, but if he could make her feel sorry for him, her heart might soften about taking off his head. He'd do anything to soften her heart.

Hugh's mind wandered back to that terrible night six weeks ago.

****

Hugh had enjoyed a night of dice at the Glory Star Tavern in a dodgy section of London. His winning streak held true for him most of the night, putting a considerable amount of money into his pocket and almost as much ale into his mug, but when Barnaby Radford joined the game, Hugh's luck turned sour. Still, the changing winds of fortune didn't bother him. He had made a good living over the last five years off his gambling winnings and had a fine time doing it. Tonight, he could ride out the storm. Everyone enjoyed Hugh's familiar laughter and spirited camaraderie, but those winds of fortune continued to blow in Barnaby's direction until Barnaby announced he'd had enough. He scooped up his dice and headed for the door.

That's when the false confidence of the ale made Hugh blurt out, "I'll wager Ruffian. Ye know the horse, Barnaby. He's the three-year-old that won the steeplechase at the Midsummer Festival last year, the one I won off William Barrow. That against the entire pot. Agree?"

With a crooked grin, Radford agreed, and a few minutes later he owned an exceedingly valuable horse. An hour after that, with two of his London gambling friends, Garret Hamlin and Murdock Weathersby, at his side for support, Hugh handed the reins of Ruffian over to the gloating Barnaby Radford.

"Dash it all, Hugh," said Garret afterwards. "You had to surrender the only thing of real value you had because you made a foolish bet. How could you have let that happen?"

Hugh's fists clenched under his friend's scolding. "So I can be more like ye? I would ne'er be able to live if I bet as cautiously as ye. When was the last time ye won a pot worth taking home? Yer only luck is that ye have a family willing to support ye and yer habits."

"Hugh, don't start in. You're angry at yourself. Don't take it out on me."

"And ye, Murdock, I canna believe that yer woman doesna care that ye lose every week. That she supports ye with nary a complaint."

"You leave my woman out of this, Hugh," said Murdock. "At least I winna be the one walking all around London from now on."

Hugh pounded his fist into his palm. "Dinna worry, I winna be walking for long. The next roll of the dice is mine."

The Wood's Edge, another busy, crowded tavern on the outskirts of London, was one of the few places a man could go and be relatively certain not to leave with a rotten stomach from spoiled food or poorly brewed beer. It had a large following of regular local customers, Hugh being one of their favorites.

Sounds of voices floated out from inside, but before he joined them, he brushed back his hair and straightened his shirt and breeches to look more presentable. He'd be more comfortable in his plaid, but in London looking Scottish meant trouble. His brogue could be ignored if he kept his mouth shut until he earned the other gamblers' confidence, usually by letting them win for a while.

On the rare occasions he had tried his hand in the more high-class gambling houses, he tried to imitate the English accent of those around him, but he could never keep it up for very long. So he avoided the high society places. The low-class ones suited his friends better, too.

Stepping through the tavern door, he took in a deep breath. The smell of ale, mutton stew, and freshly baked bread made him immediately relax. Here people appreciated his talents for conversation, riddling, and friendly wagering. He belonged here.

Although he would bet on almost anything, passé-dix was his game of choice. It required only three dice and people who wished to be separated from their money. He'd played it since he was a child, and he played it very well.

****

"Do ye ken how to play passé-dix, mistress?" he asked the woman standing outside his jail cell.

She rolled her eyes to indicate her boredom and impatience. "Explain it to me."

" 'Tis a verra old game. The Roman guards played it at the foot of the cross during Christ's crucifixion."

"I doubt that makes it more honorable," said Katherine, rolling her eyes again.

"Nay, probably no'. Ye play it with three dice. Any number can play, but one person is designated the banker, and he holds all the bets. Another is the roller. Everyone throws down their money and makes their bet. If the roller tosses under a total of ten on the dice, the banker collects all the bets. If the roller rolls above a total of ten, the banker pays double all the bets. The banker changes after each roll, and the roller changes after three losing rolls."

Hugh scooped up the dice from the floor and held them out. "Care to play a round? Let's say the stake is my head in a jar."

"Dinna be ridiculous," she replied. "Go on with yer story."

****

Hugh winked at Cathy, the tavern owner's youngest daughter, and sat down on a bench beside one of the half-dozen wooden plank tables scattered haphazardly around the room. She took a leather mug from a shelf on the back wall and filled it with ale from one of the five kegs sitting on sawbucks beneath the shelves. Behind her hung two swinging doors. One led to the kitchen while another opened into a gaming room, the most lucrative source of income for the proprietor.

"We haven't seen you in a long time, Hugh," said Cathy as she handed him the frothy ale. Ducking her head into her shoulder, she looked at him from under pale eyelashes. "I have missed you." Cathy, a homely girl of fifteen, made no secret of the fact that she fancied Hugh as the love of her life.

Hugh took a long drink. "Has anyone been bothering ye, Cathy?"

"Nay, there aren't too many drunks tonight. Mostly they stay to the back room, and Papa brings them their drink. Will you stay out here and talk with me?"

Hugh flashed a smile and patted her on the hip. "After I've won enough money to buy me back a horse and ye a fancy gown, I'll spend the rest of the evening with ye. All right?"

****

Katherine curled her lip. "Do ye think I'm interested in what ye mistakenly imagine is charm?"

"Nay, mistress," said Hugh. "But Cathy did have something to tell me that matters to the story."

Katherine gave a curt nod for him to continue.

****

Cathy pointed to the back room. "I wish you wouldn't go in there, Hugh. 'Tis the Blackwood brothers. The Blackwoods hate you."

Picking up his mug, he winked. "They dinna hate me. They just think they can beat me, but we ken they canna."

Kneeling in the center of the stuffy and crowded back room were the Blackwoods: the two brothers, Rutherford and Putnam, and their cousin, Walton. Everyone in this part of London knew that the Blackwoods and Hugh wagered on everything from draughts to dominoes, from foot races to arm wrestling, even to how many flies would land on a piece of pie. Each year the stakes became higher, the risk greater, and the ill will blacker.

"Need another for the game?" asked Hugh from the doorway.

Rutherford, a swaggering tree trunk of a man, who enjoyed intimidating others with his physical strength and his considerable force of personality, stood up and grinned. "Would we like to take more of your money? Without a doubt. Right this way."

About an hour later, the once raucous noises coming from the gaming room turned deadly quiet. The patrons in the main room scattered to the outer walls

33

when Walton, the youngest of the Blackwoods, bolted from the room with Hugh right on his heels.

"I canna let ye take it!" said Hugh, grabbing Walton's arm and whirling him around. "Give it back to me. Ye canna take my dagger!"

Two pairs of hands locked onto Hugh's arms. Rutherford and Putnam had come to their cousin's defense, and the brawl began.

Cathy screamed as a fist rammed into Hugh's eye, followed in quick order by a blow to his jaw and a knee thrust into his stomach.

Hugh crumbled to his knees just as Garret and Murdock appeared in the doorway of the tavern.

Garret said, "Hugh, we thought we would find you here."

Murdock asked, "Garret, have you noticed that Hugh is outnumbered?"

"Do you want part of this?" asked Rutherford, taking a short breather from the fracas.

"Nay," answered Murdock casually. "I was just making an observation. He may be my friend, but 'tis not my fight. Sorry, Hugh. I'll loan you my coin, even my dice, but not my fists."

In three long strides, Garret crossed the room to the bench and raised a beefy hand signaling for a mug of ale while Murdock leaned against the door frame.

Hugh flung out his fists again, knocking Putnam over a table and rolling him into the other two Blackwood men, who ended up flat on their backs on the floor.

Hugh pleaded to his friends, "Help me!"

Garret raised his mug and shook his head.

Hugh called out desperately, "Murdock! The

Blackwoods started it. I'm innocent!"

Shaking his head, Murdock said, "Look out behind you."

Hugh turned around just in time to avoid Rutherford's two-handed fist coming down on his shoulder. Knocking the swinging arms aside, Hugh twirled and leaped up on the bench and then onto the table.

"I'm begging ye, Garret, Murdock," said Hugh.

The younger Blackwood brother, Putnam, grabbed Hugh by the leg, jerking him down onto his back on top of the table, sending wooden mugs and bowls of half-eaten food scattering noisily across the floor. Rutherford landed another commanding blow to Hugh's cheek while Walton held out Hugh's right arm, trying to smash it over his knee, but Hugh jerked it away.

Murdock raised his eyebrows in Garret's direction to ask if now might be the time to step in and rescue their friend like they had so many times before. Garret shook his head.

Seconds later, Hugh lifted his hand between Rutherford's legs and squeezed what he found there. The stocky, black-haired man squealed in agony and fell to the floor in a dead faint.

Rolling off the table, Hugh swung his fist into Putnam's face. Putnam stumbled backwards in the direction of Murdock, who shoved him hard against the wall, and Putnam slid slowly to the floor in a heap.

That left only Walton to defend his possession of Hugh's lost dagger, the one bearing the Makgullane crest on the hilt.

"Ye dinna understand," said Hugh quietly, his eyes locked on the knife. "I canna leave without my dagger.

If I lose the dagger now, I'll lose the last thing my da gave me. 'Tis all I have left from my home."

"For crying out loud, Hugh," said Garret. " 'Tis only a dagger. 'Tis not worth getting your throat slit."

"Mayhap no' to ye," said Hugh, "but 'tis to me."

Using his forefinger, Hugh wiped off the blood dripping from a cut under his left eye and gingerly touched his swollen lower lip.

"Walton, 'twas a mistake for me to wager my dagger, but ye're refusing to be reasonable. Take something else for it in exchange."

Walton, now outnumbered, barely kept the tremor out of his voice. "I don't want anything else. I won this knife, and I intend to keep it."

"Nay," said Hugh, clenching his jaw until a small knot of muscle appeared at the joint. "I canna let ye take it. I will make ye a pledge of anything ye want. Ye name it, I will get it for ye, but ye canna have my dagger."

Walton sniffed haughtily. "This knife is nearly worthless, but the fact that you want it makes it priceless. I'm keeping it." He smiled at his victory until his gray eyes flickered toward Garret and Murdock now both standing behind their friend.

"Hugh is good for his word," said Garret. "You know that. We'll make the pledge with him. Just say the word, and the three of us will get you what you want in exchange for the dagger."

Murdock put his hand on Hugh's shoulder. "We all know that a lost wager can be exchanged. An honorable gambler will take something else for the dagger and be done with it. If you don't accept something in its place, especially something of greater value, no decent man will wager with you from now on."

Garret said, "You know that a reputation for fair play is worth more than that dagger, even if it has been won in a fair wager. What will you take in its place?"

Walton looked around the room. He had wagered with almost every man here. What was more important, winning a bet with Hugh or continuing to play with the others?

" 'Tis yours," said Walton as he jammed the foible of the dagger into the wooden table. "It seems you get to keep the knife, Hugh. But I'll not forget this. You cheated me, and that is how you will be known all over the district, Hugh Cullane, a cheat!"

Grimly, Walton made his way around the table to Rutherford as his cousin rose unsteadily to his feet. Clutching himself between his legs, Rutherford leaned heavily on his cousin's arm.

"A blackguard and a coward who has to depend on his friends to stand up for him. A cheat!" said Walton as he dragged Rutherford, wincing with each step, toward the door.

The tavern owner, a burly man called Dobbin, stepped in front of Hugh. "I will not have the reputation of my tavern ruined because of a dispute over a fairly won wager. I don't care a whit about anything but that the Wood's Edge be known as a decent and fair place to enjoy an evening. I make my living here, and I'll not have the likes of you take that away from me. Hugh Cullane, tell me true. Was the dagger lost in a fair contest?"

When Hugh didn't answer, Dobbin stepped even closer, breathing his sour breath right into Hugh's face. "You have never been a cheat, nor have you ever niggled out of a bet. You win and lose with a smile, and you always come back for more, until tonight. Did these pieces of road rubble cheat you?"

Hugh set his eyes on the window to his left, trying to avoid Dobbin's piercing gaze.

"Tell me the truth about what happened!"

Hugh stepped back and straightened his shoulders. "My coin was gone, and the only thing I had with me was my dagger. I kenned my luck would change. I could feel it in my bones. I could no' lose."

"So you wagered your dagger," said Dobbin, shaking his head.

"Aye," said Hugh. "Walton was the banker, so I spit on the dice."

After a moment of silence, the older man asked sharply, "And then what happened?"

Hugh hesitated. "It came up seven, and the knife was gone to Walton."

"Whose dice?" he barked. "Whose dice?"

Hugh said very slowly, "Mine."

Spitting with disgust, Dobbin pulled the knife out of the table and handed it, hilt first, to Walton. "The knife is yours. This tavern runs an honorable game, and I never want to see any of you in here again. Out, all of you!"

"I canna let ye do that," said Hugh firmly. "I canna let ye give him my knife."

Murdock put his hand against Hugh's chest. "He won it fair and square. You lost, so accept it."

Hugh shook his head, pushing Murdock's hand away. "I'm asking ye to take something else, Walton."

"The knife is mine," said Walton. "I will not exchange it for all the gold in the crown jewels. I won,

Hugh Cullane. I won!"

He and Rutherford slowly made their way to the door while Putnam eased himself up to standing and took his brother from Walton.

"The next time your da sees the dagger, 'twill be in my sheath," gloated Walton.

"Nay!" cried Hugh. His cheeks flushed with determination. "Ye canna take it. Give me my dagger or I'll kill ye!"

Immediately, Walton darted out the door with Hugh on his heels.

Walton plunged into the dark depths of the cluster of trees, sidestepping the brush. Hugh stayed close behind him.

"Stop, Walton," called Hugh to the fleeing figure ahead of him. "Let's talk like men."

Walton stopped running in a leaf-blanketed gully at the foot of a hill and turned around to face his adversary. Hugh stood a few yards above Walton on the rising slope. The trees and their low-hanging branches were close here, making the woods dark and unnerving.

Hugh said, "I'll tell everyone how ye beat me tonight. Ye won, Walton. Ye beat me and I lost, but the prize has to be something other than my knife. That knife means more to me than it will ever mean to ye."

The image of his da handing the dagger to him on the day he left Makgullane flashed through his mind.

"I had this knife forged for ye," Robin had said, "and now I give it to ye, my first son. Ye were ours first and will be ours forever. Use it only in defense of yer life, kenning that the love of yer family will see ye through whatever else may come until that love brings ye home again."

Hugh swallowed back the memory. Robin had trusted him with something of great value, and he had squandered it. He could not let that happen. "Whatever ye want, Walton, ye name it, and 'tis yers. I mean it, whatever ye say in place of the knife."

Walton, with malevolent glee, said, "I do enjoy watching you beg, my man, but I don't give a horse's fetlock about the dagger. I'm keeping it out of pure spite. I'll throw it in the lake before I give it back to you."

"Ye canna do that!"

"In fact, 'tis where I'm headed now, to throw my dagger into the lake." Walton turned to run again.

"Stop!"

The next few minutes passed in dazed horror, brilliant in their clarity, yet grotesque in their substance.

An owl, startled by the shouting and commotion at the foot of his tree, soared off his branch, flapping his wings wildly and screeching in protest. The crazed bird swooped down right at Walton's head. Lurching backward, Walton flailed his arms around his face to protect himself, but the bird dug his talons into Walton's waving arms, shrieking furiously.

Letting out an incoherent shout for mercy, Walton twisted and circled in a vain attempt to hurl off the winged banshee. A cloud of fallen leaves and branches whirled up around them, creating a terrifying mixture of beast and man, one nearly indistinguishable from the other except for the pitch of their screams.

The frenzied bird screeched one last time and, as suddenly as it had attacked, flew away. Walton, stunned and confused, stumbled backwards, his feet tangling in the thick underbrush. With his arms still flailing he fought to regain his balance, but his ankle caught on a tree root, and he fell to the ground, his skull slamming into a rock and splintering into lifeless shards.

The deadly sound of bone against rock ripped through Hugh's mind like an ax. He wanted to scream, but his throat had no voice. He could only stand and watch silently as Walton's life spurted out of the shattered shell of bone and flowed over the ground into an ever-widening river of black, syrupy blood.

Walton's dead eyes stared back at him.

****

Without a word of comment about his story, Kit said, "The English navy is anchored in the Edinburgh harbor. Are they coming this way with orders to capture the queen? Were ye sent ahead to ease their attack?"

"Nay, mistress! I came with a proposal, nothing more. I am only to ask, and then send word back to Somerset with yer answer."

"Three days ago, a man infiltrated our guard and tried to stab me and the babe while we slept. I stopped him. Our young queen isna safe here."

"Mistress," he said, "I had naught to do with that."

"My duty is to protect the queen above all else. Do ye understand why my judgment against ye is so harsh?"

"Nay, mistress, I dinna. I ne'er tried to kill ye. I ne'er would."

"But ye killed that Walton."

"Nay, mistress!"

Katherine locked her hands around the bars of the window in the door of the cell and said in clipped tones, "The Duke of Somerset sent ye, a murderer, to get his king's bride." Her face twisted as she shook the bars.

"He had no faith that ye would be successful, so he sent another killer ahead just in case, to end the need for a proposal once and for all. Then naught would stand in his way to conquer Scotland."

"Nay, mistress, 'tis no' true!"

Turning, she stormed down the passageway and out the door. One of the guards stationed there pulled it shut, and it clanked loudly behind her, sealing Hugh's fate.

Chapter Four

Kit stomped across the gravel in the courtyard, trying to release her anger and confusion. The events of the last few days had crumbled her normal confidence and strength. Today she questioned if her leadership skills were real or merely a façade, a false front to hide her weaknesses. She felt like she'd been pushed onto a frozen pond with the ice cracking below her feet and the icy water pulling her under.

Sitting down hard on the steps, she put her head in her hands. She regretted her harsh judgment against the auburn-haired man in the prison cell, but he'd made her choose. If he hadn't come north for King Edward, Hugh would have lived to see another day, and she wouldn't be carrying this heavy guilt around about what she had ordered done to him.

Her fingers went to her lips. She could still feel the prisoner's kiss, still feel his tongue sliding over her mouth. The skin was sensitive like she'd been out in the sun too long.

Curse it! His kiss turned everything she knew into a chaotic muddle of true and false, right and wrong. Her first obligation, in truth her only obligation, was to care for the young queen at all costs. She'd been trained for that. She knew she could defend herself and her young charge against all attackers, except the man in the prison cell below. Since he had jumped down from that tree, she felt unsure, doubtful, and, dare she say, helpless. These were all things she couldn't allow.

Before he landed at her feet, she'd known what to expect and what was expected of her. Everything she thought or did centered around caring for the young girl, Mary, but now, after condemning the prisoner to die, she had no idea how to move forward. She needed to concentrate her attention on finding a new place to hide the queen, but she found herself thinking more about the fine-looking man in the prison cell than the bright-eyed girl in her charge, and this frightened her. She had a job to do. Her duty came first.

The only thing she knew for certain was that she wanted another one of his thrilling kisses.

A hand on her shoulder broke Kit's concentration. Juliana stood next to her.

"Juliana, what are ye doing here? Who is with Mary?"

"I left Agnes to sit with her while she naps. I felt well enough to take a short walk. I saw ye here. Ye look troubled. Are ye all right?"

Kit stood. "Let me get ye to a chair inside and out of the breeze."

Juliana put her gnarled hand into Kit's and let Kit guide her to one of the high-backed chairs along the wall of the inside corridor.

"I kenned a man from London once a long time ago," she said. "His name was…I dinna remember his name, 'twas so long ago, but he was an honorable man, as I recall."

"Our prisoner is no'," said Kit. "He's a messenger from King Edward who has come to take our Mary away. I'm certain he understands now that willna be

44

happening."

"He's quite handsome," said Juliana, her voice still firm despite her age and illness, "the prisoner, I mean."

"Good looks mean naught when it comes to character, and this no-good has naught resembling character." She couldn't bring herself to tell Juliana that their prisoner had been found guilty of murder or that he'd been forced to come here under the terms of a royal pardon. For some reason, she didn't want Juliana to think worse of him. Let her think him an ill-advised messenger, but she needn't know he was also a murderer.

"Captain Rand reports that English ships have gathered at the mouth of the Firth of Forth. We'll have to leave here verra soon. He kissed me," said Kit.

"Rand kissed ye?"

"Nay, the prisoner kissed me. He jumped out of the tree and kissed me."

"Oh," said Juliana, looking at her curiously. "Was he any good at it? Kissing, I mean?" The smirk on her lips matched the twinkle in her eyes. "The man I kenned all those years ago was verra good at kissing."

Kit answered as if the priest had just asked her a serious question about the meaning of life. "I dinna ken. I have no' had enough kisses to judge properly. I liked him kissing me, but 'twas wrong for me to like it."

Juliana reached out to touch Katherine's wrist. "Let me see yer face, Kit."

Kit turned toward her, and Juliana put her swollen hands against her cheeks. After a moment of gazing into Kit's wide-set eyes, she said, "Dinna apologize for liking the stranger's kiss. 'Tis something over which ye have no control."

"But I should have control. I need to have control. I've been trained to be a soldier so I can protect Mary. I canna let my guard down for even a minute."

Juliana shook her head slowly. "I admire every quality about ye except one, the hardened heart that has been forced into ye. Yer duty should be tempered by a generous spirit."

Jerking her head out of Juliana's hands, Kit said, "I have to be strong to keep the guard in order and to keep my charge safe. There is naught more important. Ye ken that. I'm no' allowed silly gushing outbursts of emotions. I must be logical, and I must be strong. My duty is to Scotland's queen, and that is paramount, or have ye forgotten?" She glared at her mentor.

Juliana answered with an equally strong glare at Kit. "I have no' forgotten for a moment."

Kit hung her head. "I'm sorry, Juliana, I didna mean disrespect. I ken that ye have dedicated yer life to caring for royal children. It has no' always been easy, but ye did it well. I have made the same decision. Even now I dinna regret it."

Looking away, Juliana said very tenderly, "But ye may. Many years from now ye may regret no' taking a chance on a stranger." When Kit didn't respond, she asked, "Are ye really going to cut off his head?"

"I have to," said Kit. "I must show the English king that I can defend little Mary. If I kill all his couriers, he might decide we're no' worth the trouble." Gathering cloth from her skirt in each hand, she flung it down in an angry gesture. "I dinna have to like it. I just have to do it. I have no choice."

"There are always choices, my child, even when there seem to be none."

"Yer hands look swollen today," Katherine said as she pushed another chair next to Juliana's. Taking one of the older woman's hands, she began lightly massaging her swollen knuckles.

"That feels good, dear," said Juliana. "Let me tell ye a story, Katherine, a story I hope ye understand. I was seventeen years old when Queen Margaret Tudor, queen to King James IV, decided that I would make a proper nurse for her about-to-be-born babe. She didna ask me if I wanted it. She didna care what my feelings were, only that for some reason I looked like someone to care for the child."

Kit switched her massage to Juliana's other hand.

"Have ye ever thought how yer life would be different if ye werena charged with the care of a queen?" asked the older woman. "If ye had a choice?"

Kit stayed silent for a long time before sighing. "The child queen has no choice but to be queen, so I have no choice but to watch over her. She has her duty, and I have mine."

Just then Rand's footsteps echoed against the stone floor as he approached Juliana and Kit from the hallway. He stopped in front of them and held his chin up at attention. "Mistress Katherine, the man who attacked ye in yer bedchamber three nights ago is dead. We will bury him in an unmarked grave. Ye dinna have to be afeared anymore."

"I'm no' afeared," Kit said, "no' anymore."

"Simon confessed to being part of a patriotic faction of men from the northern Highlands who disagree with how Lord Arran is handling the English incursions. They believe Arran to be too lenient. Simon's mission was to murder young Mary and force

Arran to engage fully in a war. Forgive me for allowing that spy to become one of our guard." His eyebrows formed almost one continuous line in a scowl.

"Rand," said Kit, "there was no way for ye to read his mind or his intentions. No one blames ye. Do ye suppose Simon and Somerset have some connection?"

" 'Tis possible. Who kens how far Somerset would reach to get what he wants? I also must beg yer forgiveness for leaving ye unattended when our latest prisoner attacked ye in the woods."

" 'Twas not so much an attack as…well, I dinna ken what it was, but I am no worse for it. Besides, I made the choice to go walking in the woods alone."

"He will also be dead by tomorrow," said Rand, "and these assaults will have been disposed of with finality. Mistress, I promise ye that I will increase my vigilance, and no such attacks will happen again."

"It means that we must act quickly to move Mary. We need to be gone from here within three days. Have ye found a safe location?"

"I am going ahead to see about the suitability of one of the islands in Loch Menteith. There is a priory there that might serve us, at least temporarily. I will ken more by the day after tomorrow, and ye can make the decision at that time."

"I will await yer report on Lake Menteith," said Kit, adding, "I put my faith in ye, Rand. Ye have served our queen well. Dinna let me keep ye from yer duties."

Bowing sharply, Rand strode away.

Juliana watched Kit's eyes for a moment before her lips curled upwards in a smile. "Ye ken, I have been looking for a husband myself now that ye have taken over my duties. I'm quite taken by the look of our unwilling visitor in the dungeon. Perhaps I'll encourage the young man. He might save his neck by marrying me. What do ye think?" She winked at Kit.

"Juliana!" Kit's smile vanished. "That wouldna be possible. He dies before midday."

Chapter Five

Hugh paced in and out of the sun's first rays shining through the bars of the small prison cell window, his mind racing.

"Think!" he muttered. "Think!"

Blessed with a quick and agile mind, he needed to use it now to save his neck. As a child, his sharp wit, combined with his independent and stubborn streak, led him to speak or act without thought, getting him into trouble just as it had yesterday.

His da, Robin, discovered that the worst, or perhaps the best, punishment for his oldest son's misdeeds was to force Hugh to apologize face-to-face to everyone he had wronged by what he had done or said. Robin hoped that if Hugh saw how his actions hurt others, he might learn something, and quite often he did. He wished he had remembered those lessons yesterday.

This morning Hugh began rehearsing the sincerest, most desperate apology he would ever make. He had every word worked out when the door at the end of the short hallway of the three-celled prison clattered open. A stooped, elderly woman followed by three guards stepped within sight of his cell-door window.

"Bring my chair," the woman said. One guard quickly placed a carved padded chair just outside Hugh's door, and the old woman sat down stiffly. "Tell me yer name again," she said to him.

"Who are ye?" he asked.

Her sharp blue eyes narrowed, and her throat barked out, "Tell me yer name!"

He stood up straight as if his own father were scolding him. "Hugh, mistress, Hugh Cullane of Makgullane in the southern Highlands."

"I understand that ye're to be beheaded before midday."

"Aye, mistress. Is there anything ye can do to stop it?"

"I dinna ken. I dinna think so. Tell me what the king promised ye to come north. Was money the reason ye agreed to force our young queen into marriage?"

"I didna agree to force her into anything," Hugh protested. "I thought a marriage would be a good thing."

"How much is the Duke of Somerset paying ye?"

"He's no' paying me anything. He promised me a pardon if I delivered the betrothal. If I dinna deliver his message and send back a true answer, I'll be a hunted outlaw for the rest of my life, which at this moment looks like it will be so short he'll have no need to hunt for me."

Hugh began his rehearsed apology. "I am truly sorry to have brought this trouble to everyone in this house. I regret—"

Juliana interrupted him. "And yer crime was?" She shifted her weight in the chair to ease the pressure on her hips.

"My crime?"

"Aye!" Juliana snapped. "What crime did ye commit?"

Hugh sighed. "I already told the whole story to Mistress Katherine. A man accidentally died, and I was blamed. I swear 'twas an accident. I didna kill him. An owl did."

Juliana's eyes twinkled. "An owl, ye say. Am I to assume that the owl didna testify?" One of the guards suppressed a giggle. Suddenly the old woman's expression turned somber again. "Tell me why ye were found guilty."

She didn't want to hear his apology. All he had left was another sorry and shameful tale to tell, but if it would save his neck, he'd do it gladly.

****

The steward of Blackwood Castle called out in a raspy voice, "Hugh of Makgullane, are you here six-handed to acquit yourself of the murder without cause or reason of Walton of Blackwood?"

"Willingly," replied Hugh as firmly as he could with twelve pairs of eyes staring back at him, the eyes of the men who would determine if he lived or died.

A royal court, convened at the request of the sheriff, was held in the inner bailey of Blackwood Castle ten miles north of London. Twelve free landholders sat in wooden chairs under an ancient ash tree while the steward, who would serve as judge, stood beside them. Everyone else, be they witnesses or curious onlookers, had to find room wherever they could, on the ground, in the branches of the ash tree, or even on the wall surrounding the bailey.

Reading aloud from an official court document, the steward shouted to the crowd, "Sir Rutherford of Blackwood complains that three days ago his cousin, Walton of Blackwood, was going his way in the peace of God and in the peace of the lord, which is within the surety of your franchise, when he was assailed and done bodily harm unto death by Hugh Cullane. Before this court is Hugh Cullane, who by all that he surmises denies the deed. He is ready to acquit himself in all such wise as this court, as he ought."

Rutherford testified first. Stepping out of the crowd, he paced in front of the jury, telling in passionate details about the game of passé-dix and how Hugh tried to renege on a fairly placed wager. The most damning piece of evidence was the rock, still covered with Walton's blood. As Rutherford held it high over his head, every face in the jury turned to look at Hugh as if the rock itself had spoken.

Putnam then confirmed all the same details in a strong, compelling voice, repeating almost word for word his brother's account. Some on the jury looked to be sleeping through Putnam's testimony. No need to listen if they had already made up their minds.

Finally came Hugh's turn to speak. He reluctantly repeated what Rutherford and Putnam said about the events at the tavern. Then he related Walton's accidental death in the forest. He ended with, "I swear on my soul what I say is true."

A woman shouted out, "We all know about your soul. You're bound for Hell for your gambling ways!"

****

Mistress Juliana interrupted. "I have heard that gamblers are refused entry into Hell."

"Really?" Could this be the first hopeful news Hugh had heard in a long time?

"Aye. 'Tis told that a demon brought a gambler to Hell and left him in charge of all the poor souls condemned there so the demon could go out and look for more souls. While the demon was gone, St. Peter showed up and played highest point, or it could have been passé-dix, perhaps hazard, but no matter the game, St. Peter bet for all the souls the gambler was supposed to be guarding. St. Peter won and took all those souls up to Heaven. The gambler might have been in serious trouble when the demon returned to find Hell empty, but the demon didna want to admit that he'd left his realm in the care of such a rotten servant, so he threw the gambler out. The gambler ran straight to Heaven where St. Peter let him in, and so it goes that Hell willna take a gambler."

"Ye might think that would ease my mind some, but nay," said Hugh. "The demon could find many other sins besides gambling to take me."

"No doubt." She nodded for him to continue his story.

****

The steward silenced the crowd with a wave of his hand. "If there is no more testimony, the jury will discuss the case and a judgment will be discovered."

The jurors talked openly among themselves and with everyone else around the ash tree. Immediately, a loud, acrimonious discussion began about Hugh and his ignoble reputation. People who hadn't actually lost a wager to him knew of others who had. Bitter young women told how his handsome face and charming ways had taken them in, only to discover that his commitment to them was as empty as his pockets after a night at the gaming table. The fathers of these daughters protested the loudest. Nothing but a cad who abused their innocent maidens! Their shouts of disapproval of his character and his devil-may-care lifestyle fell one on top of the other, burying Hugh in an avalanche of rancor.

"Where's Murdock?" Hugh asked Garret, who had sat beside him through the whole trial.

"Murdock rode to see the Duke of Somerset yesterday morning to ask if anything could be done. Quiet, the jury is ready to speak. Listen and pray."

"Hugh Cullane, approach the front," said the steward.

Hugh took a deep breath and stepped up to face the jury. He would hold his shoulders high regardless of what came.

"The jury has reached a verdict. How say you, each one in turn?"

Each juror repeated the same single word. "Guilty." Twelve times the word "guilty."

The steward declared, "So say you all. Hugh Cullane, you have been found guilty by a jury of your peers, all free landholding men. Rutherford of Blackwood as the principal accuser will secure a hangman or perform the office himself by tomorrow morning at first light, when the guilty party shall be hanged by the neck until dead. This royal court is closed."

****

"I went numb," Hugh said to Juliana. "They were leading me away to the Blackwood prison when a rider raced into the bailey. 'Twas my friend, Murdock."

Juliana's expression didn't change.

****

"Wait! I have news! Wait!" Murdock shouted as he leaped off his mount. "Wait! There is more business before this royal court. Steward, call the jury back."

Rutherford answered impatiently, "This court is finished. The verdict is given and cannot be altered. There is nothing more to say."

"Except that Hugh has a royal pardon," shouted Murdock, waving a royal document. "The royal regent, Somerset, has offered a king's pardon in exchange for Hugh's service. 'Tis all right here. You must honor it."

Rutherford protested vehemently, demanding that the original verdict be upheld, but the royal decree had to be respected.

****

Juliana massaged her aching hands. "Why a royal pardon for ye? What did the king expect in return?"

"The king expects me to come back to London, or at the verra least send another messenger, with a signed letter of betrothal from Queen Mary to marry King Edward VI. If ye agree, I am to bring the queen herself. After that I'm free to do what I want, which is to go back home and ne'er venture to England again."

"If ye go home, 'twill be good riddance to ye, but as for the rest, do ye think ye're telling me anything I dinna already ken?" snapped Juliana. "What I want to ken is what does this betrothal have to do with ye? Why ye?"

"Treaties and marriages between Scotland and England have naught to do with me."

"Stop being so ignorant. I want to ken what yer bargain with Somerset was."

"I'm sorry, but I am ignorant. My only thought is that Somerset assumed my Scottish heritage might make it easier for ye to agree to the proposal. Ye might trust a Scot before ye trust a Sassenach with the same message. My only instructions were to secure a betrothal."

Juliana pointed a contorted fist at Hugh. "Ye say ye want to go back home. Will they welcome ye with open arms? Does yer family ken of yer disgrace? Did this pardon cost yer father anything? Perhaps his loyalty to the English against the Scots?"

Hugh nearly choked. He never thought that somehow Robin might be dragged into this fiasco. It would be easy enough for Somerset to find out that Hugh was from Makgullane, and even easier to find out that his grandfather, Bretane, represented the Highlands in the Scottish parliament. Could their loyalty be the cost of Hugh's pardon?

For the first time, he acknowledged that his had been a life of utter selfishness. Until now he believed he alone was responsible for everything that happened, and he alone had to endure the consequences. Could Somerset have put his father and grandfather in his debt for what Hugh had done? He felt his stomach contents edging up to his throat. If he ever got home, he'd fall on his knees to beg forgiveness from both of them. He'd spend the rest of his time on this earth trying to earn their trust again, but he'd never have that chance if he lost his head here at Fawside Castle.

"I dinna think…they ken of what has happened." Looking toward the ceiling, trying to keep his composure, he said, "But now no one would ken what became of me until my head arrives in London, and then it will be too late. My father and grandfather will be so ashamed of me. I canna face them."

"Ye ne'er think about anyone but yerself. Ye thoughtless, ungrateful…" She snapped her jaw shut and rubbed her temples trying to calm herself.

"I am so sorry, mistress." Hugh hung his head. " 'Tis my fault. No one else is to blame and no one else should take the punishment." He kept his eyes on the floor, his shoulders slumped in humiliation. "But to be hanged as a murderer…or executed here and ne'er have the chance to tell my da the truth or beg his forgiveness. I canna bear to break his heart after all he did for me, after taking me in, after…" Hugh swallowed hard.

Juliana sat still for several minutes before saying, "I have instructed these guards to prepare ye a hot bath. Ye're to wear these clothes."

She whistled, and a soldier appeared holding a bejeweled, pale green tunic with puffed sleeves at the shoulder, a pair of yellow-green linen breeches, and matching hose. The woman whistled again, and another guard presented her with fur-lined shoes and a black woolen cloak trimmed with gold brocade.

"I found these clothes in a trunk in a closed room here at Fawside," said Juliana. "They may be many years old, but they're no' moth eaten or moldy."

Hugh wondered if the old woman had turned mad. "I'm in no position to complain, mistress," he said, "but I would rather wear my own clothes to my execution. It seems foolish for a soon-to-be dead man to wear an already-dead man's things."

Juliana straightened up as much as her crooked spine would allow and fixed her gaze on him. "These are no' for yer execution, ye foolish child. Ye will be given a bath and these clean clothes to make yerself presentable."

"What? Why?"

"Ye said yer name is Hugh. I believe it means

something like 'heart, mind, and spirit.' Ye will need a strong heart, mind, and spirit to survive this when clearly ye've been thickheaded and addled all yer life. Stop it! Ye will do as I instructed, or I'll have ye beheaded within the hour. Is that understood?"

He nodded sharply. "Aye, mistress."

She whistled again. Two soldiers stepped closer to help her out of her chair and to the door.

Hugh looked at her in bewilderment. "Why are ye doing this?"

"I have raised Mary from the moment she was born. She has a fine spirit that needs to grow up free, and no' be traded like a cow. I would do anything for her."

At last, the voice of reason. "Then ye must be in favor of her marriage."

With great effort, Juliana hobbled around to face him. Her resolute voice echoed in the small area of the prison cells. "Simpkin! I wouldna sentence a goat to that wretched fate, let alone the queen of Scotland."

"Then what is this all about?"

"When the time comes, use whatever gifts God gave ye to improve yer situation. Dinna use yer shandy mouth to say any more foolish things."

Hugh started to ask again why she was doing this, but Juliana proved quicker. "If ye say another word, I'll sit back down and supervise yer bath myself." The soft skin around her eyes crinkled amusingly at his horrified expression. "I may be an old woman, but I would still enjoy watching a young, well-built man, such as ye, being scrubbed down."

Hugh clamped his mouth shut. Not that he minded a woman seeing him naked—many had since he was fifteen—and he didn't mind that she was as old and wrinkled as the cook, Marta, at Makgullane, but he did mind her being so brazen about it. She'd enjoy seeing him naked, and that thought embarrassed him.

"Take me to my chambers," said Juliana to one of the guards. "I'm verra tired."

"Aye, Mistress," said the tallest guard, named Miles. To the other guards, he said, "Prepare the bath and see that the prisoner is properly washed and dressed."

Hugh scanned the guards' faces. He didn't like their eagerness to follow the old woman's orders. They were clearly a loyal crew who thought their mistress had suffered at his hands, and they'd already been taking turns reaching through the bars and hitting him with sticks. So far, he'd been able to duck into the corner to escape most of their wrath, but he would be at their mercy during a bath.

To Hugh's relief, Juliana said sternly, "If the prisoner is injured even slightly, I will see that ye all suffer for it."

The guards, sounding like unrepentant children, said in unison, "Aye, Mistress."

During the bath, Hugh had a few tense moments when a barrel-chested guard came at him with a razor to shave him and again when another trimmed his shaggy hair, but all the men stayed reluctantly obedient.

Amazingly, the clothes fit Hugh perfectly, and when he completed his dressing ritual, the guard named Miles said brusquely, "I have no idea why ye need to look like a coxcomb to have yer head chopped off, but Mistress Juliana does, so 'tis done."

Alone in his cell, Hugh wore an out-of-style but

elegant outfit, smelling and looking better than he had since the last time he'd been at Makgullane for his mother's Twelfth Night banquet. Afraid to sit down and wrinkle his tunic or breeches, he stood in the center of his cell and waited.

Two anxious hours later, the guard Miles entered the door leading into the prison corridor, followed by four other guards in their dress uniforms.

This is it. 'Tis the last hour of my life. He suddenly felt cold and alone.

" 'Tis time to go," said Miles as he unlocked the door to Hugh's cell. "Follow me."

In a last futile attempt to avoid his fate, Hugh demanded, "Where is the captain? Ye canna take me without him."

"Captain Rand is scouting for the next place to move Queen Mary. Ye willna be coming with us. Out of that cell."

Miles took three steps back, but Hugh didn't move. If anybody thought he would get his head chopped off willingly, they were wrong.

"Take him," said Miles. He stepped aside while two guards grabbed Hugh by the arms and started to haul him out of the cell.

Bracing his legs against the floor, Hugh refused to move. The two guards tugged on his arms while the other two pushed him from behind. Progress out of the cell came by inches. When they were close to the door, Hugh wrapped his fingers around the bars in the window and held on for all he was worth.

There had never been a more hopeless battle. The guards, who not only outnumbered him but also carried sharp weapons, would eventually win, but that was just the point. He didn't deserve to lose his head, and he had no intention of being gracious about it.

"Stop fighting us," said Miles when he realized what was going on behind him, his voice dripping with unmistakable contempt. "If ye must ken, Juliana ordered that ye no' die today."

"Aye?" said Hugh as he elbowed the one on his right in the stomach. The man fell back against the wall.

"She has ordered ye to dine with them." Miles's gray eyes glowered at him. "Dinna look at me like that. I dinna ken why she wants to feed ye, but she does. My job is to see that ye cause no trouble between now and yer execution tomorrow. I'm no' required to like the task."

"Ye expect me to believe that I'm invited to eat? That the despised enemy of the queen of Scotland has suddenly become an honored guest?"

Hugh swung his leg back and kicked one of the men behind him in the shin. The man cried out in pain.

Miles strode back toward Hugh. "Get out of that cell and follow me." He raised his gloved hand to strike Hugh across the face, but Hugh swung his fist into Miles's chest first. Miles stumbled back, drew his sword from its sheath, and loomed over Hugh like the executioner himself, his blade against the prisoner's neck.

"Consider this yer last warning," snarled Miles. "If ye dinna obey me right now, I'll run ye through and tell Mistress that ye tried to escape. Killing ye would be a pleasure." Miles dug the foible into Hugh's neck. "Do we understand each other?"

Seeing the wisdom in extending his life a little longer, no matter how ludicrous the circumstances,

Hugh answered, "Aye, sir, we do." He smoothed his tunic and waited calmly for Miles to lower his sword.

Chapter Six

Kit had never heard a more shandy idea in her life! Have the prisoner for dinner? She'd like to have him for dinner all right, cut up in tiny pieces and boiled in oil. What could Juliana, her mentor and friend, be thinking?

She put her elbow on the arm of the chair, made a fist, and rested her cheek against it. "I dinna like this," she said as Lady Juliana hobbled into the small room off the main dining hall.

"I ken, dear. I'm no' asking ye to like it. I'm asking ye to do it. We owe the prisoner a last meal."

"We dinna owe that depraved sod anything," protested Kit as she stood to help Juliana into a chair at the head of the table in the center of the room. Any more serious protesting would get her nowhere since the truth was, despite anything Juliana said, Kit could refuse to eat with the prisoner. Even though she had no intention of enjoying his "last meal," the chance to see the man with the head of thick hair and the broad smile made her as flighty as a sparrow.

The room was only suitable for entertaining a few guests. No more than six could sit comfortably around the small dining table, but Kit imagined that the people who once lived here spent many afternoons eating by the fire and playing games at the table under the window.

When Miles and the prisoner appeared in the

doorway, Kit didn't know which one of them looked more bewildered.

"Thank ye, Miles," said Juliana. She pointed to the chair at the other end of the table. "Hugh, ye may sit there. Miles, ye may sit beside Kit. The other guards may go to the kitchen to eat."

"Nay, mistress," said Miles. "I prefer they remain in the hallway."

"I dinna think Hugh will do anything foolish, will ye?"

"Nay, mistress," answered Hugh. "I will be a verra good lad."

Miles scowled at Hugh before saying, "Gordon, Michael, ye will take turns with James and Marsh going to the kitchen to eat and then returning to stand where ye are." The guards and Juliana nodded in agreement.

Miles roughly pushed Hugh toward the chair Juliana indicated.

After stumbling awkwardly, Hugh smiled politely, creating two perfect crescent moon creases in his cheeks, framing his mouth. Flopping into the chair, he said, "Good day to ye, mistress, and to ye." When he looked in Kit's direction, his smile widened.

Although she would never admit it, Kit had chosen her outfit for the prisoner's benefit. A deep blue linen chemise clung to her body. Over that she wore a seven-eighths-length cotte of golden silk with a section of the hemline pulled up and draped in soft folds on one side at her fitted waist. Loose sleeves, three-quarter length and trimmed with red-flowered embroidery, finished the look. The rounded neckline, trimmed with the same red embroidery, rested just below the soft, apple-blossom-white skin of her collarbone, exactly where she wanted him to look.

"Ye look lovely today," said Hugh.

"As caretaker for a queen I must dress properly. I am a reflection of her majesty," she said, smoothing her skirt.

She noticed the prisoner tugging his tunic lower, possibly to cover a rather inconvenient sensation in his lower body, and she took some unkind delight in tormenting him. The problem was he tormented her in the same way. Too bad he would die tomorrow before either of them could take advantage of such thoughts.

"Miles," said Kit, "I dinna ken why Juliana is doing this. I would cut off his head and be done with it."

" 'Twill be done tomorrow," said Miles grimly as he took his seat.

Three serving girls appeared in the doorway, each carrying trays. The first girl had a large bowl of water boiled with rosemary for each guest to wash his or her hands. The second one placed a pigling stuffed with nuts, cheese, eggs, and spices in the center of the table while the third ladled a serving of lamb stew into the day-old bread trenchers already at each place setting.

"We will be back with the rest as soon as we can," said the youngest of the servants, a girl of about ten. "Cook's made frumenty pudding and fine, sweet pastries. I had a bite."

"Hush, Josie!" said the oldest servant. To Katherine she said, "I'll see she minds her manners from now on, mistress."

"Dinna scold her on my account," said Hugh. "I believe a meal tastes better when ye ken what is coming. Ye can get yer tongue ready." He smiled at the young girl before she curtsied and dashed from the room.

"Frumenty pudding, wheat, cream, eggs, whatever fruit is in season, and, of course, nutmeg," Hugh said. " 'Tis my mother's favorite. She always said she could eat her weight in frumenty pudding."

"Is she a large woman?" asked Juliana with a smirk.

"Nay, mistress, she is verra small, but no' delicate, and she has a will of iron."

"No doubt she will mourn for her son," said Kit.

"Katherine!" scolded Juliana.

Kit rolled her eyes and pursed her lips at the reprimand. " 'Tis ridiculous. We're discussing frumenty pudding with a man sent to steal our Mary away."

"Katherine, where is yer mercy?" said Juliana.

Sighing, Kit asked the prisoner-turned-guest, "What is yer name again?"

"Hugh Cullane."

"Hugh, I'm sorry for what I just said. I have no right to be cavalier about someone else's death, but ye do understand why it must be."

"Nay, mistress, I dinna."

Kit felt a twinge of regret. Beheading seemed a waste for a man who created such luscious feelings in her every time she looked at him, but it had to be done for the safety of the young girl in her charge.

Quickly, Juliana asked, "Will ye say the grace, Miles?"

Miles's prayer was short and simple, but Kit didn't hear it. Her eyes lingered on the prisoner even after the "amen." There was so much about him that she had never noticed before.

He had the most beautiful hands. His long slender fingers moved with care and ease over everything he touched. She watched as he tore off a piece of his bread trencher and dipped it deep into the stew. With exquisite slowness, he brought the dripping piece to his mouth and pushed the bread past his lips. His finger lingered there for a brief moment as his tongue darted out of his mouth ever so slightly to lick a drop of gravy off his fingertip.

Kit took in a long slow breath. A simple act of eating, one she had seen others do a thousand times, but the way he did it completely captivated her. In the forest, his fingers had touched her hips in that same fascinating way, carefully, but with a firmness that wasn't crude or rough. She imagined those fingers touching her in places that were not her hips. Her heart fluttered in her chest, and she tried to swallow it down.

"Mistress Katherine," asked Miles, "are ye all right?"

Suddenly realizing that all eyes at the table were upon her, she shook herself out of her meditation. "Aye, I'm fine." Picking up her wine glass, she took a large gulp.

The conversation during the rest of the meal proved pleasant and ordinary. After all the courses had been served, Hugh swallowed the last of his pudding and wiped his hands on the cloth spread over the table, as was customary.

"Does anyone here like riddling?" he asked. "I ken many good riddles, some I heard from others and some I made up myself. Would anyone like to hear one and try to guess it?"

"I would," said Juliana as she leaned forward

against the table. "I have no' heard a good riddle in a long time. If we canna guess yer riddle, Hugh, ye will receive a reward. I hope ye tell a juicy one." She winked at him.

Hugh put his finger to his lips, pursing them in thought. "Perhaps this one will interest ye. It goes like this." Leaning back in his chair, he steepled his fingers. "A lass, young and lonely, often locked me in a chest. She took me out at times, lifted me with fair hands and gave me to her loyal lord, fulfilling his desire. Then he stuck his head well inside of me, pushed it upwards into the smallest part."

"This is no' a tavern!" said Miles. "These are ladies."

Kit giggled at the exaggerated look of innocence on Hugh's face.

"The riddle doesna offend, I promise ye," said Hugh. "Hear the end of it first. Where was I? Pushed it upwards into the smallest part. 'Twas my fate, adorned as I was, to be filled with something rough if that person who possessed me was virile enough. Now guess what I am." He turned to Kit, raising his eyebrows. "Can ye guess, mistress?"

"Give me time to think," said Kit. "Juliana, what do ye think it is?"

"Many things come to mind, but I'm certain none of them is the correct answer," she said with a grin. "Could it be a drawer?"

"Nay, mistress. Try again."

"Could it be an axe at the woodpile?" asked Kit. "Or a treasure chest? Nay, I have it. 'Tis a helmet! Aye, a helmet. Pushed into the smallest part is the pointed top of the helmet, and the rough part is the man's hair.

His full head of hair would be virile. Am I right?"

"Aye, mistress, ye are," said Hugh, touching his fingers to his forehead as if tipping his hat to her. "How about another?"

"No more riddling," said Miles. "The prisoner should go back to his cell."

Before Miles could move to take Hugh away, Juliana said, "Hugh, do ye like to play games? Kit is quite a competitor at draughts."

"Is she now?" said Hugh. "Would ye honor me with a game, mistress?"

Kit glanced up at Miles standing behind her chair like a sentry, but the decision was hers.

"Please, mistress, one game of draughts," said Hugh, pushing the loose curls of hair off his forehead. "I couldna beat ye at riddling and win my reward. Perhaps I could at draughts."

The corners of Kit's lips turned up. "Ye willna beat me. Set up the board."

The pair moved to the gaming table under the window, and Hugh placed the draughts board with its alternating squares of light and dark wood on the table between them. He dumped out the round playing pieces that had been haphazardly heaped in a wooden box with a sliding top and began passing them out. "Which do ye prefer, mistress?" he asked.

"The light colored. Ye may take the dark." As she gathered her pieces, Hugh's hand brushed against hers, and a curious tingling sensation shot up her arm. She looked to see if he had pinched her. He hadn't.

Hugh's moves across the board appeared impulsive and often risky. He moved his wooden circles from square to square toward her side, seemingly not giving any more than a second's thought to each move. Her moves, on the other hand, were deliberate and cautious, each requiring considerable thought. When waiting for her to finish her turn, he leaned his elbow on the table and rested his head in his hand, staring at her.

"Would ye stop that?" she asked, without looking away from the board.

"Stop what?"

"Stop looking at me while I think."

"Ye may look at me while I think, if ye wish. Care to guess what I'm thinking now?" he asked, grinning at her with those charming creases in his cheeks.

She looked up at his eyes, the color of fresh earth ready for planting, of oak bark in the spring, of a mourning dove's feathers. All colors of things she loved. One of those eyes winked at her.

"I would no' have any notion what ye might be thinking," she said, moving one of her pieces diagonally to the right. "Nor would I care."

Hugh sat up straight in his chair and said quietly, "I was thinking that ye're a most beautiful woman, but that ye dinna ken it or rather ye dinna believe it. Ye're uncommonly lovely, and I canna take my eyes off ye."

" 'Tis enough talk," said Miles. "Play draughts or back to the cell with ye."

Immediately, Hugh picked up a wooden disc and jumped it over three of Kit's pieces, all evenly spaced apart. Collecting her pieces, he placed them on his side of the table.

Kit heard the clicking as he jumped the disc across the board, but she didn't see it. She saw only him. He had called her beautiful in a way that, for the first time in her life, made her believe it might be true. He had said it plainly with no flowery words or implausible exaggerations. He had said it straight out with all the seriousness of taking an oath. He had declared her a most beautiful woman, not a protector or a caretaker, but a woman.

Before she could fully take in that revelation, Miles's hand came over the back of her chair, making her remember that this prisoner named Hugh remained dangerous to everything she held dear. His very presence meant peril to little Mary, something she had sworn to prevent with her last dying breath.

"I concede the game to ye," she said. "Take him back to his cell. The execution will be tomorrow at yer convenience. I dinna wish to be informed of the details."

Rising from her chair, she strode from the room without looking back.

Chapter Seven

Hugh couldn't sleep. Flashes of long past memories from his childhood darted through his mind. How he had enjoyed playing games in the yard at Makgullane with his longtime friend and adopted brother, Fergus, and then teaching his younger brothers and sisters how to play the same games as they were born to Suannoch and Robin. He recalled how he loved training the estate's stallions and racing them against lads from the nearby manors. He could almost hear his father's voice reading aloud to him at night by the fire, with Homer's tales being his favorites, and he remembered his mother patiently trying to teach him to read. It proved a daunting task at best, one he never fully mastered. For him, the letters jumped around on the page, although if someone else read it aloud, he could repeat every word.

He also remembered what he didn't have: a wife, children, or a purpose. He had squandered his life, his only life, on amusement, gambling, and drinking, and that insight tore at him. He didn't want to die before he made up for wasted time, before he proved to Robin that taking him in had not been a mistake.

The next morning Miles delivered another suit of old-fashioned clothing to Hugh's prison cell, this time a suit made of heavily embroidered woolen broadcloth called "scarlet" in a watchet sea-blue color. New clothes meant new hope.

Miles ordered him to put them on.

"Where am I going today?' asked Hugh as he finished dressing and tying the cloak around his shoulders.

"Ye can pray for Heaven, but for the likes of ye, most likely 'twill be Hell," said Miles.

"Perhaps no'. Mistress Juliana assures me that gamblers are no' accepted in Hell."

"Mayhap those without heads will be."

Hugh's heart sank. No reprieve today. Today she would execute him.

" 'Tis time to go," said Miles as he unlocked the door to the cell. "The executioner's blade is sharpened, but he has no' had much practice lately." Miles manacled Hugh's hands in front of him. "Sometimes he misses."

Hugh's heart stopped beating. "What?"

"Sometimes he misses the neck. He might just lop off yer hair or maybe an arm. Then he has to try again. Once he took off the man's jaw, and the poor bloke couldna even scream while he waited for the second blow to finish him off."

"Ye canna mean it," said Hugh, his knees wobbling under him.

"Mistress Katherine is a kind soul. She only allows three swings of the ax. If ye're still alive after three tries, ye're set free. Want me to slip the executioner a bit more ale? He has been drinking steadily all night, but a little more might give ye a fighting chance."

Hugh put his hands against the door, his head reeling. *Lord, have mercy!*

With two guards holding his arms and two more

following closely behind, Hugh trudged out of the prison basement, around the castle, and across the yard. The execution party continued marching down the dirt road away from the castle.

Hugh asked, "Are we going straight to the graveyard?"

The guards didn't answer.

"Ye're probably right," continued Hugh. "There is no need to lug my body all that way when I can walk there by myself first."

"We dinna bury the likes of ye," said the guard on his left. "We leave ye for the wolves and maggots."

Another sickening wave shot through Hugh's belly.

The execution procession marched along the road for about three furlongs until they came over a hill out of sight of the castle. Ahead on the road sat a carriage drawn by four matching blue roans, each one a rich brown color with a sprinkling of white hairs and shiny black manes, tails, and fetlocks. The lead horses snorted, anxious to show their passengers their lively stride and energetic spirits.

Hugh's face brightened. More than anything he wanted to stroke their muzzles before he died.

"May I see the horses?" he asked. When he had no reply, he said, "I ne'er saw a more perfectly matched team. We breed horses at home, for racing mostly, but some coach horses, too. 'Tis my last request. I'll no' speak another word if ye let me spend a minute with those magnificent animals."

The last of Hugh's hope drifted away with their silence. Not wanting his final glimpse of this world to be of the horses he longed to stroke, he dropped his head and kept his eyes on the dirt at his feet.

The opening of a carriage door sounded.

Miles asked, "Mistress, are ye certain this is what ye want to do? 'Tis no' safe."

"Will ye be riding up top?" asked a woman from inside.

"Aye, mistress, with Peter and Rolf. James and Marsh will follow on horseback."

"Then I'll be safe enough. Take the manacles off and let him inside the coach."

Hugh's head and eyebrows shot up. *Now what?*

"I would feel better if he stayed chained," said Miles.

In a flat wooden voice, she said, "Please, 'twas difficult enough arguing with Juliana this morning over this excursion. I canna take any more from ye. We have to get this over and done with before Captain Rand returns today, so let him inside."

"Aye, mistress." Unlocking Hugh's chains, Miles leaned close to his ear and whispered, "Listen to me, ye waste-from-a-pig, I'll pull out yer tongue and strangle ye with it if so much as a hair is out of place on my lady."

"Not a hair out of place," said Hugh with as much respect as he could muster for this pitiless guard. "I promise."

The shackles fell away, and Miles shoved Hugh onto the floor of the carriage. He landed with his face buried in the corner and his feet halfway out the door.

"Get up on the seat," said Katherine curtly.

Hugh righted himself as the carriage began bouncing over the bumpy road away from the castle. Scooting onto the bench seat across from her, he took a long look at the lady opposite him. *Katherine, ye do make my blood to run!*

He had never before experienced the kind of instant attraction he felt toward her. With other women, he wanted one thing from them, a kiss, or more if they would give it, and he was the one in control. But with this blue-eyed beauty, she held all the dice, and in some unexpected way, that didn't matter to him. This morning more than ever, perhaps because he was so close to death, he wanted only to taste this exquisite woman.

She wore a burnt crimson gown with stark white lace draped around the neckline and bodice. Wide sections of lace, stitched around her arms above the elbow, hung in gentle folds past the mid-point of her hands. The dress took full advantage of her height by placing alternating panels of crimson and green in her flowing skirt, which would swirl together when she walked.

"Yer gown is most fetching," he said.

She sighed before saying, "And what do ye think of Mary's gown?"

All at once Hugh noticed the four-year-old queen of Scotland on her knees in the corner of the seat beside the window, her light red hair blowing in the wind.

"Hello, Yer Majesty," he said.

"Hello, yerself," replied the child as she seated herself properly on the bench. "Is this the man we are going with?" Before Kit could answer, Mary went on. "We're going on a hunting feast. Do ye ken what a hunting feast is?" Again, before anyone could respond, she said in her high-pitched voice, " 'Tis when we eat outside, but we have to mind our manners just the same as if we were at the table. Can ye mind yer manners?"

"Of course, I can. I have verra good manners."

Mary got on her knees to look out the window again.

Hugh's eyes wandered back to the woman in front of him. He looked upward past her round hips and narrow waist, to linger on her firm bosom for a moment, and he felt a familiar surge of desire. His eyes moved to her face. She held her mouth in a tight grimace, but there was no mistaking her ethereal beauty. He might fall in love with her, if it weren't for the fact that the object of his affection had every intention of cutting off his head.

He returned to his accustomed casual banter in hopes of winning the fair lady over. "I'll admit I have ne'er been beheaded before, but this is the oddest execution I have ever heard of. Mistress Juliana orders me dressed in this fancy outfit, and now we're in this carriage with royalty, no less. Is this the way 'tis done in this part of Scotland?"

Her lips twisted into a patronizing smile. "Nay, 'tis no' the way 'tis done here or anywhere else. As long as Captain Rand is away, I choose to indulge Juliana. 'Tis her request that yer death be delayed one more day. 'Twas my request that Mary come along with us as a chaperone. I think she will enjoy her own small hunting feast."

Hugh laughed out loud. "Are we really going on a hunting feast? Surely ye jest."

"If ye dinna want to go, I'm certain we can rouse the executioner and take yer head right now."

"Nay, mistress," he said quickly. "I love to eat outside. What will ye tell yer captain when he returns?"

Katherine shifted uncomfortably in her seat. "We

will tell him naught. Despite what he thinks, I'm perfectly safe from the likes of ye."

"Perfectly safe," Hugh assured her, but he so wished she weren't.

Katherine and the old woman had given him another chance to save his neck, and he had better not waste it. He had one more day to convince Katherine that he was more valuable to her alive than dead. One more day to use his celebrated charm to its best advantage.

Hugh, spreading out his arms and trying to appear as if he were enjoying a perfectly ordinary day and a perfectly ordinary carriage ride, asked, "How is it that ye came to be the protector of a queen? Lord Arran made an unusual choice in a woman, especially since I've been told he is in line for the throne himself."

"So ye do ken a little about the succession of the crown," she said, rolling her eyes, "but no' enough to make sense of it. Mary's regent is the great-grandson of King James II, who is also Mary's great-great-grandfather. Until Mary was born, the earl was next in line for the throne after her father, James V, but now as her regent he has responsibility for all royal decisions."

"That makes his choice of a woman guardian even more absurd."

Hugh didn't notice her shoulders stiffen or her eyes narrow as she said, "A woman was King James's request. He wanted a specially trained protector, and he didn't trust male guards and soldiers who had no' protected him when he was held captive by his stepfather. King James specifically wanted a woman."

"But how can a woman defeat a man in a contest of strength?"

Leaning forward, Kit pointed her finger at his face. "Do ye think a woman canna do the job? I'll have ye ken that I am more than capable. Rand trained me well, and I am as qualified, if no' more so, than any man. Especially a bampot like ye."

He bolted up straight. Hoping his face didn't give away his alarm at having angered her, he held her gaze with steady, warm eye contact. "I have no doubt ye are, but ye must admit, 'tis unusual for a young woman to have so much responsibility. It doesna leave ye much time for, shall we say, personal amusement."

"I'm certain ye make up for my lack of amusement."

So far, his very last chance to keep his head was not going well. He would try to assuage Mistress Katherine another way. "Mary, if I may call ye that…"

The child got off her knees and sat down, snuggling beside Katherine. "Ye may," she said. "What is it ye want to say?"

"I would like to ken what yer favorite pastime is."

Mary's finger went to the corner of her mouth as she folded her lips inward in thought. After a moment, she said, "I like it best when Kit teaches me things like how to ride the horses. The next best is when we go for walks, and she tells me all about the different trees and flowers. Did ye ken that I can name thirty-seven different kinds of trees?"

"Nay, I didna ken that. Thirty-seven is quite a few."

The queen scrunched up her face. "There are many, many more than that in the world. Someday I want to ken all of them."

Suddenly an idea came to Hugh. "Perhaps we can

get out and walk, and ye can show me some of the trees and flowers ye ken. Would that be all right, mistress, if Mary and I walk?"

Several things wandered through his mind in asking Katherine to get out and walk. It might be easier for him to escape, though that prospect didn't look too promising with so many guards close by. His other thought was that his natural charm might be more potent in a natural setting. A stroll through a sunny meadow often brought on romantic feelings in a woman, generous and forgiving feelings, especially if a child were nearby.

After some hesitation, Katherine called out, "Miles, stop the carriage. We will walk for a while. Stay close to us."

"Aye, mistress!" said Miles, bounding down from the driver's seat and ordering the other soldiers to dismount.

Quickly, Hugh opened the carriage door and jumped to the ground. Roughly pushing Miles's hand aside, he extended his own. He would be the only gentleman Katherine saw today.

"May I escort ye and the child, mistress?" he asked.

She nodded, took his hand, and stepped out. After Hugh lifted Mary from the carriage, the three of them walked across the lush meadow where the sweet smell of grass and brush filled the air. Mary pointed at and named all the trees she recognized. Then she ran ahead to pick some grass and blow it into the wind.

" 'Tis a prestigious job ye have been given," Hugh said, "one that other women must envy, living in the luxury of court, having servants to work for ye."

Slowly, she turned her head in his direction, and in a voice that pinned back his ears, she said, "So other women envy me? Why? Because 'tis an easy job to care for a child? Because I get royal favors for doing naught but living with the queen? If ye think that's true, ye're as addled as a blind squirrel!"

Immediately, he gave her a deep bow. "Please, forgive me, mistress, for my ignorance."

"I am a trained soldier, trained the same as any man in service. I am bound to keep our queen safe and alive against armies of men who want to harm her. A responsibility ye canna handle. How dare ye think I am like ye, a ridiculous skamelar, a parasite, living off other people's hard work and none of yer own."

He straightened up. "On many occasions I have been told I'm a fool, this being one of them. I sincerely apologize."

She turned her back on him, breathing heavily.

He had made a fine mess of this. Glancing back at the guards following them, Hugh gave a questioning shrug. *Now what?*

Miles, his lips curling in disgust, waved for Hugh to come over to him. "Against my wish to be rid of ye, I have a bit of advice. Let her be until she calms down. She'll speak again when she's ready, but no' before. If ye interrupt her now, ye will suffer for it."

"Thank ye for the advice."

Miles bit out the words but kept his voice low. " 'Tis no' for yer good I say it. 'Twill save the rest of us getting on the wrong end of her tongue as well."

"She is fierce, then?"

Miles gripped the hilt of his sword and rattled it in its scabbard. "She is in command of the house. She has to be fierce. Men try to trample all over her to get to the queen, so she doesna have a choice. She can ne'er relax, ne'er enjoy herself. She has to be always on her guard, to be always one step ahead of the queen's enemies, so hence yer beheading. Mind yer tongue if ye ken what's good for ye."

Hugh waited patiently until Katherine eventually turned back to face him. Even with her obvious resentment toward him, she was still the most beautiful woman he'd ever seen. Her cheeks, showing a rosy glow, accentuated a silky neck that longed to be kissed. Her collarbone called for him to run his thumb softly along its rounded edge.

She pointed across the field. "Do ye see the River Esk on the far side of the hill?"

It took him a second to pull his gaze from her to the river. "Aye, mistress."

" 'Tis a kind of dividing line that marks the boundary of Pinkie Cleugh. A messenger arrived a sennight ago with news that Mary's regent wants Mary to wed French royalty and has begun negotiations."

"That means he will reject any proposal from the English King Edward, so why send me with one?"

"The English havena given up on arranging a marriage, but my job is to prevent any marriage to anyone and to keep her safe from being kidnapped and forced to wed or, worse, being murdered. I dinna ken why Somerset sent ye, but I am prepared to defend Mary from all sides."

Katherine motioned for the guards, Marsh and James, to bring two heavy chests over to her. "Mary," she called, "come back to me. We are about to eat."

Without looking back at her, Hugh said, "That

reminds me, I haven't eaten anything today. I hope the cook made something good."

"She always does. Marsh, please, open this chest with the food for me. Now hand me the quilt."

"Aye, mistress," said Marsh.

The breeze ruffled Hugh's hair. Sunshine and food were just what he needed, and, of course, a reprieve from his execution.

"Help!" she cried out.

He turned immediately.

A three-way battle raged between Katherine, the quilt, and the wind, and so far the wind had the upper hand. She wanted the quilt on the ground at her feet, and the wind preferred somewhere over the next hill.

"Help me with this!" she ordered as the quilt whipped over her, covering her completely. All four guards stepped forward, pulling the obstinate cloth off her face, but the wind continued to plaster it across her body, delineating her curvaceous figure.

"No' ye," she said sharply to the guards. "Him! What is yer name?"

"Hugh."

"Get over here, Hugh! Can ye no' see I need help, or do men no' practice chivalry where ye come from?"

The wind blew long wisps of her hair across her face as if begging him to brush them away. Her azure eyes squinted against the sun while her fingers gripped the insurgent quilt as if determined to show it her strength of will. He saw her mouth turn down in a frown, and he still wanted desperately to kiss it. He suspected that even if she never surrendered her body to him, he would still want her.

He bounded up the hill and, grabbing a corner of

the quilt, wrestled it to the ground. She flopped down on another corner and brushed the hair out of her eyes.

Mary, who had giggled delightfully through the entire episode, jumped down and sat on the third corner. "We won!" she exclaimed.

"I'm sorry, mistress, for no' coming to yer rescue sooner," said Hugh. "Please, forgive me again." He smoothed out the quilt before saying, "Let me help ye unload the chest."

Hugh lifted a variety of crockery dishes out of the ornately carved container. One held salted beef, another salted fish. Carrageen jelly filled another bowl while others held stuffed eggs, and still others carried cooked spiced apples and pears sprinkled with nuts. The last two crocks nearly overflowed with apple beer and spiced wine.

"All this food and there are only three of us?" asked Hugh.

Kit looked at him from beneath long, dark lashes. "I count eight unless ye feel 'tis proper to let yer guards go hungry. No wonder they're so anxious to execute ye."

Hugh's stomach tensed again. By now any other lady's heart would have melted, but his formerly reliable boyish appeal didn't work with this woman. Although, he did understand why she was so cold toward him. He'd been sent by her enemy to do her and her young charge harm, and he proved his evil intentions by stealing from her what she should have freely offered, her kiss.

In her mind, he was nothing but a problem to be eliminated without a minute's sorrow. He needed her to understand that, although he might be a man flawed in many ways, he deserved her kindness and her mercy. Only complete truthfulness remained for him. He needed to speak with the kind of honesty previously reserved only for when his father disciplined him. Perhaps it was time to admit that his father was right.

"Mistress Katherine," began Hugh, "Mistress Juliana warned me to no' let my mouth say careless things, and I beg yer pardon." He nodded to the soldiers standing behind her. "And yers as well."

They halfheartedly nodded a reply.

"I have made many mistakes in my life," said Hugh as he spread out the crocks of food. "I'm a gambler and a rogue, and since I was twenty years old, I have spent too much time drinking and wagering. I am sorry to have hurt anyone else, but the truth is the person who lost the most was me."

Her expression reverted to one of total indifference.

"Please, believe me when I tell ye that I have no interest in the politics that call for a marriage between little Mary and the king of England. Honestly, I dinna ken or care anything about the reasons for it."

"I believe ye're as uninformed as ye say," she said. She took the lid off two dishes, stuck her finger in one, and licked off the sweet jelly.

He slowly dragged air in through his nose. This woman demanded more from him than his charm. She required candor and sincerity, and he had better be prepared to give it. She had to know the whole truth about him and nothing less.

"Ye ken that sending me north was a condition of my pardon," he said.

"Pardon?" said Miles, moving closer with his hand

on the hilt of his sword. "Ye're a murderer?"

"Nay," said Hugh quickly, putting his hand up to keep Miles back. "A man died accidentally after an argument with me. He fell and hit his head on a rock. I didna touch him, I swear. 'Twas an accident."

Kit said, "Ye told me the story, no' that it makes any difference. The man is still dead."

" 'Twas my fault it happened, and I'll regret it for the rest of my life." He lowered his eyes.

Smearing a slice of bread with jelly, she handed it to Mary, who gobbled it up, covering her chin with the yellowish sweet. Kit prepared one slice for him and then more for each of her guards.

Looking up at her again, he said, "I have had a lot of time to think since I left to come here, mostly about how much I want to get back north to Makgullane. The last words my father said to me were 'Take this dagger to keep ye safe until love brings ye home.' I want to get home to him and my family more than anything. I dinna have the dagger anymore, but I will always have his love."

Without acknowledging Hugh's remarks, Kit picked up a knife and cut eight hunks of cheese off the small wheel. Taking one for herself, she passed the rest to the others. Wiping off Mary's face, she asked the child, "Do ye want some cheese?" Mary took a small piece from Kit's hand.

Hugh went on, wondering if anyone listened to or cared what he had to say. "If I dinna complete the pardon, I'll be a hunted outlaw for the rest of my life. I'll ne'er see my family or my home again."

He bit into the cheese, but he couldn't swallow it. His story sounded so poor, not at all like the man he needed to be for her, the man she wanted him to be.

When had this change come over him? This desire to please another more than pleasing himself? All at once he knew. It happened in the woods when she punched him in the jaw and kicked him in the gut. She had bested him, and instead of it making him angry, it made him understand she was the kind of woman he needed by his side if he was ever going to find his place in the world.

"If ye're looking for sympathy here, ye willna find it," said Katherine bluntly. "Consequences for mistakes are often serious. If ye had no' led a life of depravity, ye would no' have ended up here. Ye brought this on yerself, and whining about it willna help."

He gritted his teeth. He wanted her to rescind her order of execution because she admired him for accepting responsibility for his actions, not because she felt sorry for him. He had already chastised himself endlessly over Walton's death. He didn't need any more of it from her!

"I'm no' looking for yer sympathy." He jumped to his feet, surrounded seconds later by Miles and the rest of the guard with their weapons drawn.

Fixing a stare on Katherine's startled face, he said in a heated voice, "Juliana sent us out here because she hoped it would make it harder for ye to execute me. Well, I'll make it easier. I'm tired of that sick feeling in my stomach every time somebody doesna approve of me. I'm tired of humiliating myself to plead for my life. Kill me! Lop my head off and send it to the king! I dinna care! Just do it!"

He whirled away from her.

Chapter Eight

Mary's brilliant blue eyes widen in alarm. "Stop! Dinna hurt the man! He wants to ken the names of the trees. I must tell him."

Quickly Katherine pulled the child into her lap. "I willna let the soldiers hurt him. I promise. Would ye like to lie down on the quilt and take a nap while Miles sits here with ye? When ye wake up, ye can tell the man all about the trees."

Wiping her eyes and her nose with the back of her hand, Mary nodded and curled up on the quilt. She was asleep almost immediately.

Kit walked up behind Hugh and touched him on the shoulder. She said quietly, "Ye dinna mean that."

His head dropped back in exasperation. "Nay."

"Perhaps there is a true man beneath the rogue, a man capable of real emotions, instead of covering them over with clever words and an easy smile."

He didn't answer.

To the soldiers, Kit said, "Miles, sit on the quilt beside Mary. The prisoner and I are going over the hill. Watch from the crest, but dinna come any closer."

"Mistress," Miles protested, "I'll no' leave yer side. I'm sworn to protect ye."

"Miles, please, we will no' move out of yer sight, I promise. I only want to honor Mistress Juliana's request by talking to Hugh privately. I'm confident that ye will see to Mary's and my safety."

Miles nodded, knowing his first duty was obedience to his mistress even if it meant bearing Captain Rand's wrath later, which he was certain would come when the captain arrived back at Fawside.

Miles barked at his soldiers. "Spread out along the ridge. Arm yerselves and be prepared to kill if he does anything suspicious, and I mean anything!"

"Thank ye," said Katherine.

Taking Hugh's hand in hers, she led him down the hill to the clear, flowing stream in the gully below. Squatting at the water's edge underneath the canopy of oaks, she pulled him down to his knees beside her. Leaning over, she dipped her hand in the stream and let the water gently ripple over it. Without warning, she splashed cold water on his face, soaking his tunic.

He reeled back, sputtering, "What the...?" He laughed with her. "I canna believe ye did that."

"Do ye want to splash me back?" she asked, still laughing and waving her hand through the water. "Answer me true."

His eyes crinkled with his smile. "Aye, I do."

"Then do it."

He glanced back up the hill at the grim-faced soldiers standing in a line, their swords drawn and crossbows loaded.

"Marsh," Katherine called out to Miles's second-in-command, "if I get wet, ye will no' do a thing. Do ye understand?"

Marsh nodded, but his face looked black with doubt about his mistress's judgment.

"Do it," she said to Hugh. Her rosy cheeks and beaming smile engulfed her face.

He couldn't refuse, and soon the unquestioned mistress of Fawside Castle dripped water from her face to her waist.

Laughing, she fell back on the grass as she wiped the water from her cheeks. "Tell me about yer family, the one ye miss so much."

He sat back on his haunches. "I am the oldest of now seven bairns of Robin and Suannoch of Makgullane. They adopted me when I was ten at the same time with my adopted brother, Fergus, who was seven. Before that I was an orphaned street urchin."

"So that's where ye learned to gamble and shame yer family?"

He answered sheepishly, " 'Twould seem so."

"Tell me more about this Robin and Suannoch." She pulled up some grass and tossed it in the air, smirking as the wind caught the blades and blew them into his face.

Spitting grass out of his mouth, he answered, "Ye dinna want to hear about them. Ye only want to hear what a terrible person I am."

She sat up, and their eyes met. "Aye, at first, I did only want to hear terrible things about ye, but now I want to ken who ye really are."

"Only if ye tell me who ye really are."

"All right, I dinna ken who my birth parents were, but they were of some means, since I was left with the church when I was verra young. Whatever dowry I had was given to the king in return for his support of the church, and he in turn gave it to his captain of the guard as a reward."

"Ye were sold to the captain of the guard?"

"No' exactly. I wed him. I had ne'er met him, but

my sixteenth birthday and my wedding were the same day."

Hugh came up on his knees, his fists clenched. "Was it Rand?"

"Nay. 'Twas Rand's brother, but four years later, when he died, Rand saved me from being given to another man when he took me to train to protect the infant queen."

"I am sorry," whispered Hugh.

A soft chuckle left Kit's mouth. "Dinna be sorry. I was treated well, far better than many lasses. At least my original dowry kept me safe in the convent. Other orphans are abandoned to the streets as ye were."

Hugh nodded.

"In many ways, I am much better off than the queen of Scotland." She glanced over at the still sleeping Mary. "She is trapped by her crown. I would no' wish anyone to be queen."

For nearly two hours, Katherine and Hugh exchanged stories of their childhoods.

"I dinna remember much that was good until I came to live with Robin," said Hugh. "He showed me that no' every day had to be a fight. He is a verra fine man, and my mum, Suannoch, is an equally fine woman."

"I ne'er had to fight for anything until I met Rand," said Kit. "Everything around me was quiet and calm...so dull. Some days the spoon clicking against the bowl when I ate was the only sound I heard all day. Sometimes the only excitement came when the soup burned my lips."

Hugh chuckled. "I often prayed for days when the only excitement would be hot soup."

"Rand changed everything for me, and I'll be forever grateful that he did."

"Robin changed everything for me, too, until that old itch reared up, and I left for the freedom I thought I was missing. Life in London in the taverns was ne'er dull, and I thought I could control it, but it turns out I couldna."

A pair of little arms wrapped around Kit's neck.

"Ye're awake," she said to a smiling Mary.

"Aye! What are ye doing? I want to do it."

"Have ye heard of the Midsummer's Eve custom of the wet fire ceremony?" Hugh asked.

"Have I?" Mary asked Kit. "I dinna think so. How do ye play it?"

"First, everyone carves a small wooden boat. Then we write wishes on a small piece of paper that we put in the boats under a lighted candle. We set them adrift in the stream, and whichever one reaches the other side first with the candle still lit, that wish comes true. I'm always verra lucky. My wishes come true almost every year."

Jumping up and down and clapping her hands, Mary said, "Can we, Kit? Can we play? I have my wish already. Please!"

"All right," said Kit. "We will each make a wish, but dinna tell anyone, and since we have no boats to carve, we can play with leaves and acorn tops."

"One wish," said Hugh. "I ken exactly what mine will be." She would have to grant it, and he would keep his head. "Mary, may I help ye choose yer leaf and acorn?"

"Aye," the girl said, taking Hugh's hand.

Hugh scoured the ground and the branches of a

half-dozen trees close to the stream. The leaves were all too small or too thin, but he finally found one for Mary and then another one just right to save his neck. The acorn top was easier. He picked the two smallest ones he could find.

"Are ye ready?" asked Katherine.

"Almost," said Hugh. He carefully laid his acorn top on his leaf and then helped Mary get hers ready.

"Make yer wish," said Katherine, "but keep it to yerself until we see who wins."

Mary scrunched her eyes tightly shut before saying, "I ken my wish."

"Ready? Launch."

Three broad, green leaves with tiny acorn tops in their centers floated gently into the water. The current pulled them downstream, around rocks and over the burbling white water, while Hugh, Katherine, and Mary trotted along the bank beside them. Soon the leafy boats left the shaded canopy of the small grove and floated into the bright sunshine.

"Mary, did ye ken that the sun makes a halo of reddish gold around yer hair?" he asked.

"Aye. Juliana calls it my crown. 'Tis no' as heavy as the real crown. Look! The leaves are almost to the other side."

Each leaf took a turn coming closest to the other bank, but then floated away. In complete unison, all three leaves landed on the other side.

"Look!" Hugh cried.

Kit hadn't seen the end of the race. She had been staring at his face and his smile.

"Look," he said again, pointing to the opposite side of the stream.

Her eyes followed his finger to the leaves. When she saw them pushing against the bank, side by side, she shouted, "We win! We all win!"

Whooping a cheer of victory, he hugged his arms around her waist, picked her up and spun her around. They fell over each other into the grass and down the gentle slope. "Huzzah! Both our wishes will come true."

Mary raced after them and jumped on Hugh's back as he sprawled across Kit.

Kit and Hugh's eyes met and shouted hundreds of secret wishes, dreams that neither of them dared express as long as she was the guardian and he was the man sent to steal the child from her.

"Mistress!" shouted Miles.

"I'm fine. Dinna come closer!" she shouted back.

Her breath came in jagged gasps. When her breath steadied again, she asked, "What is yer wish?"

"What I wished for when I set the leaf in the water is no' the wish I want granted now," he said, sweeping a wisp of damp chestnut hair off her cheek with his forefinger. "I want something more important."

"Tell me what ye wished."

His thumb stroked her cheek. Leaning in, his mouth nearly touched hers as he said, "My wish is to call ye Kit."

Stretching her neck toward him, she said, "Call me Kit? Is that all?"

"It would mean a lot to me."

"I grant yer wish. What is yer wish, Mary?"

"I want ye to kiss! I want ye to kiss! Kiss the man, Kit! Kiss him!"

A blush rose in Kit's cheeks. Turning her face

95

toward his ear, she murmured so only he could hear, "I, too, wished that ye would kiss me."

He leaned in. "I surrender my life for yer kiss." That is exactly what he did now. He traded his chance at freedom for one more taste of her soft, rich lips, traded it for one more minute close to this incredible woman. He slowly caressed her cheek until their mouths met. "My life for yer kiss, mistress."

"Kit," she corrected as she began tasting his mouth.

He whispered the words slowly and distinctly, "My lady, Kit."

Their kiss began soft and delicate, sweeter than the one in the forest. She gave what was rightfully hers, and he didn't have to steal it. Their mouths teased and tempted each other, sometimes lightheartedly and other times intimately. They became part of each other as their tongues exchanged passion and joy. She arched her back to press her breasts and hips into him while she wrapped her arms around his neck, pulling him even closer.

Moving his hands gently, he stroked his thumb along the top of her shoulder and along her collarbone.

"Let me give ye a thousand kisses," he whispered, "A thousand and then a thousand more."

Suddenly Mary stopped clapping her hands.

"Release her," said Captain Rand, pressing a cold blade of steel against Hugh's neck. "Right now! Take him!"

Two pairs of rough hands grabbed Hugh's arms and lifted him to his feet, but he didn't even try to shake off his captors. Instead, he looked at Kit, waiting. All she had to do was say the word, and they would release him. He cocked his head, waiting for her to explain that everything had changed between them. He waited.

"Mistress, may I help ye up?" said Rand, offering his hand to Kit.

She nodded and was soon on her feet, brushing herself off. Taking the hand of young Mary, she let Rand lead her toward the carriage.

Now Hugh strained against the guards' tenacious grip on his arms. "Kit?" he pleaded. "Kit!"

Rand turned back and growled, "Chain him and take him to the dungeon. Tomorrow he dies."

Kit walked silently up the hill, not looking back.

Chapter Nine

Rand's anger boiled like gravy in a pot. "How could ye go anywhere with him?" he roared as he tore open the carriage door and guided her none too gently inside. "I'm the captain of the guard. Ye had no right to put yerself and our queen in danger. Ye will no' ignore me!"

Before Kit could answer, Rand slammed the carriage door shut and turned his anger on his guards. "Tie yer horses to the back of the carriage so ye can walk back to Fawside. That will give me time to think of a suitable punishment for yer disobedient actions." Spittle gathered in the corners of his mouth. "I am appalled at yer stupidity. Take off yer boots. Ye will walk home in yer stocking feet."

Kit stuck her head out the carriage window. "Dinna blame them. They obeyed my orders."

"They ken better! A condemned man is dangerous because he has naught to lose."

The furious captain grabbed Miles by the shirt, jerking him back and forth like a torn blanket. "Ye will suffer for this foolhardy expedition. I'll see to it," he shouted.

His wrath turned full force on the other soldiers and on Hugh. One by one, Rand struck each soldier and Hugh in the mouth, knocking each to the ground.

"Do ye intend to beat us all to death?" asked Hugh,

rubbing his jaw. "Because if ye are, I'll fight back, chained or no', even if the rest of them are too afraid of ye to defend themselves."

Rand's fist convulsed with suppressed rage, and his mouth tightened into a hard line. "Fight back? We'll see if ye can fight back." Grasping the chain on Hugh's wrist manacles, he dragged him over to a tree at the edge of a grove some fifteen yards off the road.

Rand unlocked one wrist manacle, pressed Hugh's face against the tree with one hand, quickly tugged the chain around the tree, and secured the metal band around Hugh's wrist again. This forced Hugh to stand, hugging the trunk with his face scraping the bark.

"Fight back now, will ye!"

To his soldiers, Rand said, "Start walking!" as he climbed into the driver's seat in the front of the carriage and slapped the reins on the horses' rumps. The carriage jerked forward.

" 'Twas no' their fault," said Kit, still leaning out the window. "They did as I told them."

"They are my soldiers, and 'twas their fault, and they will pay for their disobedience."

Little Mary clung to Kit and cried all the way back to Fawside Castle. Kit held the girl tightly and shivered herself at the consequences of her decision to give the prisoner one more day. Rand's fury at finding the man unshackled and kissing her sealed Hugh's death sentence once and for all. She had made a terrible mistake. She should have taken his head days ago and saved herself the pain of now caring for the man only to lose him anyway.

Mary stretched up and kissed Kit on the cheek. "Will Captain Rand bring the man home?"

"Aye, he will," answered Kit, sniffing to avoid her tears. No sense in telling the girl that bringing Hugh home meant his death. Or in telling her that the man and the ones who sent him were dangerous, and she should be afraid of him.

"I am sworn to protect ye," Kit said to Mary. "I will ne'er let anyone hurt ye. Do ye believe that?"

Mary nodded.

"Sometimes I have to do things for the best even if they seem bad at the time. I have to make decisions that are verra hard. Ye might even say they're cruel, but they have to be made. Sometimes they break my heart, but I do them for ye because ye're the most important person in the whole world to me."

Mary nestled against Kit.

Katherine remembered her pledge on the day she first became Mary's guardian, and she whispered it now. "I pledge on my honor and my life to forfeit all I am, and all I have, in the protection of the life and well-being of Queen Mary of Scotland. From this moment on, my life belongs to her, and no sacrifice will be too great."

Today the full impact of that lifelong promise hit her hard.

The rain started just as the coach entered the yard around the castle, and it continued throughout the night.

The rain with its continuous lightning and thunder showed no sign of abating at midnight when Kit gave up trying to sleep. She dressed and went to the kitchen to find something to eat for herself and little Mary, who had also tossed and turned all night.

Lost in thought about the man chained to a tree, she sliced off large chunks of cheese to have with leftover bread. Suddenly she felt a strong hand on her shoulder.

"We need to talk," said Rand, "now that I have regained my composure."

"Aye, we do," said Kit. "I couldna sleep either. I'm sorry for what happened yesterday."

"That isna our worry right now. Have ye looked out the window toward the River Esk?"

"Nay."

"Come with me." Rand led her to the top of the tower on the west side of the castle. Pointing out through the open window, he said, "Do ye see that? When the lightning flashes can ye see it? The dark mass in the distance?"

"Aye, what is it?"

" 'Tis the English army. Lord Arran has negotiated that the English may come as close as the River Esk just west of this castle. 'Tis too close, and we must be gone by first light. We'll head to Inchmahome Priory in the middle of the Lake of Menteith. 'Tis about sixty-two miles to the northwest, so pack only the essentials, as we may have to move around battle lines."

Kit began to work as she'd been trained. She gathered the guards and her staff around her with her plan to get the household ready to travel while she supervised every detail in an orderly fashion. She ordered that food be prepared that did not need cooking and could be eaten quickly, preferably without utensils. It also had to be in numerous small packages so that each person could carry their own food in case anyone got separated. Travel clothing had to be simple, sturdy, and made for easy movement through rough terrain, and all women had to wear breeches and oversized tunics.

She reminded the women to bind their breasts for their comfort when moving quickly and to carry extra rags if their womanly courses should come before they reached safety. All the women's usual slippers and soft shoes had to be traded in for sturdy, waterproof boots, and their hair had to be pulled back into a braid that could be tucked under a shirt or secured in a hat.

It was especially important that Queen Mary be disguised as a servant child. Absolutely nothing could be carried by anyone that might alert an enemy that she was royalty. Even the guards were to wear civilian clothing, as anyone recognizing their uniforms would know that the queen was nearby. By sunrise, all those within Fawside Castle had passed Katherine's inspection and were gathered in the stable ready to mount and leave at Captain Rand's instruction.

Kit searched the stable, looking for Juliana, who would need extra care in order to travel.

"Mistress!" cried the maid, Agnes. "Mistress Juliana is gone! She sent me to fetch her something to eat, and when I came back, she was gone. Joshua is gone, too, and in this storm. The stable boy said he took a cart. I'm sore afraid for her."

Kit stopped saddling her horse and dashed toward Agnes, shaking her by the shoulders. "Tell me what ye ken."

****

All night the rain poured down in cold streams, and the thunder sounded as if the gates of Hell opened with every lightning strike. Hugh, still chained to the tree at sunrise, shivered and prayed that someone would come back for him.

Then someone did.

Chapter Ten

"Where is he?" Juliana muttered from her seat in the back of a small covered cart.

The early morning sun, peeking through the sheets of rain bucketing down, allowed her only a wisp of hope that she'd find him, but she refused to go back to the castle until she did.

"Do ye see him, Joshua?" she asked the driver of her cart. "Where is he?"

"I dinna ken, mistress, but we must go back. Rain is washing the road away. The mare will lose her footing, and we'll all take a spill."

Just then the wheel on the cart caught in one of the many muddy, water-filled ruts and cracks in the road and threw her painfully to the floor.

"Sorry, mistress," said Joshua, the avener of the stable, as he reached over to lift her back onto the seat.

The horse had already reared back a half-dozen times when a lightning strike came too close for comfort, and although the driver, a strong young man of thirty years, had been able to keep the beast under control, the mare grew more skittish the longer they stayed out in the downpour.

The rain fell in unceasing rivulets over Joshua's eyebrows and down his cheeks, and as the droplets reached his mouth, he licked them away. "We have to go back, mistress. 'Twill be easier to find him after the bloody rain stops."

"Nay," said Juliana firmly. "Something terrible has happened. I can feel it, and I'll no' go back until we find him."

"Mistress, why do ye care about a man who's to be executed?"

"Dinna worry about why. Just do as I say."

"Aye, mistress."

Juliana had to find him. If only those two foolish people could give themselves a chance, Hugh would love Kit as she deserved to be loved, completely, absolutely, and until the end of time. If Juliana could bring him back, Hugh might be able to offer Kit the chance she never had—the chance to live a normal life with family, children, and love.

No one knew better than Juliana that if Kit stayed bound to little Mary for the rest of her life, she would never complete the soul God gave her on the day she was born. Kit deserved to know the joy of Heaven on earth with a man who cared for and protected her, and above all others, loved her.

Many years ago, Juliana had found perfect love with a young man named Thatcher, an apprentice blacksmith, who courted her in secret until the day Juliana's mother discovered them and, using her influence as a royal maid to the queen, had Thatcher imprisoned. Her mother told her that he'd been conscripted onto a sailing ship headed for the Indian continent, and Juliana never saw him again. Seven months later, the queen, James V's mother, chose Juliana to spend the rest of her life as nursemaid and companion to the prince, never again to call her life her own.

Sustained by only her memories of Thatcher's warm kisses and soft words for the last thirty-five years, Juliana vowed that if she had anything to say about it, Kit would have more than memories to sustain her. But first she had to find Hugh.

About two miles from the castle, she heard the call over the pounding rain.

"Over here!"

Juliana strained her ears. "Did ye hear that, Joshua?"

"I hear naught but the voice in my head saying we should go back while we still can, mistress."

"Over here! Over here!"

Through a flash of lightning, Juliana caught sight of someone beside a tree off to the side of the road. "I see him!" she said. "Over there!"

"I see him," said Joshua. " 'Tis the prisoner. I dinna think we can help him. He's chained to the tree. We should turn back right now."

"We will do no such thing. Go over to him and bring him back to the wagon. He has been out in the rain since yesterday afternoon. He'll catch his death."

"He's going to die anyway. Mistress Katherine and Captain Rand decreed it."

"Do as I say!" she ordered, shaking her cane at him.

Shrugging, Joshua did as he'd been told. He returned a few minutes later without Hugh. "He's shackled to the tree. Got no key."

"Help me down," said Juliana. Painfully, she grasped Joshua's arm and hobbled on crooked legs over to the tree where Hugh sat chained. "Did Rand leave ye here to die?"

"Nay, mistress. He'd take too much pleasure in seeing me lose my head. It seems he doesna like outings by the stream."

"Oh, dear," said Juliana. "It seems that no one does."

Hugh smiled through teeth that chattered relentlessly. "I enjoyed it up until the part where I had to walk home in irons. Do ye have a key to these shackles?"

"Nay. Joshua, give me yer pick for cleaning out a horse's hoof."

Joshua handed her a narrow, pointed tool with an iron grip from his belt. Barely able to force her twisted fingers over the hand grip, Juliana pushed the pointed end into the keyhole on one of the wrist manacles. Concentrating, she twisted the tool, pulling it up and down, and twisting it again.

The manacle fell from his arm. Quickly, he jumped to his feet, rubbing that wrist. "Can ye do the other one?"

Again, Juliana inserted the hoof pick and released it.

"Thank ye, mistress," said Hugh with a bow. "I'll be out of sight afore ye ken it. I'll remember ye!" he shouted as he started running up the road. "Ye saved me from losing my head, and I'll be truly grateful wherever I go for as long as I live."

He had only gone a short way when a flash of lightning touched the earth mere yards in front of him, and the accompanying rumbling thunder sent him reeling. Seconds later, the horse and wagon raced toward him from behind as the terrified mare ran for her life. The cart brushed past him, and as he fell to the ground, the wheel of the cart rattled over his ankle.

"Can ye walk, lad?" asked Joshua as he ran by chasing after his runaway mare. "The cart's no' heavy, and if yer boots are strong, ye'll be all right. 'Tis Mistress Juliana's wish to set ye free, so be off now. If ye come upon my horse afore I do, tie her to a tree."

"What about Juliana?" asked Hugh, sprawled out in the mud and rubbing his tender ankle. "She should no' be out in the rain."

" 'Tis what I been telling her, but I have to get the horse and cart afore I can take her back. She canna walk, ye ken." Joshua started down the hill after the horse already nearly out of sight.

"I'll get her back to the castle," shouted Hugh through the downpour of rain.

Joshua turned back to look at him. "Captain Rand says he's taking yer head. Ye best be away while ye have the chance. Mistress will be all right under that tree."

"No' in this storm. I'll get her back to the castle."

Joshua shrugged and took off loping after the runaway mare and cart.

Slowly, Hugh sloshed through the mire back to the tree where he'd left Juliana.

"Mistress," he said when he reached her crouching under the meager shelter of the branches, "yer carriage awaits." He held out his arms.

Between coughs, she said, "Ye came back."

"I couldna leave ye. Ye're lame from the rheumatism and helpless against the elements. Besides, if I can see ye back to the safety and warmth of home, I can repay ye for the faith ye've shown in me by trying to get Kit to let me keep my head. I'll leave ye in sight of the gate and then be gone meself."

"I would rather ye go free now."

"And I would rather take ye home." Scooping up her tiny body, he headed in the direction of the castle. Hoping it might be drier under the cover of the trees, he entered the woods with Juliana in his arms.

After the pair struggled through the thick underbrush for almost an hour, Juliana said, "Put me down for a bit. Ye need to rest."

"I'm fine," said Hugh. "How much farther is it to the castle?" He pushed a low branch out of the way with his shoulder and stepped around it, releasing it only when the two of them were past it.

"Another mile. Put me down. I want to rest."

Hugh set his would-be rescuer on a stump and stretched his arms behind him to ease his cramped muscles. Twisting his head from side to side, he let out a low moan of relief.

"I kenned ye needed a rest," said Juliana. "I might no' weigh verra much, but ye have barely shifted my position since ye picked me up. I wish we could go faster, but I'm no' up to it." Her body shook with a shiver that rattled her teeth, followed by a deep cough.

Taking off his cape, really another dead man's bright blue-green cape, Hugh draped it over her shoulders. " 'Tis just as wet as every other piece of our clothing, but its thickness might keep ye a little warmer."

"Thank ye, lad. It does help."

Rubbing his arms to get his blood flowing, he said, "Would ye happen to have a loaf of bread hidden anywhere? My stomach is growling."

"I wish I did, lad, but those blackberries over there

are edible." She pointed to a bush a few yards ahead of them. Lifting the edge of his tunic, she said, "Fill this, and bring some back to me."

He nodded and forced his way through the dense underbrush to the berries.

Juliana looked back to the road. There sat Kit on her horse with her outer cape soaked with rain and a panic-filled look on her face.

****

As soon as Hugh was a few yards away with his back to her, Kit jumped down from the horse and dashed through the thicket toward Juliana, only to come to a sudden stop when Juliana put out her hands and waved her back. Kit opened her mouth to speak, but Juliana quickly put her finger to her lips and mouthed the words, "Go back." She repeated the phrase three times, before Kit glowered and walked back to her horse.

Kit leaned against her saddle and watched as Hugh returned to Juliana with the hem of his tunic loaded with juicy berries. Carefully, he took out a handful and presented them to Juliana, who nibbled at them one by one. When she'd had enough, she motioned for Hugh to take his share, and in three mouthfuls the berries were gone.

He had fed an old woman first. Could there be other kindnesses lurking beneath the quick-tongued, wayward exterior he presented to the world? What courage it took for him to carry Juliana back to the place where he'd been condemned to death. This kind of selfless act didn't appear randomly. Such a characteristic had to be inborn, and not every man had such traits.

Then Kit remembered her pledge to protect young Mary. She could wish that Hugh might become the man she wanted in her life, but some things could never be.

****

"She's following us," Juliana whispered in Hugh's ear after he picked her up, and they started walking again.

"I ken," said Hugh, stepping over a fallen log. "I saw her when we got the berries. Why does she no' call for help? There must be others out looking for ye. After all, I'm a desperate man."

Juliana's twisted finger touched Hugh's cheek. "Love her," she said, and his startled expression told her what she wanted to know, that he already did. "Tell me how she makes ye feel."

He scowled. "She turned me over to Captain Rand and the guards."

"She was afraid. Tell me what ye feel for her."

Hugh ducked his head to avoid a low hanging branch. After a moment's hesitation, he said, " 'Tis odd, and I canna explain it. I ne'er felt this way about any woman afore, but the first time I saw Kit, I saw such extraordinary beauty and wonder in her eyes. When I saw her looking back at me, it somehow changed me, ye ken, inside. Has been like that every time I see her."

"Any man can see beauty in a woman's eyes, in her face, in her body," said Juliana in a scolding tone.

" 'Tis more than that. She makes me catch my breath, and the only way I can breathe again is when she smiles. 'Tis odd, but right now all I want to be is the man she sees, the man she needs me to be."

"Do ye love her?"

110

He paused again. "If what I feel for Kit is love, it must be true. I have ne'er been in love. Still, what good would it do if I were? She needs to protect the wee queen, and as long as she thinks I'm a threat, I have to accept that we're no' meant to be together."

"Set me down again," said Juliana sharply. "I have to talk to ye face to face."

Hugh found a fallen log to put her on and knelt before her.

"The only choices a woman in royal service has are those allowed her by the queen or king, but many years ago, I found love, true, deep love," began Juliana, "and everyone said it could ne'er be, that I was too young, that he was no' of my station, that he had no right to want me. I started to believe what they said was true, but when I finally decided his love was worth the taking, it became the experience of a lifetime."

"Was it with the man whose clothes I'm wearing?"

"Nay, dear lad. Thatcher and I, we were young, but we wed secretly. I only kenned him for eighteen months. 'Twas no' easy, but I listened to my heart, and the passion I had for him, and he for me, still burns in me after all these years. Do ye ken how a woman becomes a nursemaid to royal princes?"

He shook his head.

"She has a bairn, and the milk in her breasts meant for that bairn is given to another."

"Ye have a bairn?"

"Nay, my wee boy was stolen from me. I ne'er held him or saw him or his father again." Juliana seemed to drift away, lost in a memory. In a voice so soft, Hugh almost couldn't hear her, she said, "Thatcher taught me how to love and laugh and live, but I ne'er learned to forget him."

She snapped her head around to face him. "Dinna let that happen to Katherine. She has her duty, but ye have her heart. Dinna leave her with only memories."

Although stunned at the intensity of her words, Hugh said, "I want to get ye out of this rain." He lifted her into his arms again.

"I have more to tell ye," said Juliana. "If ye are to be strong enough for Kit, ye must understand what she faces. Listen carefully."

He stepped over yet another low bush, easily lifting Juliana's small frame around the obstacle.

"Kit has led a sheltered life."

"I ken. She told me how she was orphaned and sent to a convent and how the church gave her inheritance, or at least part of it, as her dowry to a man she didna even ken."

"Aye, all that is true. The man was older and set in his ways, but he treated her kindly. All she was required to do was service him on occasion and knit shawls for the poor. The life nearly bored her to death. Then he died, and Rand, seeing the strength of her personality, saved her from another possibly worse marriage by convincing King James and Queen Margaret that Katherine would make a protector for the infant not-yet-born. No one would expect a woman to be guarding the babe, but Rand could make Kit capable enough to keep the child safe.

"Even though Kit leads the guards and servants and they obey her, her life isna her own. Queen Mary owns Kit's life, and Mary will ne'er release it. Even if Mary dies, Kit will still be bound to her. Her fate is no different from mine."

Finally, the rain started to let up, and sunshine and its warmth found its way through the wet leaves. Juliana stopped shivering.

"I dinna ken how I can change that," said Hugh.

"I am an old woman, and I dinna have much time to do what I can for Kit. She needs someone to stand beside her, to work with her, to share her burden. It has been all on her shoulders long enough."

"Why me, the man she condemned to lose his head?"

"Because ye're clever enough to be trained."

His brow knitted into a tight line. "Trained? Like a schoolboy who needs a good thrashing to set him on the right path?"

"If I could thrash ye myself, ye would be the better for it," she said, shaking her finger in his face. "Ye have to show Kit that behind that handsome face is a hard-working, honest, resourceful young man. She will sacrifice her heart before she sacrifices her duty. Ye must prove yer worth before ye can prove yer love, and ye must do it soon. The threats to the queen grow more terrible every day."

"If I stay with her, 'twill no' be because of politics."

"Aye, lad, I ken why ye'll stay. Ye're young and full of vigor, and ye want to make love to her. Every time ye think of her, yer body shouts for ye to make love to her."

He stopped walking and looked her squarely in the eyes. "I was going to say that I would stay because she is a woman who needs my help." With a wink and a sly smile, he added, "But ye're right, I do want to make love to her."

"There is plenty of time for that," she said, "providing ye ken how a woman takes her pleasure."

"Juliana!" He hoisted her higher in his arms and continued walking. "I am no schoolboy."

"But dinna do it until ye're ready to be everything she needs. Ye have a great deal to learn first. There are tales to be told, and ye will have to work harder than ye ever have because of them. Ye will be bruised and battered inside and out before 'tis over, and ye still may no' win. I canna fight this battle for ye. The only thing I can do is give ye a bit of time to show her what yer soul is really like. The rest is up to ye."

The forest and the rain ended at the same time. Hugh set Juliana down on a large moss-covered rock under a knotted oak tree.

In front of them, atop a tall, steep hill sat Fawside Castle. To their right along the edge of the cleugh flowed the River Esk. Closing in on the flat plain on the other side of that river marched the English army, and the rumbling of their wagons, cannons, and troops filled the air.

"They're nearly to the river," said Juliana. "We haven't much time. They'll take the advantage to attack the castle before the Scottish troops get here. We have to hurry, or we'll be caught in the middle. Quickly, one more thing for ye."

Juliana reached into the lining of her overdress and pulled out an orange scarf with a yellow full moon and three stars embroidered on either end. She handed it to Hugh. "I made this for Thatcher, and I have carried it ever since. I want ye to have it."

Hugh eyed her skeptically. "Why do ye keep giving me things from dead men? It doesna bode well for my success."

Her sky-lit eyes blazed at him. " 'Tis a great treasure of mine, but if ye're going to be ungrateful, I want it back." She snatched at the scarf, but Hugh hastily lifted it out of her reach.

"I'm no' ungrateful, mistress," he said as he tied the favor around his neck. "I thank ye for this remembrance. Do ye think we can make it up the hill to the castle?"

"I can make it. Are ye ready to face what's ahead? Do ye understand everything I have told ye, and ye're no' afeared?"

"I understand, mistress, and 'tis why I am afeared. There is danger here outside and even more once we get inside the castle door, especially for me. Ye're asking me to risk my life to take ye there."

She wagged a crooked finger at him again. "I'm no' asking ye to do anything, lad. Ye're asking it of yerself. Dinna ever make me choose between Katherine and ye because…" She didn't finish her statement, but Hugh knew what she would say. *Ye will lose.*

He grinned, and two half-moon creases appeared in his cheeks around his mouth. "Mistress, I am facing the worst odds of any wager I have ever made."

Her swollen fingers stroked his cheek. "Keep yer wits about ye, lad."

Hugh scooped up her small body in his arms again and started running up the grassy hill, only to be stopped by a horse pulling up directly in front of them.

"Far enough!" the rider shouted.

Hugh swung around to avoid the horses' hooves coming down on his head.

"Katherine!" cried Juliana. "Ye're here. We have

to hurry."

In a voice laden with vehemence, Katherine asked her friend and mentor, "Why did ye come out here? Risking yer life for a condemned man?"

"We have no time. Canna ye see the English army coming?" said Juliana. Her voice may have been weak and shaky, but her determination shone through.

Looking toward the river, Kit continued to sneer. "We would have been long gone from here, if ye hadna gone out in the deluge to find him. Now we're trapped."

"No time to scold me. Let us get on the horse so we can reach the castle in time."

Without waiting for Kit's response, Hugh hefted Juliana onto the horse behind Kit. "Hold tight," he said as he positioned Juliana's arms around Kit's waist. With a quick slap on the rump of the horse, he sent the women up the hill in the direction of the castle and safety.

He watched them for minute before he started to run up the hill himself. On his second stride, an arrow from an English archer across the river struck the ground beside him.

Chapter Eleven

Another arrow came flying across the cleugh to lodge in the dirt in front of him, then another and another. He tried picking up his pace, but after a day chained to the tree in the rain, his legs refused to cooperate.

At the top of the hill just outside the entrance to the castle, Kit reined her horse to a stop, dismounted, and lifted Juliana into her arms to help her inside.

His legs burned, and his energy waned with every step, but he had to reach Kit. It would be smarter to run back down the hill and hide in the woods, but he had a powerful need to get to her. Her well-being had become more important than his own, and it could only be because Juliana was right. He did love her.

At first her beauty attracted him, but now her strength and courage drew him in. She was a woman like no other he'd ever known. She wasn't compliant or biddable or eager only to please, but strong enough in her own right to be his counterbalance. He needed someone like Kit, someone strong enough to withstand his restlessness and his strong-willed, often reckless, temperament. He did love her, and he had to get to her. Not to save her—she could do that herself—but to stand with her and help her protect those in her charge. To be her partner. To be her lover.

A musket shot sounded, and the gunpowder smoke

rose from the muzzle of the English-held gun in the distance. The musket ball hit his shoulder, knocking him to the ground. He fell flat and struggled to catch his breath as pain shot through his left shoulder and down his arm, but he couldn't let it stop him. He had to reach her. Slowly, he came to his feet and started moving up the hill again with his left arm dangling at his side.

He was more than halfway to the safety of the castle when the English cannon fire started. The first cannonball landed some thirty yards behind him, but the shattering debris of dirt and iron bits from the shrapnel included with the ball fell over him, digging into his back. He put up his right arm to shield his head and his eyes, but he kept moving through the smoke.

The next cannonball landed closer to him. Fortunately, it hit behind him again, but the vibration of the ground made him stumble. He forced himself to his feet and kept moving.

Through the ringing in his ears, he heard voices. "Ye're nearly here! Faster!"

He looked up to see Rand and Kit standing well outside the safety of the Fawside walls. Rand used his longbow to shoot arrows in rapid succession toward the English artillery, and several soldiers fell when Rand's arrows hit their targets. Kit braced herself behind a standing musket cannon to load it, and after balancing it on the stand, she fired. Her first shot must have fallen short because she adjusted her angle, and then raised her arm in victory when each of her next two musket balls found their marks. With no time to bask in Kit and Rand's victories, Hugh kept moving toward her.

By this time, he struggled to keep control of his legs. He stumbled and fell often as every step jolted his wounded shoulder, and his arm became a useless weight. One more step. One more step.

The whistle of another incoming cannonball told him that this one would be right on target. He charged forward with the last of his remaining energy. Through the smoke and cinders, he ran straight to her, swept her up with his uninjured right arm, and carried her through the open door into the safety of the castle with Rand right behind him. The explosion hit and shook the ground, landing right where she'd been standing.

Once safely inside, with all Hugh's strength depleted, he collapsed on the floor with Kit under him fighting her way out.

"Get off me!" she cried, pushing against his chest.

His agonizing moan stopped her.

"Rand, Rand!" she shouted. "Can ye see where he's hurt?"

Rand leaned over both of them. " 'Tis his shoulder. Looks like he's taken a shot. Hold on to me, lad, and I'll help ye up." With Kit pushing and Rand pulling, the two of them lifted Hugh and carried him to a cot in a nearby interior room.

One quick rip of his tunic exposed his back riddled with jagged cuts and scrapes from the debris of the cannon explosions and one large gouge in his left shoulder from the musket ball.

"The ball isna in his shoulder, just a deep slash through the skin," said Kit. "I'll clean it out, and Rand, ye tend to the rest of the wounds. Agnes, get me my bag."

As Agnes scurried up the stairs to get Kit's bag of salves and medicines, Rand washed each of the two dozen cuts and scrapes on the younger man's back.

"There is dirt and iron bits in each one," he told Hugh. Running his finger over one, he squeezed it until the shard of iron oozed out.

Hugh groaned.

"Ye'll have to endure it, lad, or they'll get poisoned, and that's no good."

Rand worked his way along Hugh's back while Kit cleaned out the musket ball wound. The ball had torn the skin apart in a wide swath in the muscle that couldn't be stitched closed, so Kit packed the deep gouge with strips of cloth soaked in diluted saltwater, tying long cloths over it and around his shoulder.

The cannon fire stopped.

An hour later Hugh lay on his stomach, his chest wrapped in strips of cloth. The only wound that still bled was the one on his shoulder, despite the thick pad covering it. Hugh could no longer identify where each throb of pain came from. His entire body had become one tormenting pounding of hurt.

"Ye're taking it well, lad," said Rand. "We're finished, and ye can rest. Katherine, I'll see if there is any other damage to the castle or to our people."

"Lie still," she said to Hugh, "and dinna roll over. I winna have time to repair yer bandages if ye tear them open." She spoke firmly, but at the same time stroked his forehead with a gentle touch, brushing his hair back. "Do ye hear me?"

He nodded.

"Ye saved Juliana's life," she said, retying the orange scarf loosely around his neck. "This is her precious token, so wear it proudly."

"I will."

Putting her hands on her hips, she stood and asked

in the same stern voice she used with the guards, "Why didna ye save yerself by going back into the woods?"

He twisted his head as far as he could to see her. "Because ye are here."

"I dinna understand."

"Because *ye* are *here*."

Kneeling beside the cot, she spoke softly. "It took courage to carry Juliana back to the place where yer death was a foregone conclusion." She paused. "And it took forgiveness to come back to the woman who abandoned ye to the soldiers by the stream, but ye made me choose between my duty and my heart."

He tried to lift his head off the cot. "Yer heart?"

"I am forced to admit, against my better judgment, that I want to find out more about ye, who ye really are. I want to ken what is hidden beneath yer quick tongue and knavish exterior."

With a sly grin, he said, "So I get to keep my head while ye figure it out?"

She lightly flicked her finger against his cheek. "Aye, ye do. My head tells me that ye brought trouble to my door, and ye should be dispatched before Mary pays the price. But I now believe ye're a man caught in something beyond yer control, something ye regret, and something ye want to make amends for. But because of ye, the enemy is quite close now. If Juliana had no' gone after ye, we would be away from here and out of danger."

"I am grateful that Juliana came for me, and I am glad ye waited, but I regret that we're under attack. I am sorry for that."

She sniffed. "Ye're sorry quite often." Moving her fingers over his cheek and chin, she wiped off some of the sweat and dirt. "The cannons have stopped. I'll be back to check on ye."

"Wait," he said, struggling to pull himself up on his right elbow. "I want to thank ye for treating my back. It does hurt some, but no' like it did afore."

Reaching up as far as he could with his injured left arm, he pulled her down to join his mouth with hers. The kiss began as softness, then followed with intensity, and she responded by leaning over him. He dropped his head back onto the cot, and she followed him. He inhaled the unique fragrance of lavender in her hair that floated over the scent of soap and the natural sweat from all she'd been through this morning.

Her breath quickened. Lifting her head, she murmured, "When I saw ye coming up the hill, I was frightened, and I havena been frightened in a verra long time. Ye can ne'er do that to me again." Her lips returned to his as her tongue quietly stroked his mouth.

"By promise made, I will ne'er do that again," he said beneath the kiss. His body wanted her so badly, and he was glad he lay on his stomach so she couldn't see just how badly.

Her head lifted. "Do ye understand my duty is to protect Mary? That comes before all else. I canna be distracted."

"I understand yer pledge to the lass, and I want to help ye. We can take care of her together."

She pushed away from the cot and squatted on her knees before him. "I dinna need yer help. I have Rand and Juliana to do whatever else needs to be done."

He was losing her. When would he learn that instead of a quick, glib tongue, he needed a sincere and truthful one? "I ken, but they dinna love ye, no' like I do."

"Aye, but they do love me!" Her eyes flashed.

His words came understated and compassionate. "No' like I do. Meeting ye was fate, and falling in love with ye I had no control over." Putting his hand behind her neck again, he pulled her mouth toward his. She did not resist. "I can tell ye with my words, but my kiss will say it all."

His kiss didn't demand anything from her but gave to her like the rain gives to the flower. Her mouth blossomed, inviting him in, deeper and fuller. When the kiss ended, as all kisses must, he brushed his finger over her mouth to feel the wetness lingering on her lips.

With hooded eyes, she took in a quiet breath. "Ye had already proved yerself to Juliana when ye carried her back here, and even though I saw a different man from the rogue who showed up with the message from our enemy, I…" She raised her gaze to the ceiling and took in another breath before looking back at him. "I dinna trust easily. I have no' been able to be certain of anyone but myself all my life. I grew up alone in the convent, and alone in my arranged marriage, no one but me. I want ye to be…I dinna ken exactly what I want ye to be, but I will ken it when the time is right."

A dry wind blew from the hallway into the room, no sound, no whistle, just moving air.

"I can wait," he said. "I have found my place with ye. Even though no one who kenned me afore would believe it, 'tis true. With ye, I have found what I've been searching for all my life, even when I didna ken what it was."

"But will ye give it up if the worst comes? Will ye go back to the easy life ye lived afore? Will ye choose it again?"

He searched his mind for a way to tell her that what he had looked for, the calmness, the surety, the peace in his own soul, he had found with her, and he would never give it up, no matter what he had to do.

"Anywhere with ye is better than anywhere I have ever been without ye. Words may ne'er be enough for ye to believe me, but by a promise made, even if ye ne'er love me, I will stay. I will stay."

He kissed her again. "Because ye are here."

Into their reverie came a small, high voice. "Kit, Kit, where are ye? I need ye!"

Kit sat up. "I am here, Mary," she said with a wink for Hugh.

Mary appeared in the narrow doorway and dashed into Kit's arms, knocking her across Hugh, who grunted when he was forced onto his back.

The little girl said, "I hid where ye told me to until the loud noises stopped. I looked for ye. I was frightened, but now I am no'. Ye and the man are here."

"Aye, the man and I are here. I have to go help Captain Rand. Will ye sit with the man and keep him company?"

"Aye!" exclaimed the girl as she jumped up on the cot, jostling Hugh again.

Kit situated her in a more comfortable spot for both of them, saying, "Dinna let him roll onto his back. He's hurt."

Mary's blue eyes popped open wide at the red stains on the bandages. "He's bleeding."

"Aye, but it will stop soon if he doesna roll on his back. Can ye take good care of him?"

"Aye," said Mary, sitting up proudly.

Hugh, who held Kit's hand through this whole exchange, tugged her near to him and whispered again, "Because ye are here."

With a smile, she tenderly brushed her fingers through his hair again. "And now ye are here." Her gaze lingered on his face as she straightened up, saying, "Dinna lie on yer back."

He smiled back at her, watching her leave before turning his attention to little Mary. "I willna. Mary willna let me, will ye?"

"Nay, I will tell ye a story so ye willna roll over," said Mary in her soft, high-pitched voice. " 'Tis one of Aesop's, and 'tis about a wolf and a nurse." Without waiting for Hugh's response, she started her tale.

"This story is about a child, her nurse, and a wolf. The wolf came outside the door of the cottage and heard a nurse scolding a child. Kit scolds me sometimes, but only when I deserve it."

Hugh nodded, glad for the distraction from the pain of his injuries.

"The nurse said, 'If ye dinna behave, I will throw ye out to the wolf.' "

"Oh, dear," said Hugh with a look of utter horror on his face. "That would be terrible."

"Dinna worry. The nurse didna mean it. 'Twas an empty threat. 'Tis something ye dinna really mean, like when Kit saw ye running up the hill and said, 'I should lock the door and let the English have him.' She didna really mean it. She told Rand to shoot his arrows, and she shot her musket until ye got inside."

"Thank goodness for that," said Hugh.

"So the wolf, being a greedy fellow, sat outside the house and waited for the nurse to throw out the girl so he could eat her and have the best meal he'd had in a verra long time. I wouldna eat a girl!" She pulled a face.

"Nor I," said Hugh.

"But then the wolf heard the nurse say, 'That's a good lass now. If the wolf comes for ye, we will beat him to death!' When the wolf heard this, he ran away and ne'er came back to that cottage again. Kit will beat to death anyone who tries to hurt me. She is stronger than any wolf."

Mary looked around as if checking for anyone who might be near enough to hear her. She whispered, "The wolf is like the men who shot arrows and cannonballs at us." She raised her eyebrows. "I am no' their queen, and they dinna like it, but Kit willna let them hurt me."

"So ye are a queen?"

"Aye, Juliana told me," she said, "but we have to keep it a secret. Someone told the king of England that I am the queen, and now he wants to marry me." She scrunched up her face. "But I am too young to marry anyone."

She looked around again. "Ye're why we had to wait at the castle. Kit wouldna leave until she found Juliana, and Kit had to go out in the rain to find her. That made Kit verra angry." Putting her hand up to shield her mouth, she said in a low voice, "She called ye names I am no' allowed to say. Want to hear some of them?"

"Nay!" said Hugh. "I apologized to Kit, and I made a promise ne'er to do that again."

"Ye may have to go to bed without yer supper, but then Kit will forgive ye. She always forgives me, and sometimes she brings me a treat so I willna be so hungry."

"Kit loves ye."

"Aye, and I love her. She is like my mum. Do ye have a mum?"

"I do. Do ye want to hear about her?"

Mary nodded eagerly.

"I didna always have a mum. I was an orphan until Suannoch, my mum, and Robin, my da, took me in. Suannoch is small in size, but she is like a giant in how she loves me and all my brothers and sisters."

"I dinna have any brothers or sisters."

"I want to tell ye about mine." And he told her tales of all his siblings, and her laughter bounced off the walls of the small room.

****

Kit moved down the hallway in long strides before stopping to press her back against the wall. She could scarcely draw in a full breath. Her body ached to feel that man close to her, to feel him making love to her. When he kissed her, his touch on her neck sent a warm rush through all of her, and she struggled to keep her knees from buckling. When he smiled, her heart melted.

She wanted more of him. She never wanted to leave his side. As long as he looked at her with those soft, rich eyes, as long as he gently touched her hand, her neck, and her face, she wanted him so powerfully it reached her soul.

Her eyes closed as she whispered, "I didna want to fall in love with him...but he smiled, and now I am losing myself to him."

Her eyes sprang open to a strong odor of smoke filling the hallway.

Chapter Twelve

Hugh struggled to sit up. "Do ye smell that, Mary? 'Tis smoke. Where is my tunic?"

She handed him the torn blue tunic from the floor. He put it on, but with the back ripped open, it would never stay on his shoulders.

Mary squinted and studied the problem. "Put it on backwards," she said. "Then ye can tie it shut with this." Quickly, she unwrapped the cloth belt that had been wrapped six times around her waist.

"Ye're indeed a smart lass," said Hugh, tying his torn tunic closed.

"I ken," she answered with her chin in the air.

Taking the girl by the hand, Hugh leaned out the doorway into the corridor where a thick layer of dark smoke floated near the ceiling. "Stay down. Do ye ken which way to go?"

She nodded and tugged Hugh down the hall. With each step, the smoke grew thicker and lower.

Out of the haze, Kit darted in front of them from a corridor on the left. "This way." Together they ran down the side hallway. "The English shot burning pots of oil at the castle. Some hit the walls and fell, starting the grass ablaze outside. Three others came through the windows and set the rushes and rugs on fire. They mean to burn us out and destroy the castle."

"Kit, I'm afeared!" cried Mary, doing her best to

keep up with Hugh's long strides.

Reaching down, Kit picked up the child, setting her on her hip. "Be brave, little one. I ken a way out that the English dinna. Hold tight."

The three weaved through corridors and rooms, all the while moving downward, level by level. In the last room, a tall cupboard against the wall had been shoved aside, revealing a rough, passageway carved out of the stone. Already waiting in the room were four of the guards, the cook, the steward, and the three maids. Rand arrived moments later carrying Juliana, who looked pale and weak. Frequent coughing came from deep in her chest.

Tugging a large brown cloth bag out of her waistband, Kit guided Mary to step into it. The girl did so easily. Her legs and arms now dangled out holes in the sides while Kit slipped the straps over her own shoulders, settling Mary on her back with the child holding her legs around Kit's waist and her arms around her guardian's neck. With the carrying sack, Kit still had her hands free, and if Mary lost her grip, she would not fall off.

"Can ye carry her like that?" Hugh asked.

"Of course. We've done this many times. Right, Mary?"

"Aye," said the girl. " 'Tis fun, and we can move verra fast this way."

"Where are the rest of the guards?" asked Hugh.

"Six of them stayed to fight the fire and to stop any English soldiers from following us."

Hugh grimaced. These men faced certain death by volunteering to be the last line of defense to protect their queen. If they escaped being burned alive, which was doubtful, they would die at the hands of the invading soldiers, and all so the small queen of Scotland would live to see another day.

"They are verra brave men," said Hugh, stroking Mary's damp hair.

"Aye," said Kit. "Rand, ye ken the gates that must be opened so we can get through the tunnel." Reassuring the others, she added, "This old tunnel will take us underground to a hidden opening at the base of the hill on the other side, along the road. From there we will move in different directions without the English kenning we are gone. This tunnel is verra old and has no' been used in a verra long time. 'Twill no' be easy to manage, but 'tis the only way."

Pointing at the two burliest guards, she said, "Go with yer captain and make certain the way is cleared for us." The guards stepped through the opening.

"I'll take Juliana," said Hugh. "Mistress, yer carriage awaits." He squatted down and motioned for her to climb on his back. "I can move faster this way."

She shook her head. "But yer back. 'Tis bleeding through the bandages."

"No matter, except the blood will ruin yer gown."

"No matter," answered Juliana as Rand helped her up onto Hugh's back. He braced himself against the pain of the bandages scraping his wounds. After Juliana wrapped her arms around his neck, Hugh lifted her legs and straightened up. "We're ready. Lead the way."

Rand disappeared into the tunnel and, after a few tense minutes, called back, " 'Tis open! Come ahead!"

The cook, the steward, and the maids ran into the tunnel, followed by the remaining two guards, then Kit and Mary, with Hugh and Juliana at the last.

Fawside Castle's location high on a hill was its only real defense. The residents could see who was coming, but without extensive weapons or even a surrounding moat or thick wall, they could be easily overrun. If invasion looked imminent, their only possible escape had to be to follow the River Esk through Pinkie Cleugh to the Firth of Forth that drained into the sea. If getting to the sea also proved impossible, this tunnel became their last option and their last hope.

As the tunnel narrowed, it became harder and harder for Hugh to keep Juliana on his back. Every time she coughed her frail body shook, and Hugh had to stop and wait so she wouldn't lose her grip.

"Keep going, lad," she said between coughs. "I'll be all right."

Still, she often slid down his back, and he had to reposition her to keep her from landing in the moldy water covering the floor.

"I've got ye," he said. "I willna let ye fall."

"Yer faith impresses me," she said, leaning her head against his shoulder. Her grip weakened.

The two guards carried the only lanterns, and they soon moved out of sight in the dark and mildewed tunnel. Hugh and Juliana only went forward by Hugh feeling his way along the damp walls. Neither of them could see any light coming from the exit out of the tunnel. While Hugh couldn't see much more than his next step, he followed the fading voices of Kit and Mary up ahead.

All at once Rand appeared out of the dampness in front of them. "It gets narrow about fifteen feet ahead, too narrow to carry Juliana. Hugh, ye will have to lead her while she walks. Do ye think ye can do it, mistress?"

This time her cough brought up globs of red mucus. "Nay, Rand. I canna make it any farther than this."

"Ye can do it," said Hugh, hoisting her up on his back. "Together we can make it."

"As I said, yer faith impresses me, lad, but my journey ends here."

"Nay, mistress, we can do it together."

Rand put his hand on Hugh's shoulder. "Ye dinna understand. She is dying. She has kenned for a while now that her time was short. That is why she risked going after ye in the rain. It didna matter if she got cold and wet because it couldna make her any worse. She only let me bring her into the tunnel for Kit and Mary's sake. If they think she's still behind them, they'll keep going."

"I winna leave her," said Hugh. "Kit and Mary need ye, mistress. Please, try."

Juliana reached out for Rand, slid off Hugh's back, and Hugh reluctantly helped her set her feet on the slippery floor of the tunnel. Rand put his arms around her and held her up despite having to stoop over himself. "Go ahead, lad. I'll stay with her."

Juliana reached up a gnarled finger and stroked Hugh's cheek as if to erase his lost expression. "I have done all I can for wee Mary and Katherine. Now 'tis up to ye."

"Please, mistress, we can make it together."

"Nay, lad. They dinna need me any longer, but they will need ye for a long time to come. I am trusting ye to take care of both of them." The sound of her next coughing fit echoed in the narrow space. When it was over, she said, "There is something else I must tell ye before ye go." She looked up at Rand. "We must tell him."

"Ye're right, mistress," said Rand. "Hugh, listen carefully. This secret has been well kept for all these years, but it canna be any longer. If the English army discovers the truth before ye, Kit, and Mary are gone from here, all of Scotland will pay dearly, especially Mary."

The sounds ahead of them vanished.

"We must hurry," said Juliana. "I dinna have much time." Her eyes closed, and she sucked in a shallow breath, barely enough to fill her lungs before she spoke. "Ye have been played for a fool, Hugh. Aye, ye were sent here, but no' to bring a proposal of marriage." The next cough drained even more of her strength as she slumped against the captain. Her voice weakened. "Rand," she whispered.

"Yer task was to find our Mary," said Rand. "The Duke of Somerset couldna be certain of where she was, so he gave ye several places to go, didna he?"

"Aye. Fawside was the first. Another was Craigmiller Castle. The third was Lochleven Castle, both farther north."

"He had spies tracking ye the whole time. Ye were to lead him to her. He is desperate to find a way to stop Scotland from signing a treaty with France, and there are only two ways to prevent that. One is to have King Edward marry our little babe. The other is to kill her. Setting the castle on fire proves that Somerset has chosen the latter. With Mary dead, Scotland would have no bargaining tool to bring France over to its side."

"Using the lass in that way is beyond

understanding," said Hugh.

"There is more," said Juliana. The rattle in her chest as she expended air echoed in the narrow space. "Listen." She closed her eyes again, and her head fell on her chest.

Rand kept talking. "Here is what ye must ken. I swear what we say is true. The little girl we have taken care of for the last four years is no' the real Queen of Scotland."

"What?" Hugh knew Rand couldn't see the shocked expression on his face, but he was certain Rand could hear it in his voice.

"She is an imposter, a decoy, a pawn to be easily discarded."

Hugh's jaw dropped. "How can that be?"

"We dinna have much time," Rand said. In as few words as possible he explained the plan for the protection of the real baby queen. He told the story of Mary's birth and how the babies had been switched at King James's dying request and about how Rand and Juliana had taken our Mary into hiding. They leaked word about Mary being moved, so the rumors followed them, and thus the true queen would be safe.

"But right now, our Mary is a liability. If our Mary is believed to be the true queen, England must be rid of her to stop a Scottish/French treaty. However, if England finds out she is an imposter, that puts the real queen in even more danger, and if the true Queen Mary willna marry the English king, she also must be eliminated. Two innocent babes dead for naught but a chance to govern the land."

"Does Kit ken?"

Rand shook his head. "I didna like deceiving her,

but 'twas the only way to keep the secret safe."

"Does Lord Arran ken the truth about our Mary?"

"Of course."

"But winna he protect our Mary in order to protect the real queen?"

"Ye truly are as ignorant of royal politics as Juliana says ye are. Nay, he cares naught for our girl. If our Mary is killed, he loses nothing, and the world might praise him for having such a clever plan as two Marys. Even so, there is always a chance that by eliminating one or both of the Marys, Arran might maneuver himself or his son onto the throne."

"How?"

"Royal succession can be a complicated thing if a direct line from parent to child is no' established. James had many illegitimate children, but none could inherit. After Mary, the next closest relative is Arran, as the great-grandson of James II."

"But what about the true queen? Will he protect her?"

Rand shrugged. "Right now, Arran wants to marry her off to the five-year-old dauphin of France. At the verra least, he will negotiate with the French for a position of power for himself in Paris."

Hugh paced back and forth in the narrow space, shaking his head and rubbing his forehead. "It makes no sense."

"When royalty has absolute power, nothing has to make sense."

Turning back to them, Hugh asked, "What can I do? I'll do whatever it takes."

"Save our Mary!" gasped Juliana. Her body collapsed to the floor, and her breathing grew shallow.

Falling to his knees, Rand held her to keep her out of the water.

"I will stay with Juliana until the end," said Rand. "Then I will follow ye. Go now, go quickly while there is still time. Save our Mary!"

The walls of the tunnel shook as yet another English cannon found its mark near the castle walls. Rocks and mud crumbled on their heads.

"Go!" shouted Rand.

Hugh stumbled through the narrowing opening, unable to see what lay ahead. Finally, he heard voices calling as a pinpoint of light grew larger and larger until it became an opening the size of a beer barrel. Just outside stood Kit, reaching in for him. "This way! This way!"

He grabbed her hand and wriggled his way into the sunlight only to find four soldiers, carrying spears, swords, and longbows, standing there.

Immediately, he pulled Kit, with Mary still on her back, behind him.

At that moment, he'd give anything for a weapon!

Chapter Thirteen

"Who are ye?" Hugh snarled at the men. "What do ye want with us?"

The tallest soldier with bright red hair chortled. "Ye're right, mistress. He will fight for ye. If I were ye, I'd keep him close."

Leaning her head around Hugh's shoulder, Kit said, "These men are part of the proud legions of Scots who have come to push the Sassenachs off our land, starting here at Pinkie Cleugh. Look!"

She pointed down and around the hill into the glen at several thousand Scottish men, horsemen, and foot soldiers alike, many in yellow Scottish army tunics, and many more in Highland plaids.

"The English Somerset's army is entrenched around the hill in front of the castle," said the soldier. "Our Scottish Earl of Home is already engaging in a cavalry battle with the English Lord Grey. Can ye no' hear the clamor?"

Hugh now recognized the roar of clashing swords with the cries of horses and men coming from the glen behind him.

"Ye need to get away from the fighting as far as ye can," said the soldier.

"We canna leave without Juliana and Rand," said Kit as she lifted Mary out of the carrying sack.

"They willna be coming," Hugh began,

"Juliana…"

With the set of her jaw, Kit said, "We will wait until I ken they are safe. Do ye see that outcropping of rocks over there?" She pointed to the north up another hill. "We'll wait there out of sight until Rand brings Juliana."

"They willna be coming," repeated Hugh.

" 'Tis no' safe, lass," said the soldier. "Ye need to leave."

"We will wait," said Kit. She took hold of Mary's hand and marched up the hill toward the rocks.

Hugh watched her go before asking the man, "Do ye have a dirk or a sword I could use?"

" 'Tis no' safe," said the man as he drew a dirk out of his belt and handed it to Hugh.

"I ken."

"Ye're putting the wee lass in danger."

"Right now, she's safer with us than anywhere else in this world."

Hugh trotted after Kit.

It felt good to have the knife safely tucked into his belt. His grandfather, Bretane, a warrior battling for Scottish freedom since he'd been twelve years old, had spent many hours teaching Hugh how to use a variety of weapons, and Hugh proved himself to be a gifted fighter. He struggled to learn to read, but with a dirk in his hand, he proudly established his skill.

The outcropping turned out to be several tall, thick rocks spreading out from the hill to form a nearly closed circle with a rocky floor in the center. After slipping through the narrow opening, the three of them were virtually hidden. An entire army could pass by and not see them.

"How did ye ken this was here?" asked Hugh.

Kit gave him a scorching look. "Did ye no' think I scouted the area around the castle afore I brought Mary here? I ken every inch of this land for five miles."

Mary climbed into Kit's arms, nearly knocking her down. "Dinna fight with the man," the child whined. "The noise from the fighting hurts my ears."

"My dear girl," said Kit. "Let me hold ye." She sat down and curled her arms around the trembling child. "No one can get to us here. I promise that ye are safe. The man and I will protect ye. How about an oatcake?" Kit reached into the rucksack she carried across her belly and handed an oatcake to Mary, who munched on it and lay back on Kit's shoulder.

Hugh scooted next to her and put his arm around both of them.

They sat quietly for nearly an hour before thundering hoofbeats pounded the ground in front of them. Horse after horse, most of them bleeding and some riderless, raced passed their hiding place. First, came the Scottish mounts, immediately followed by charging horses and riders in English dress.

"The English have routed them," said Hugh. "They'll chase our lads until they have killed every one of them. Scotland has lost the first battle."

"We will wait," said Kit.

"Will we spend the night here?"

"We have no choice." Using her carrying sack as a blanket, she tucked Mary into the far corner of the circle and covered her with it. "She is exhausted."

"We all are," said Hugh. "Come sit with me, and we can keep each other comfortable while we wait."

Kit snuggled next to him. This was how he wanted

things to be, with her near him, safe and close to sleep. Her body warmed his, and she relaxed as his body did the same for her. They would be all right through the night, but who knew what the morning would bring? He didn't want to know. He wanted her beside him.

"I have something to tell ye," he said.

"Can it wait?" said Kit in a voice slurred with fatigue.

"Nay." He touched her chin with his finger. "Ye have to ken."

"All right, what is it?" She closed her eyes.

"Juliana and Rand willna be coming."

She sat up. "Ye canna be certain."

"Aye, but I can." He cleared his throat in a vain hope that he wouldn't have to tell her news that would surely break her heart.

"The last time I saw Juliana she was dying, and Rand was going to stay with her. They sent me on ahead."

"It canna be. Neither of them would leave me or Mary."

"Juliana's been sick for a long time, and she kenned she didna have long to live. She made her way to the tunnel for yer sake and for Mary's. She didna think ye would leave without her if ye kenned the truth. When 'twas too late for ye to turn back, she told me that she wasna going any farther, and Rand vowed to stay with her. I suspect he intends to die with her."

Kit's face twisted as the reality of his words sunk in. "Rand loved her, ye ken. He was younger, but that didna matter to him. He loved her, but she didna love him in return. He always hoped that someday she would. He'll stay with her as long as it takes."

When her mind finally accepted that no matter what she said or did, she would never see Juliana or Rand again, she buried her head in Hugh's torn tunic and let the wet tears pour down her cheeks. Her words came out in bitter sobs. "I kenned...she was sick, but I...didna ken how bad."

"Ye loved her." Hugh held her close and softly rubbed her back. "And she loved ye. She and Rand trained ye well. They kenned ye would take care of Mary."

Kit wiped her eyes with the heel of her hand. "Did she say anything else? Any last advice for me? Juliana always had more advice."

"Aye, but that can wait until morning after we've all had some sleep."

"I canna sleep. Was she in pain?"

"I dinna think so. She couldna stop coughing, though. It made her weak."

Hugh tugged her closer. "She told me about Thatcher," he said, "how they wed when she was verra young, and how she had to give him up, and her babe."

Suddenly Kit pushed away from him. "She told ye what she ne'er told me? I kenned there was a man, but she ne'er spoke his name, and she ne'er said a word about a babe, only that the orange scarf belonged to someone she kenned when she was young." She tugged on the orange scarf around Hugh's neck. "I thought it to be a brother or a friend." Her tears came again. "She didna love me enough to tell me the truth! She told ye. A stranger."

Hugh tried to pull her into his arms to comfort her, but she fought him. "She died, and I didna ken her!"

"Juliana did love ye," he said. "She didna want yer

fate to be the same as hers. She wanted ye to live yer own life, mayhap make other choices."

Kit didn't answer.

Knowing that nothing would make things easier for Kit now, he shared the rest of what Juliana and Rand had told him. "There is something else."

When he hesitated, Kit slammed her fist into his chest. He grunted. "Tell me!" she cried.

Just then Mary rolled over and opened her eyes. "Kit, dinna cry."

Quickly Kit scooted across the stony floor and laid a hand on Mary's back. "I winna cry if ye go back to sleep. Ye need yer rest so ye winna be cranky tomorrow."

Mary yawned, and her eyes closed bit by bit. Her breathing slowed as the silence and Kit's loving touch lulled her back to sleep.

Hugh reached out his arms to Kit, and slowly she moved back to his side, where she twisted and turned under his arm to get comfortable.

After a few minutes, she lifted her face to his. "Tell me the rest, and I promise I winna cry."

Hugh held her tight. "I'll just say it out. Our Mary isna the real queen."

Kit's forehead furrowed. "What do ye mean? How can that be? She's been in Juliana's care, and then mine, since the day she was born."

"True, but she hasna ever been the real queen."

Kit put up her hand to protest.

"Wait," said Hugh. "King James thought that having two Marys would protect his daughter, and by coincidence, a girl babe from one of his mistresses was born two days later. That babe is our Mary. He took that babe and hid his real daughter out of sight."

"I ne'er saw another Mary."

" 'Twas all verra well planned. Ye took our Mary into hiding right away, so ye ne'er saw another child."

"Where is our Mary's mother?"

"She died in childbirth."

An involuntary whimper escaped Kit's lips. "Why was I ne'er told? Did Rand think he couldna trust me?"

"Nay, nay. He didna want to burden ye with the secret, kenning how great yer responsibilities already were. Much has been happening that we didna ken until today. Rand got word that Lord Arran has said that Somerset of England sent a spy, me, to find out where Mary was. Arran reported to all who would listen that I had exposed her secret hiding place, which is why Somerset attacked Fawside. Arran is trying to capture and hang this traitorous spy, me. By the way, this will make the third time my neck has been in danger."

Kit leaned out of Hugh's arm, stood, and started pacing in the small space between the rocks. "But if we tell everyone that our Mary isna the queen, and if we can show that our Mary is alive and well, then Scotland will still have her true queen living somewhere else, and ye will be proven innocent."

" 'Tis a bit more complicated than that." He cleared his throat.

Kit gritted her teeth. "Tell me!"

"In truth, Arran and Somerset plotted together, but then they double-crossed each other. Sending me was only a ploy. Arran intended to keep Somerset busy looking for her while he negotiated with France to marry the true queen into the royal house there. And Somerset followed me while negotiating to set up his army here."

"So why try to kill her now and ye along with her?"

"Because Arran is verra close to completing the negotiations with France. All he had to do was keep Somerset out of the way. However, if Somerset can defeat the Scots and capture our Mary, Somerset can present her as the true queen, and the French will then have doubts about any young girl's identity. Arran needs to find our Mary and eliminate her and banish any doubts that the girl he wants to send to France is the real queen."

" 'Tis so complicated, so full of trickery and lies. How could they use Mary like this?" She went over to Mary, tucking the makeshift blanket tighter around her, and kissing her on the forehead before kneeling again in front of Hugh.

Hugh took her hand. "That is true for them, but no' for us. Let Arran and Somerset fight it out. Our only concern is getting our Mary to safety. I've been thinking. We should take her to my family home at Makgullane. That's where I wanted to go in the first place, and 'tis isolated enough that all three of us will be safe there."

"Where is Makgullane?"

" 'Tis in the southern Highlands. It would take us two or more weeks to walk there, but if we can find a wagon or a horse…"

"I canna think anymore tonight. There is too much to put in order before I can decide what we do next. I need to find a way to calm my thoughts and to heal my grief." Tears formed again in the corners of her eyes. "I will miss Juliana and Rand for the rest of my life."

Those tears spilled over.

Tucking her under his arm, he made soothing sounds. "Ye dinna have to do this alone. I am here, and I promise to always be. Have I told ye that I love ye?"

"Nay," she murmured. "Do ye love me?"

"Aye, I do, and that is 'the verra first time I have ever said that to a woman. 'Tis the first time I have ever felt it about a woman."

She lifted her head to look into his eyes. "Truly?"

"My da and mum pledged their love with the first two lines of a Findern poem, and the whole poem is painted on the wall in their bedroom. The first lines are 'Where I have chosen, steadfast will I be, ne'er to repent in will, thought, nor deed.'

"For ye I pledge my love with the last two lines of the poem. 'While in this world I have strength and might, which is in duty, of very due right, by promise made with faithful assurance, ever you to serve without variance.'

"Ye're the first I have ever loved…and by promise made, ye are the last. I love ye, Katherine Payne, with all I am and all I will ever be, by promise made."

Hugh delighted in her first genuine smile since they had escaped the burning castle.

"I need ye," she said, coming up on one knee and straddling his lap. "I need ye in a way only someone who loves me can give me. Please."

Her lips were inches from his. "I canna think anymore tonight. I need ye."

Their kiss deepened as Hugh's hands caressed her hips and bottom, and she held her palms on each side of his face.

Hugh waited for her to say that she loved him, too,

but he soon realized it wouldn't be tonight. She looked for escape and release from all he had told her and from all that had happened in the last few days. She told him she would know when she felt the same for him, and he said he would wait. He'd given her his promise, and he would wait for as long as it took. Until then, he would give her whatever she needed and be grateful that he could. She needed his touch, and as she smothered him with her kisses, he gladly returned them in kind.

"Kit, I canna bear to see ye hurt. 'Tis worse than if it happened to me. I'd take a flogging if it would save ye pain."

"It wouldna." She continued to kiss and caress him. "My pain is mine, and I wouldna want ye in pain because of it." Tugging open the shirt he had on backwards, she kissed his neck and shoulders. Pulling it down, she slid it off his arms and began to suckle his chest around and under the orange scarf tied around his neck. A deep hum came from the back of her throat.

All at once she sat up straight. "I am sorry. I dinna want to start something that makes a promise I canna keep, no' with Mary so close. I want ye, I truly do, but no' here, no' now. I'm sorry." She started to move off him.

Holding her fast, Hugh said, "Then let me keep the promise to ye."

One hand drew her back into his kiss while his other hand slid slowly up her thigh over her breeches until he reached her waist. He moved his hands ever so softly under her loose tunic and up her bare skin to her breasts. Kneading them, he sighed under her kiss, and she answered with a deep sigh of her own. Now, knowing that she would not pull away, he massaged her firm breasts until her nipples peaked and throbbed.

She whimpered, "That pleases me."

"And me as well. Tonight, my pleasure will be to give ye pleasure. I want nothing else and nothing more."

She rested her hands on his shoulders.

Lifting her tunic, he ducked his head under it, licking and kissing both her breasts, one at a time, as Kit sighed and moaned softly under his tongue. Then, he unlaced her breeches and opened them.

Sliding his hands into the opening, his fingers moved down, separating the cloth as he went lower and lower, until he touched her most intimate spot. He moved his thumb over that nub as she squirmed and arched herself upward so he could reach more of her. Her head fell back when his finger slid down and slipped inside the wet, warm space between her legs.

Closing her eyes, she gasped, "Hugh."

He didn't speak. He only watched in wonder at this woman who had made him love her.

His finger and his thumb pleasured her with rapid and then slow, deep movements until she felt the world open up before her, and she spiraled out of control. "Hugh!"

Mary stirred.

Quickly, he covered Kit's mouth with a kiss to muffle her cries as she soared and then gradually came back to earth in his arms.

Unhurriedly he withdrew his hands, retied her breeches, and tucked in her tunic. She kept her eyes closed the whole time until she slumped against his chest.

They both slept peacefully until dawn, Hugh a little

less peacefully until his wanting her subsided.

At first light, the explosions and roar of battle started up again.

"Stay here," said Hugh, "while I go see what's happening."

"Nay," said Kit. "I'm the trained soldier. I'll go."

Putting his hand on her arm, he pointed to Mary crawling over to them. "And ye are the trained guardian. She needs ye."

Kit nodded her consent, brought Mary into her arms, and whispered reassuring words to the frightened child who held her hands over her ears while Hugh crept out of their hiding place in the rocks.

The stench of smoke, sweat, blood, and fear even this far from the battle threatened to choke him, and he tugged the collar of his tunic over his mouth and nose. Lying flat on the ground, he crawled around the hill and peered over the ridge into the cleugh at the heart of the battle.

The Scottish troops had crossed the Esk River bridge during the night in an attempt to overrun the English before they could use their artillery, but the narrow bridge hindered the speed needed to get large numbers across in time. The Scots, preferring a close combat fighting style, could not withstand the barrage of cannon fire from the English ships at sea or the artillery across the river. The bodies of men and horses killed or maimed, too many to count, possibly in the thousands, littered the ground on both sides of the river. Legs, arms, and heads blown off both men and beasts soaked the ground with their blood. The river ran red.

Hugh watched as Scottish troops running back across the bridge to escape were easily caught by the

English cavalry and slaughtered. Others drowned in the fast-moving Esk River, and as their bodies dammed up the water, the river overflowed its banks.

Hugh gagged and vomited into the grass.

Crawling back the way he had come; he passed the exit to the escape tunnel from the castle. Peering into the hole, he called out, "Rand, Juliana." His voice echoed against the walls, but he heard no reply.

With careful steps he entered the tunnel and squeezed his way through the narrow passage until it gradually opened up to where he could almost stand straight. The early morning sun, at just the right angle, shone into the tunnel, and Hugh could make out the passageway. Water soaked his feet as small rocks and pebbles fell on his head.

In the shadows, a gruesome sight appeared.

Rand lay crumbled against the wall, his stomach split open from his neck to his legs, his innards spilling out as if someone had pulled them from his body. He'd been gutted.

Juliana lay curled in a ball a few feet away, her head severed from her body, but there was no blood.

"Thank Heaven she was already dead," Hugh said. "I wish the same had been true for Rand."

Knowing that nothing could be done for either of them, not even a proper burial or words spoken over them, he ducked down and went out the way he had come in. As he approached the opening, the sunlight at the exit of the tunnel blinded him, so when he crawled out, he couldn't see the soldier. Instead he heard him.

"What have we here?" muttered a man with an English accent.

Hugh felt the end of a musket rifle pressing against

his chest before he could see it. Rubbing his eyes, they gradually adjusted to the light, and an English cavalry man glared back at him. The man, in a blood-covered chest plate and tunic over baggy short pants and high boots, roared in laughter. "Were you looking for a friend in there? There is naught but bloody Scots in that tunnel. We had a fine time cleaning out the guts of one of them. The woman was already dead, or we would have done the same to her."

Loathing welled up inside Hugh. It was one thing to kill a man in battle, but quite another to torture a helpless enemy for the sheer pleasure of doing it. War was cruel, but what this soldier had done was beyond the pale.

"They were my friends, and ye had no right!" cried Hugh.

Before the English could answer, Hugh latched onto the barrel of the musket with both hands and shoved it as hard and fast as he could back into the man's chest, pushing the man onto the ground. In one smooth motion, Hugh flipped the musket around and aimed it straight at the stunned soldier. Before even one more outraged thought formed in Hugh's mind, he pulled the trigger, shattering the man's chest with the exploding musket ball. The backfire of the gun set Hugh on his backside.

When he realized he'd been holding his breath, he sucked in a noisy gasp. The sound of the gun would be lost in the noises of the battle on the other side of the hill, but was this man alone? Had anyone seen him? Hugh scanned the area. No one in sight.

He threw the musket, now useless without more ammunition, back into the tunnel as far as he could.

Then he grabbed the soldier under his arms and dragged him inside, too. Hugh struggled with the body at the narrow opening, but he had to get the man completely out of sight. Wrenching, pushing, and shoving, Hugh forced him inside far enough that he couldn't be seen with just a quick glance.

There would be time enough to tell Kit the awful things that had been done to Rand and Juliana when Hell froze over, along with every English bastard trapped in the ice.

He and Katherine had only one choice now—to get Mary to safety.

Chapter Fourteen

Kit, with Mary already on her back in her sack, stood in the center of the circle of rocks when Hugh slid in through the narrow opening.

"There's blood on yer cheek…and yer tunic! What happened to ye?" she said, reaching for him.

He brushed her hand away. Wiping both sides of his face, he tried to clean off the evidence he'd missed.

"Are ye hurt?"

"Nay, but I killed someone."

"An owl didna do it this time?"

He glared at her. "Nay, this time I killed someone. I went looking for Juliana and Rand, and an English soldier found me at the tunnel."

"Are they…?" she asked with both hope and grief in her voice.

Leaning in so only Kit could hear, he said, "They're dead, buried inside the tunnel." To the child hanging on Kit's back, he said gently, "Juliana and Rand willna be coming with us."

"I ken," Mary replied. "Kit told me this morning that if I couldna see them anymore…" She pointed to her chest. "I can always remember them in here. I can see them in my dreams. I can ne'er lose them."

"Kit did a good job of telling ye about it," he said.

"She always does," answered Mary. "And dinna try to keep things from me. I am four years old, and I need to ken everything."

Hugh nodded.

The trio left by the slim opening between the rocks and hurried to reach the wide road of pounded dirt that wound around the hill directly behind Fawside. In reality, it was two roads, one along the top of the ridge of a steep cliff, and a parallel road at the bottom of the cliff. Ten miles to the north, the upper road came downhill to merge with the lower road, and it eventually led into Stirling. The three travelers walked on the upper road, and before long the battle noises lessened.

"From what I could see of the fighting, the Scots have been soundly defeated," said Hugh. "Thousands are dead, so many on top of each other ye canna walk across the battlefield."

"Mary doesna need to hear this," said Kit. "Ye can tell me later. Besides, we are no' safe here from either side. How long will it take to get to yer Makgullane?"

"Depends on how well Mary does with the traveling. 'Tis north of Stirling, northwest of Perth."

Kit bit her upper lip in thought before saying, "I wish we had a horse, but until then we have to walk. Mary is strong. She can make it."

When Mary's weight slipped, and Kit realized the child was asleep, she put her hand on Hugh's shoulder. "I...I want to thank ye for last night. I needed yer comfort, but ye understand 'twas only comfort. Until Mary is safe, that's all it can be."

He wanted so much more from her—he had so much more to give her—but Mary's safety needed to be the most important thing on her mind. He could wait. He was sure of himself, and he was sure of her. He could wait.

They walked in silence as Kit kept up a quick pace for the next few miles. Along the side of the road, pools of blood congealed, left from men and horses, after the disastrous cavalry battle the day before. After the third mile, a wide path of grass and dirt trampled by horses and men left the main road and disappeared over the hill.

"They must have tried to escape that way," said Kit. "I wouldna want to have to take Mary through a battlefield of dead and wounded."

"Is today Saturday?" asked Hugh.

"Aye."

"A black day for the Scottish army," he said, shaking his head.

"I hope Mary stays asleep until we're off this road," said Kit. "The roads converge about six miles ahead. The one on top of the bluff moves down to meet the one below, and that road leads away from Edinburgh toward Stirling. 'Tis no' a main road, no' many travelers, so it serves our purpose. 'Tis one reason we chose Fawside."

Suddenly the short hairs on the back of Hugh's neck stood up, alerting him to something, but he didn't know what. Turning his head back, he said, "Horses behind us."

In the distance, the bobbing heads of the horses of an English patrol headed in their direction.

"Down the cliff is the only way. Ye take Mary," she said, tugging the straps of Mary's carrying sack off her shoulders. "The wall of the cliff has a small cave in it about halfway down. We can hide inside. I'll go down first and lead the way. Ye follow with the babe.

I'll guide ye. Here." She hefted Mary and the carrying sack onto Hugh's back. "The straps will rub on yer shoulder and start the bleeding again, but there is no other way."

"Doesna matter. Are ye set, little one?" he asked Mary.

She kissed him on the cheek. "Aye, the man will take good care of me, Kit."

Kit shifted the smaller pack of food and water that she carried in front to her back before getting down and peering over the edge. Rocky jagged edges of stone jutted out along the face of the cliff.

"I think I see the cave." She pointed. "I'll start that way and call for ye to follow." Swinging her legs over the side, she quickly started the climb down.

Hugh watched her from the top, trying to memorize where she put her feet and hands. "Mary, ye watch Kit verra carefully so ye can help me put my feet in the right places. Ye can even grab hold of the stones with yer hands to help me. Can ye do it?"

"Aye. Kit and I climbed this cliff more than once. Captain Rand put a rope around her waist, but we didna need it. Kit and I climbed up and down all by ourselves."

"Are ye ready?"

"I am!"

Hugh adjusted quickly to Mary's extra weight, and he found it relatively easy to follow Kit's route down over the jagged rocks.

About halfway down the face, Kit called to him. "I see it. The cave. About thirty feet to yer left. I'll get there and lead ye to it."

"Aye," he said.

That's when loose rocks started sliding down the cliff, not the pebble or two that fell off when his hand hold wasn't secure, but bushels of debris falling fast and hard. Kit fought to find a foothold. She had a grip on a rock with both hands, but her legs swung uselessly. She grunted and strained, but she didn't cry out.

"I am coming to ye!" called Hugh.

"Nay!" she called back. "Get to the cave where Mary will be safe. I'll find a way."

Her right hand slipped off the stones, followed by her left, and she fell. Time slowed down as she flew through the air, bouncing repeatedly against the face of the cliff. Two, three times she slammed into the wall. Her tunic caught on a stone and ripped nearly off. On the fifth time, another jagged edge caught her boot and tore it from her foot and twisted her body until she fell headfirst toward the ground. She landed on her back with a sickening thud at the edge of the road below.

Mary screamed.

"Hush, Mary," Hugh said, hoping the soldiers thought the sound was only the wind whistling. "Kit's all right. I can see her moving."

The lie churned in his stomach, but he had to get Mary to safety before the patrol trapped them. He moved slowly toward the opening in the stone on the face of the cliff. Whenever he could, he glanced down at the figure at the cliff's base. Listening, he tried to hear if she at least moaned, but he heard nothing except the wind gusting around him.

Breathing hard, he moved across the face of the cliff. He had to get to safety in the cave before the approaching soldiers reached the road above them. One foothold, then another, until after what seemed like an eternity of time, he reached the edge of the cave and swung his leg inside the small space. He pulled himself and Mary inside a cavity in the stone with just enough room for him and the girl to sit up. Carefully, he got Mary out of the carrying sack and cuddled her on his lap.

She cried softly, saying over and over, "Kit, Kit."

Voices approached on the road over his head.

"Hush," he said, quickly checking to be certain his long legs were out of sight. Hugh strained to hear the words.

A deep voice with an English accent said, "It looks like they stopped here and tried to go down the cliff."

Another voice said, "Look, one of them's there at the bottom. Can you see? 'Tis the woman. Dead. We won't have to worry about her anymore."

A gravelly third voice said, "That leaves the man and the girl, and 'tis the girl we want. I doubt he'd try to climb down with her. He probably kept to the road. Let's keep moving. We'll catch up soon enough."

Hugh and Mary sat quietly for a long time as he rocked her until he was convinced the soldiers had moved far enough away. He ventured to stick his head out. The coming sunset left long shadows across the valley and across the crumpled shape of Kit.

"I see her. She's going to be fine." But to his eye she didn't look fine. Her leg twisted under her, and her head hung over the edge of a rut in the road. It didn't look like she'd moved at all from the last time he saw her. Pulling his head back in, he drew Mary close to keep her from looking over the edge.

"We canna climb down in the dark, but she'll be fine until morning. She waved at me." He hoped this lie would keep the lass calm while they waited for daylight.

"Can we pray for her?" Mary asked.

"Of course."

Mary crossed herself and bowed her head. "Hail Mary," she began in her small but confident voice. "Full of Grace, The Lord is with thee. Blessed art thou among women, and blessed is the fruit of thy womb, Jesus. Holy Mary, Mother of God, pray for us sinners now, and at the hour of our death." She repeated the prayer three times before crossing herself again and laying her head on Hugh's chest.

"Why did ye no' pray with me?" she asked.

"I did but silently." Hugh prayed that if Kit lay dead on the road, the trust he and this young girl had built recently wouldn't be shattered in the morning. He also prayed that his own heart wouldn't be shattered as well. "I have some stale bread stowed in my tunic. Want a piece? 'Twill have to last us until morning when we can get something from Kit's pack."

Mary took the chunk of hard bread from his hand, struggled to bite some off, and then struggled to chew it.

All at once thunder rumbled in the distance, and Mary buried her face in Hugh's shoulder, whimpering. The rain started a few minutes later.

"Hush, little one. We're safe and dry in here. How about a game?" Reaching through the opening in his torn shirt, he untied the small leather pouch on his breeches. He opened it and handed Mary his three small brown wooden dice.

"What are these?" she asked as she jiggled them in her fingers.

"We can play a game with them. I've played many games with them. First, ye throw them, and then I throw them, and we see who has the highest number of dots. The dots are called pips. The winner gets a reward."

"All right," said Mary, taking the dice in her hand and drawing her arm back past her head, preparing to throw them—out of the cave.

"Nay! Nay! Ye dinna throw like that. Ye toss them gently on the floor."

Startled by his rough voice, Mary replied sheepishly, "Oh." She let them roll out of her hand to the floor of the cave.

"How many pips?"

Putting a finger on each dot, she counted aloud. "Ten!" she said.

"That is a verra good roll. Now 'tis my turn." Hugh rolled a twelve. "I win. What will my reward be? I used to play for money, but neither of us has any coin, so we have to think of something else."

Mary scratched her nose in thought. "I ken! Sometimes Juliana and I played for kisses." Stretching up, she kissed Hugh on the cheek. "Now I get to roll again."

This time she rolled a sixteen, but Hugh rolled only an eight. He gave her a wet slobbery kiss on her cheek.

Giggling, she wiped it off with her sleeve. "My turn again."

When it got too dark to see the dots on the dice, Hugh returned them to his pouch.

Mary yawned and laid her head on Hugh's chest.

"Would ye like me to tell ye a story this time to help ye sleep?" he asked.

Mary nodded, put her first two fingers in her mouth and sucked noisily on them.

"A verra long time ago lived a beautiful woman named Athena," began Hugh. "She was verra strong and verra wise, and she had been trained to be a warrior."

"Like Kit."

"Aye, like Kit. She was so kind that she helped a lot of people. Once she helped a man named Hercules by holding up the world so he could search for a verra special apple. Another time she helped a man named Odysseus. He had been fighting in a war, but when the war was over, he wasna allowed to go home to his family."

"Why no'?"

"He made mistakes that he was verra sorry for."

"Like what?"

"Well, I dinna ken exactly what his mistakes were."

Hugh thought of all the mistakes he had made—gambling for money, drinking too much ale, kissing the wrong lasses—and like Odysseus, all he wanted to do now was go home.

Hugh continued his tale. "But for ten years storms wrecked his ship. He had to fight giants and monsters, and once he had to go into the dark world of the dead, and he thought he would ne'er get out of there. But Athena was his friend, and she showed him ways to escape all the dangers until finally he found his way back home. He loved Athena, and she loved him."

"Did he kiss her?"

"Aye."

"On the lips, no' on the cheek like friends, like we

do?"

"Aye, he did kiss her on the lips, but she had to leave him to help and protect other people."

"I liked that story," said Mary with another yawn. "I think Kit will like it." After a few wiggles and squirms, she fell asleep.

Hugh tried to lean against the rocky side of the hollow to sleep, but every one of the wounds on his back had been rubbed open. Some seeped, making his bandages stick to the cut and pull every time he moved. He needed rest to heal his aching body, but there was no time for that. He had to get Mary to someplace safe first, so he leaned in against her, but except for occasional dozing, sleep eluded him.

For the rest of an uncomfortable night in their rocky chamber, Hugh considered how his story and Mary's tale held truths for each of them. Mary found strength in the story of the nurse who protected her from the wolf, and his tale of Athena was about second chances. He worried that while he might be able to go home, it might be without Kit because, like Athena, she had other people to help and protect.

The sun had just begun to rise when Hugh gently woke Mary. "Time to go." He tried to wipe the tear-stained streaks off her face but ended up only smearing the tracks across her cheeks. Getting her cleaned up would have to wait.

" 'Tis light enough for us to climb down and get Kit," he said. "Get into yer sack. I'll check out the…" He peered out the opening toward the road. "Where is she? She's no' where she fell." A knot gripped his chest. "I dinna see her! Mary, do ye see Kit?"

Carefully, Mary lay on her stomach while Hugh

clutched her shirt to keep her from falling, and she peeked over the edge. "I dinna see her! Where is Kit? Where is my Kit?"

Chapter Fifteen

For Hugh, the climb down the cliff to the road was more challenging than it had been the day before. He'd been through a lot in the last few days: a night in the rain, carrying Juliana in the woods and again in the tunnel, being wounded, and now carrying Mary. In all that time, he hadn't had a decent night's sleep. What he wouldn't give for a soft bed, but that would have to wait until both Kit and Mary were safe.

With great relief he put his foot on the ground. He slid Mary off his shoulders, and she wiggled out of the carrying sack.

"Where's Kit?" the girl wailed over and over as she ran in frantic circles, waving her hands and crying. The last few days had been hard on everyone, to say the least, but even more so on a four-year-old child. Falling on her knees, Mary pounded her fists into the ground. "Where is Kit? I want Kit!"

Hugh wanted her, too. The thought that he might never again see this woman who had so quickly entered his life and so drastically changed it made him shiver despite the warm sun. He had no idea how, before he met her, he could have thought he had the right to live the useless life he did.

When did she first start to change him? Had it been the fear and shock of her threats to behead him that shook him to his core? Nay, it had started before that.

His first glimpse of her face told him she could be someone very special, and when she brought him to his knees in the woods, she convinced him. He hadn't been looking for her, but he had found her, and now she was part of him.

Where was she? What if he never found her? Without her, his heart would ache beyond imagining for as long as he lived, but now Kit's duty to protect Mary became his duty, and he would willingly care for her just as Kit had. And he would love her just as Kit had.

Mary's fury continued. Hugh tried picking her up to comfort her, but she would have none of it. She kicked and screamed until he put her down, and he let her wear herself out. That's when he spotted it.

Lying several yards ahead, in a slight gully on the side of the road, was Katherine's food pouch. Picking it up, he tore it open. As fast as he could he pulled out two oatcakes and two slices of cheese along with a flask of water.

Holding them out, he said, "Here, Mary, try this. Kit left it for us."

Mary jumped to her feet, grabbed the oatcake out of his hand, and stuffed it into her mouth. He held up the flask for her, and she gulped down the water. After wiping her mouth with the back of her hand, she said softly, "Where is Kit?"

"I dinna ken, so we have to think. Where could Kit be? We need to look for clues."

The two of them walked in different directions along and across the road, back and forth, and then again. They spotted them at the same time.

"I see them!" Mary shouted. "Wagon tracks! She's in the wagon."

"Aye, that makes sense," he said, chewing on his own portion of the food. "We should follow these wagon tracks left in the mud and see where they take us."

"To Kit?"

"Aye, to Kit." He took her hand, and the two of them started down the road.

The wagon tracks were easy to follow, but walking on the rocky, mud-covered road was not, especially for little Mary. Hugh carried her most of the time. On the way she taught him two songs, but Hugh knew better than to teach her any of the tavern songs he knew. The sun had nearly set again when Hugh started to look for a safe place to spend the night. An exhausted Mary slept on his shoulder in her carrying sack.

The wagon tracks they'd been following turned off the road and disappeared behind a scraggly copse of bushes and trees. Had these wagons picked up Kit? Or was she still out there with someone else? Hugh heard voices. Crouching behind a tree, he watched and listened.

Through the branches he saw three worn and patched tents set up around a large campfire. Two cooking pots swung over the glowing embers, giving off tantalizing aromas that played havoc with Hugh's ravenous hunger. But food would have to wait.

Behind the tents sat two dilapidated wagons, each with tall sides and a roof. Printed on one of them in faded letters was *Plays, Stories, Tales, Poems, Readings, News*. On the other wagon were the words *Countryside Players*. Two mules nibbled the grass just behind the wagons while three equally bedraggled and faded men sat around the cookfire.

One of them, a rotund barrel of a man with a thick, curly beard, had a thunderous voice. As he passed bowls of steaming liquid from one of the pots to the others, he said, "Dinna worry, lads. We'll be paid handsomely here. The fair at Stirling always draws a large crowd with coin to spare. In a couple of days, we'll dine with meat in our pot for a change."

A second man, tall and lean, said, " 'Tis what ye said a month ago, and we havena been offered a farthing in all that time, and we've only eaten what we could steal." He spit out the spoonful he'd just taken. "Onion soup again!"

The third man took a long noisy sip from his bowl. "Peter," he said, looking up at the skinny man, "if ye'd spend more time talking to those lasses ye nuzzle against, ye'd ken that this trouble with Queen Mary keeps everyone too worried to hear our stories. But Stirling is far enough north from the fighting for us to finally earn a fee."

"Who needs talk when there are lasses about?" said Peter with a wink as he brushed his unruly red hair out of his eyes.

"Anyone who cares more than a cockroach about what hole he sticks it in."

"I'd watch who I insulted, Gus." The brutal tone in Peter's voice swelled with every word. "Ye're too scrawny for decent work. All ye're fit for is playing the women's parts. If it werena for ye hanging it out to relieve yerself, nobody would ken ye were a man."

Gus stood up. A red flush rose on his neck until it burst into a brilliant scarlet on his cheeks. "Watch yer tongue!"

"If I were ye," said Peter, blowing on another

spoonful from his bowl, "and I'm glad I'm no', I'd keep my mouth shut. If ye're asking for a punch in the nose, ye might just get one."

"I'll teach ye a thing or two," snarled Gus, putting his fists up.

Peter's bowl clattered to the ground as he, too, stood up with his fists at the ready. "Ha! Save yer threats for yer wife, runt. Ye do her well enough until a real man comes along."

Hugh suppressed a giggle at the sight of these two scrawny men circling each other. Gus was shorter by a good eight inches and probably a stone or more lighter, and Peter, although taller, was so thin his arm could slip through a knothole in a tree. This would not be a contest of strength.

Just then a large dumpling of a woman ducked out of one of the tents. "Hush! I dinna want to listen to ye fussing again. Enough. If ye are no' careful, I'll take ye both on, much to yer regret." The two men stopped circling each other.

The fat man stepped between them and said in a rumbling voice, "Whoa, lads. The Countryside Players have been together too long to let a few words come to blows."

Gus backed up and sat down on the ground again. "Sorry, Damon. 'Tis just the worry and the hunger talking. No coin coming in, and we're near starving. Me and Jolene's thinking of quitting the troupe and finding work somewhere else."

"Ye canna quit the stage," said Damon. "The stage is in yer blood."

"Jolene deserves more than onion soup and apple cider. I could do better cleaning stables than I do here."

"I promise ye, we'll get paid. Just stay until after the Stirling fair. We need ye, Gus. No one puts together a stage play like ye do. Yer characters are the most original in the country."

"I like making up the stories, and if we were a bigger troupe, ye wouldna need me on stage, but I have to think of Jolene. She's been sickly."

With a sigh, Peter lowered his fists and said, "I dinna want ye to go either." He picked up his fallen bowl and locked his round amber eyes on it. "My quick tongue gets me in trouble, been doing it ever since I learned to talk. Sorry, Gus."

Damon laughed. "Ye have taken more than one beating because of that mouth of yers, Peter, but what is a flaw to the world is an asset to us. Ye ken how to make the audience laugh, but this time ye went too far with Gus."

"I ken," said Peter. "I'm sorry, Gus."

The woman said, "Ye all sound like family to me, fighting just like brothers, but ye canna quit family, just like ye canna quit each other now. We've been through a lot together, but today I made something special for all of us." She unfolded the napkin in her hand. " 'Tis an apple tart. I made it today. Do ye want a taste?"

Suddenly Mary pushed against Hugh's back. Loud enough to be heard by all, she said, "I want a piece. Let me out of this. I'm verra hungry."

Everyone around the campfire turned their heads in Hugh and Mary's direction. "Look at who found us," said the woman. "Come have a bite, lass. We have enough to share."

Hugh stood up but stayed behind the tree and did not release Mary from the carrying bag, still not sure if this was a safe place. "We've been walking for a long way," he said. "I canna pay ye, but if ye had a small piece for my lass here, we'd both be grateful."

"We share what we have with other travelers," said Damon. "It may no' be much, but we will give ye what we can. Come join us."

Hugh hesitated until the woman said, "My name is Beatrice, and while these men may bluster, no' one of them would harm a flea, let alone a child. If they did, they would answer to me."

All the men nodded quickly. "She's right," said Gus, "and dinna forget my Jolene. She may be little, but she's as fierce as any mama bear." He pointed to a tiny woman just coming out from under the flap of the other tent. He ran over to her and put his arm around her shoulders. "Is she no' the prettiest thing ye ever did see?"

Jolene's resplendent cinnamon-colored hair hung nearly to the ground, and her vivid green eyes highlighted her face. Hugh thought her to be a most beautiful woman, except for the fact that she was a misshapen dwarf. Her torso was of normal proportions, but her legs and arms were exceptionally small and malformed. Most babes born like this were drowned before the mother even saw them, so for Jolene to have survived meant that people cared for her. Gus obviously did.

Jolene hobbled over toward Hugh and Mary. "Hello, wee one," she said, reaching out her hand to the girl still on Hugh's back. Mary hesitated at first, but then took Jolene's stubby fingers in hers.

"How old are ye?" asked Mary. "Ye're little, but ye look old. I'm five. My name is Mary." Jolene smiled, showing white teeth that complemented her beauty.

"Nay," said Hugh. "Ye're four years old. Ye were born in December. 'Tis only September."

"Nay," said Mary firmly. "I want an apple tart. I'm hungry, and Kit always gives me a treat on the day I am born. That's today! Let me down! I'm hungry!"

Hugh complied and helped Mary slide out of the sack. Before releasing her, he held her by the arms in front of him and whispered in her ear, "To tell a lie is wrong."

She frowned and ducked her head. "But I'm hungry."

"All right, I will forgive ye, and I'm certain the apple tart will forgive ye, too. May I have a bite?" She smiled, nodded, and ran over to Beatrice, who scooped out a chunk of the crusty tart and put it in Mary's hands. She took a big bite.

"Who is Kit?" asked Jolene. "Yer wife? The lass's mother?" Her voice suddenly turned dark. "Or perhaps her guardian?"

At the word *guardian*, Hugh put his hand on the dirk in his belt and gave Jolene a look of uneasy caution. He did not speak.

Almost before he could blink, Hugh found himself surrounded by the three men with Jolene pressing a small knife against his stomach. "Tell us who ye're looking for, and we might tell ye who we found," said Damon.

In an instant, the narrow rope that had dangled in a loop from Damon's belt was around Hugh's chest and his hands were bound in front of him by a chain and a lock. Gus pushed him flat onto his back and sat on his chest with a force strong enough to empty Hugh's lungs. He struggled for breath.

"What are ye looking for?" said Gus. "Who sent ye here with the lass?"

Kneeling beside his head, Jolene scraped her knife across his neck, drawing blood along the surface of the skin. "My next cut will be deeper, and we will bury ye where ye'll ne'er be found. Who sent ye?"

****

Katherine awoke with a start. She couldn't draw a breath! Everything around her was dark, airless, and a thick cloud of dust choked her. Gasping frantically, she flailed wildly to free herself from the oppressive space.

Mounds and mounds of heavy, musty cloth held her in their grasp, ells and ells of it. She tore at the tattered material, but the never-ending cloth only wrapped itself tighter around her hands and her throat, clinging like a noose. Just when she thought she'd die in this tangled grave of fabric, she found an opening and crawled out. Jumping to her feet, she inhaled deeply. Air!

She looked around. Where in the name of all the saints was she?

She expected to find herself shattered into pieces of broken bones at the bottom of the cliff or in an English prison having been captured by the soldiers following them, but instead she stood in a small wagon with high sides and a roof. The interior might have once been painted a bright blue, but most of the paint had peeled off, leaving irregular patches of splintered brown wood. Scattered across these blotches jutted out more than thirty nails, and on each nail hung an article of clothing, all kinds, all sizes, men's and women's, some plain, some fancy. One even looked like a bear skin. Three large trunks littered the floor, each overflowing with dozens more tunics and robes of black, brown, and purple.

She frowned in confusion, but her heart quickened at the sight of something shiny in the corner. Weapons. Swords, knives, and lances. She could defend herself. She reached for a large sword and waved it over her head only to find it unexpectedly lightweight. It was painted wood. All the weapons stacked in the corner were the same, useless!

Suddenly she remembered.

She remembered the cliff. She remembered the fall and the excruciating pain when she landed on her back on the road. She remembered Hugh with Mary clinging to his neck above her and then only blackness. The next thing she remembered was opening her eyes inside this same wagon and five strangers staring down at her. The pain in her back had not lessened, and her every breath made it worse.

"Lie still," said a large, round-faced woman. "We're doing the best we can for ye."

"Yer back is covered with bruises, and yer hands are pretty cut up," said a tall, thin man with a narrow face and a large nose. "We put salve on them and bandaged them. Ye willna be able to use yer fingers for a while."

"Where is my Mary?" Kit struggled to ask. "My girl, Mary? She isna safe. He has her. 'Tis my duty to keep her safe." Her voice drifted away.

A woman with beautiful red hair leaned over her. "I gave ye a draught so ye'll sleep. When ye wake up, ye'll feel a lot better." The woman put her small hand over Kit's face and gently closed her eyes.

How long had she been sleeping in this mound of cloth? She held up her hands. They'd been bandaged, as had her scraped and bruised legs. Her legs? Where were her breeches? How did she get into this ragged kirtle? She flopped back on the cloth only to immediately roll onto her side because of the pain in her back. With a groan, she closed her eyes again.

The next time she awoke, she heard voices, angry voices coming from outside.

****

"Do with me what ye will, but dinna hurt the lass," said Hugh. "She's innocent."

"Ye think we would harm a child?" said Jolene. "We are no' like ye. We wouldna steal a child and hold her for ransom."

"She can tell ye who I am. Mary! Mary!"

As Mary ran toward them, Damon scooped her up. "Now, lass, ye dinna have to be afraid anymore. Ye're safe with us. The bad man winna hurt ye anymore."

Mary kicked her feet into Damon's stomach and pulled on his hair. "The man winna hurt me! Put me down!"

"If ye ken him to be a good man, tell me his name."

" 'Tis the man! The man!"

"If he is a good man, ye would ken his name."

"His name is Hugh Cullane," said Kit from the door of the wagon.

All eyes turned. With great effort, Kit stepped down the short ladder from the door to the ground. "Mary calls him 'the man,' but she kens him well."

Kit's next wobbly steps brought her to her knees and Beatrice to her side. "Sit here, lass," said the older

173

woman, helping her to her feet and leading her to a stump a few steps away.

"Let him up," said Kit. "He has helped keep Mary safe since the battle at Pinkie Cleugh. He willna hurt ye, but if ye dinna let him up, Mary might. He is her man."

Damon set Mary on the ground. She ran to Hugh and tried to push Gus off him. "Let my man go!"

As soon as Hugh was set on his feet again, she hugged his leg and then dashed over to Kit, who put up her hands before the child could reach her. "Careful. I'm hurt." Mary fell to her knees at Kit's feet and gently stroked Kit's leg.

"I saw ye fall. I screamed," said the girl, "but the man said we had to wait until morning to go get ye. When we got down, ye were gone." Big tears slid down her cheeks. "We didna ken where ye were. Beatrice gave me a tart."

Kit rubbed her bandaged hand carefully over Mary's cheek. "These people saw me on the road and picked me up. They've been taking care of me." She held up her hands. "See how Beatrice took care of my hands? She's as good as a physician."

Hugh said, "We thank ye for taking care of Kit and for the kindness ye showed her, but we need to be going. If we stay here, 'twill only bring ye more trouble than ye can handle. Ye canna take down armed soldiers as easily as ye did me."

"Ye willna be going anywhere until I tend to that wound on yer shoulder," said Beatrice as she marched toward Hugh, took him firmly by the arm, and led him to her tent.

"Soldiers searched us twice, once on the road and again after we camped," said the big man. " 'Tis no' new to us. We get stopped often. Somehow a traveling troupe of players always look suspicious to soldiers. They said they were looking for a man and lass and that the woman was dead. It didna take long for us to figure out who ye were."

"We dinna want to bring trouble to ye," said Kit, "so if ye can give us some food and a blanket, we'll be leaving."

"Nay, ye willna," said Gus. "There's no better place to hide ye than with us. Sit here and I'll bring ye a bowl of soup. 'Tis no' much, but 'twill warm ye up."

Kit, grasping the wooden bowl as best she could with her bandaged hands, sipped out of it. "I'm grateful for ye taking me in." The soup burned her lip. "Tastes delicious."

"Nay, it doesna," said Gus, "but it pleases Beatrice to hear ye say it. Let me introduce us. Damon is the big man, Peter, the tall one, and I am Gus. Ye met Beatrice, Damon's wife, and here is my wife, Jolene."

Kit nodded to each one in turn before draining her bowl of soup. A few minutes later, Hugh came out of the tent with a fresh bandage on his shoulder and wearing a clean shirt three sizes too big.

" 'Tis one of Damon's," Hugh said, tugging on the sleeves. "Seems I have some growing to do."

"There's no infection, so all he needs is a good night's sleep and he'll be as good as new," said Beatrice.

"We are the Countryside Players," Gus went on with a sweeping bow, "a proud and esteemed performing troupe of the theater. We travel across the land bringing news to astound and inform and stories to amaze and entertain."

Peter stepped in front of Gus and continued with a flourish of his hands and exaggerated facial expressions. "Our most recent tale has been of a fire in a castle and of the daring escape of Queen Mary of Scotland. We tell how she escaped from a traitorous spy, and how she led the army into battle where the Highlanders won the day. Our tale always ends with her living happily forever in a glorious land where she drives out the Sassenach invaders and heals all of Scotland's wounds. 'Tis quite a story we tell."

Hugh looked up from his own bowl of soup. "No' much of it is true."

"Nary a soul cares if 'tis true, only that it entertains and gives people hope for better times to come."

"At any time does this tale include three runaways hiding with a desperate band of players," Hugh asked, "where they could easily be turned in for a reward?"

Damon stood up and put his hands on his ample hips. His voice rumbled with indignation. "Are ye asking if we would turn ye in for a chest full of coin?"

Hugh stood and put his hand on his dirk again.

All at once every one of the Countryside Players burst into raucous laughter. Peter nearly choked on his guffaws, and Gus held his side as he rolled onto his back.

"Do ye think anyone would give us a chest of gold?" said Damon, still laughing. "Folks call us lower than snails, and what would snails do with a chest of gold?"

"They'd hang us afore they did ye," added Jolene.

"We may no' be welcome anywhere, no' even in church, but we ken justice," said Gus, coming back to his feet. "If soldiers are looking for ye, it canna be for any good reason, so we'll do whatever we can to keep ye safe, all of ye, especially the wee lass, whoever she might be."

"Hugh, what do they ken about Mary?" asked Kit sharply.

Jolene scampered over to stand beside Kit. "He didna tell us anything, but if the soldiers are looking for a wee girl, it could only be the wee queen. She has been kept in hiding for years, and now she is lost, but what better place to hide a small child than with us? Stand up, Yer Majesty."

Mary obeyed and stood beside Jolene. They were the same height.

"When I told them I was the queen, they laughed," Jolene added with an incredulous look. "I dinna ken why. We look just alike!" She reached over and tickled Mary, and their laughter sparkled over the camp.

"When were the soldiers here?" asked Hugh.

"The last time about midday. We hid Kit in the curtains after giving her something to make her sleep. The soldiers started to poke the pile with their swords, but when Peter told them the curtains were made from the robes of dead lepers, they stopped right away." The troupe laughed again at the horrified looks on Kit and Hugh's faces. " 'Tis no' true, mistress."

"Speaking of how ye look," said Beatrice. "Ye couldna have come to a better place if ye wanted to look different. Let me see here." Running her fingers through Kit's hair, she yanked a pair of scissors out of her apron and started cutting off large chunks of Kit's chestnut locks.

"Stop!" cried Kit. "What are ye doing?"

She continued to cut despite Kit's protest. " 'Twill

be easier to hide short hair under a wig. I am thinking Widow Carney. What do ye think, Jolene?"

"Perfect. I have some hair dye for the lass. A nice walnut brown will cover the red. We can also cut it to make her look younger, mayhap even a lad. Mary, do ye think ye can pretend to be only three years old?"

"Aye." Mary stuck her fingers in her mouth. "If they ask, I will say I am three. No one will ken 'tis me. Remember when we were in the wagon coming to Fawside, and I had to pretend to be Agnes's girl?"

"Aye," said Kit, "and ye did a fine job. This will be like that."

"Now as for the man," said Beatrice. "How can we hide him?" Her eyes lit up. "I ken!" She climbed the steps into the wagon and came out carrying a long brown robe. "Ye will be the monk. Have ye been to church enough to act like a man of faith?"

Hugh shook his head. "Our priest died when I was young, and no one came to take his place. My da read to me from the Bible, but I dinna ken how to bless ye or say the sacraments."

"Can ye cross yerself?"

"Aye." He quickly crossed his head to chest, shoulder to shoulder.

"Just do that all the time. No one will ken the difference, but we will have to shave yer head."

"What? Nay!" Hugh grabbed the top of his head.

"Dinna be fashious, lad. 'Twill only be the top of yer head to give ye a tonsure. Ye can keep most of those curly locks, the ones around yer face."

An hour later, three new members joined the Countryside Players: the Widow Carney, an elderly, stooped woman with bandages on her hands; Mary, a dark-haired orphaned three-year-old; and Brother Hubert, a friar with a wide smile and a twinkle in his light brown eyes, and an orange scarf tucked under his robe.

Chapter Sixteen

Kit soon found out that there was more to becoming Widow Carney than having her hair covered with a gray wig and wearing raggedy clothes. Gus and Jolene smeared makeup on her face, covering her creamy complexion with lines of wrinkles and numerous brown age spots.

"The widow is a heavy drinker," said Gus as he applied a thin slightly red-stained paste to her nose. "Now that is the kind of whiskey nose a woman like ye would have. Now I have to teach ye how to walk and talk like the poor widow."

Over the next two days and nights, Gus taught Kit how to walk with a limp and stretch her hips to ease her "pain." As she practiced, Peter helped her transform her voice from that of the young woman used to ordering people around into the weak, gravelly tones of an old hag.

"Ye're a quick study," said Damon, "and ye must ne'er forget who ye are now, not for a second. We will all be hanged if ye do. We're only two days outside of Stirling. When we arrive, the risk will be great."

"Mayhap we can return Queen Mary to her rightful place at the castle, and she will be safe there," said Jolene.

Kit said, "After the defeat at Pinkie Cleugh, Mary may no' be safe even in Scotland. We are charged with taking her somewhere no one would look. We were nearly captured at the cliff where ye found me, and we're grateful for yer shelter and care, but we will soon have to move her to a place only we ken."

"The Countryside Players are at the queen's service for as long as ye need us," said Damon.

That evening the company had visitors in the form of the same soldiers who had searched the wagons a few days ago on the road. At the sight of the soldiers standing at the edge of the camp, Kit pulled Mary into her arms. "Remember who ye are," she said. Mary nodded.

The first soldier had a scar across his cheek and a rough edge to his voice. "We're still patrolling the road to Stirling looking for the man and young lass who are wanted by the Earl of Arran, and we see ye have picked up more lowlifes since the last time. Who are they?"

Stepping between the soldiers and Hugh, Damon said, "We meet many on the road." Pointing to Hugh, he said, "We met Brother Hubert as he was walking to Stirling to join the priests and monks at the Church of the Holy Rood there. We are easing his long journey by letting him ride with us."

Hugh bowed his head and crossed himself.

The soldier snorted.

"And this," said Damon, "is my mother, a poor widow, who we canna let starve when we can care for her in her dotage." And with a third shift of his arm, indicated Mary. Before he could introduce her, Mary piped up, "I am Toby. I am three." Sticking her first two fingers in her mouth, she sucked on them.

The soldier came close to Mary, looking her over through squinted eyes. "Ye be good for yer grandmum, and mayhap ye'll grow up to be big and strong like me, right, lad?"

Mary smiled.

Spitting at her feet, the soldier stormed away, motioning for the other soldiers to come with him.

After every one of the Players breathed a sigh of relief, Kit said to Mary, "Ye did a fine job as the lad, Toby."

"I ken," said Mary with a grin, and Kit smothered her with kisses.

The only one who didn't seem relieved was Hugh, who paced around the campfire.

Beatrice asked, "What is troubling ye, lad? We fooled the soldiers again."

"That's just it," said Hugh. "We've got to keep fooling them, especially after we get into Stirling. There'll be a whole lot more of them there, and if they talk to each other, they might get suspicious about us and these wagons. 'Tis a good thing they think Kit is dead, but they winna give up looking for Mary or me. We need to think."

The three other men joined Hugh in pacing around the campfire until Jolene jumped up with her hands in the air. "I've got it! We disguise the wagons."

"As what?" said Peter. "A pony or mayhap a cow? How about a bird?"

"Dinna be a fool. We decorate them until ye canna see that 'tis *our* wagons."

Beatrice's eyes lit up. "I have an idea," she said. "Damon, Gus, come with me and help me carry out some of those old curtains. Peter, ye get out the paint we use for the scenery. Hugh, ye can spell, so ye're going to make us a sign. Move!"

By the next afternoon, the Countryside Players' wagons had been transformed.

Peter and Damon gathered up the various jars of paint. There was an assortment of colors, but not enough to do both wagons. Peter, mixing yellow with blue to make a rich green, made enough to cover one wagon. He mixed what he had left of the red, blue, and white to create a soft lavender for the second wagon while Kit and Mary wove strips of dark blue material in and around the spokes of all eight wagon wheels. Beatrice, cutting four large swaths out of the black and red curtains, twisted them together with a thin strip of yellow and instructed Gus where to nail the cloth to the edge of the roof so that it draped over each of the four sides, swooping down in the center and held up at each corner.

Stepping back, the Players admired their handiwork.

"Now," said Beatrice. "I think we should have signs we can nail to the sides."

"If we paint something different on each side, we can switch them out later. So, who do ye want to be?"

"While we're in Stirling, we have to be actors so we can put on our Feast of Fools and make some coin. Let's be something simple like 'The Company.' Can ye spell 'company'?" asked Peter.

Hugh hesitated. He'd never learned to read properly. The letters always jumbled up for him. He hoped he could spell "company."

"I think I can," he said.

"How about if Hugh does the writing and I do the spelling?" said Kit.

"Dinna care who does it, just ken it winna be us."

said Peter.

"On the other side of the sign, let's become 'Ratcatchers!' " said Gus. "I caught rats afore Jolene and me joined the Players. Nobody will ken 'tis us, and we might pick up a little more coin along the way. I still have the rat trap."

Damon cut out four square pieces of wood from the props. On one side of all four of them, Hugh, with Kit's help, painted the words "The Grand Company" while Damon painted happy-faced and sad-faced masks around it. On the other sides, Damon drew three rats hanging off a pole. No words necessary.

With the drapery and the new signs on each side of the two wagons, the Countryside Players had become all new.

"If we wear different clothes from our costume trunks, who will ken 'twas us?" said Gus.

"Nary a soul!" answered Peter.

That same night, Hugh finished a meager but still belly-filling vegetable stew by saying, "Beatrice, ye're a wizard with a cooking pot. I thank ye for sharing yer skills with us."

She blushed her appreciation.

"Now, lads, how do ye fill yer evenings when ye're no' telling yer tales?"

Peter, sitting close to the fire, drinking the last of the ale he had pinched from the shed of a cottage they passed the night before, said, "Hey, Hugh, are ye a betting sort?"

Kit giggled. "Are ye, Brother Hubert, are ye?"

Hugh narrowed his eyes at her. "I might be," he said.

" 'Twill be an entertaining way to pass the

evening," said Peter.

Hugh didn't see him wink in Gus and Damon's direction.

"I think I would love a game," said Hugh. "I have no' had much to entertain me since I arrived in this part of Scotland." He looked at Kit with a grin.

She scowled, saying, "And whose fault is that?"

"We got no money to bet, so we bet chores," said Peter. "How about it?"

"All right," said Hugh. "I'll be up for a good game of wagering. What game do ye suggest?"

Kit interjected, "Ye should ken that he made his living on dice and wagers in London."

"Mayhap he did, but he has no' played with us."

"I take that as a challenge," said Hugh.

"Have ye played passé-dix?" asked Gus.

Hugh nodded.

"Have ye dice?"

Hugh nodded again and took his three lucky dice out of his pouch.

The other men each had their own sets of three dice. Pulling them out, they handed each set to Hugh to let him examine them.

"Simple dice," said Gus. "Nothing else to it than that. Do ye agree none are weighted, and there is no trick to it?"

"I agree," said Hugh. "All three are just ordinary pieces of wood."

"Now let us see yers."

Hugh obliged, and all four men were ready to play.

"Like I said, we got no money, so we wager chores. The banker names the bet. We all roll, and the loser gets the chore. Are ye still up for a good game?"

"I am, if it means I can rid myself of hitching up those mules. They bite me every time I put the bit in their mouths. I practically have to drag them to the hitch."

"I'll go first," said Damon with a laugh, "and I'll wager burying our latrine before we leave in the morning. Is my wager taken?"

The other men agreed. All four tossed their dice onto a piece of flat wood and then leaned over to check the numbers showing.

Hugh grimaced since he was the only man with a number less than ten.

Clapping him on the back, Damon said, "Thank ye, Brother Hubert, for burying the latrine."

"My turn as banker," said Gus. "I'll wager fixing the spoke on the wheel next time it breaks."

The men tossed again, and now the next time a spoke broke, Hugh would be fixing it.

Peter, as banker, wagered dousing the campfire and spreading out the ashes every night for a sennight and a few minutes later was delighted when Hugh would also be doing that chore.

"I'm the banker this time," said Hugh, "but I want to check yer dice again." He pursed his lips. "I am suspecting chicanery."

"Chicanery?" said Peter. "Is that a fancy word for cheating?"

"Nay," said Hugh quickly, but with a slight curling smile. "I would ne'er accuse ye of cheating, no' good men like yerselves, but all the same, I want to see yer dice again."

After Hugh had inspected all the dice, he bet hitching up those blame mules in the morning. This time Peter lost.

"My luck has changed," said Hugh. Peter winked at Damon and Gus again, and by the time each had been banker twice, Hugh had five extra chores, and he still had to hitch up the mules in the morning.

"Keep this up," said Kit, "and ye'll be needing another pardon from the king."

Hugh shot her a stern look right before Peter said, "Another pardon? Pardons are for murder and heinous crimes." He stood up. "What kind of criminal are ye?" Picking up a burning stick from the fire, he took a fighting stance. "Beatrice, Jolene, get behind me. Take the wee lass with ye."

Kit raised her bandaged hands in surrender. "Nay! I spoke too soon. I only wanted to tease Hugh about his claim to be a great gambler and how he is losing so badly. Please, forgive me. He is a free man."

"What about the price on his head from the earl?"

"That's a trick to find the queen. A lie. Mary is here and verra safe. Please, believe me. Hugh is a good man, no' to be feared."

Jolene put a hand on Peter's arm. "We've been with them for days, and no' once have we doubted them. We willna start now. I believe what I see. He loves her, and she loves him, and they both put Mary above all else. Put down the stick, collect yer dice, and get some sleep."

Hugh gave a sigh of relief when Peter dropped the stick back into the fire, walked to his tent, and crawled inside.

Hugh said, "I think I'll stop losing while I still have my boots and get some sleep myself. Thank ye for giving me the opportunity to do so much of yer work."

Both Damon and Gus clapped a hand on Hugh's shoulder before they, too, went to their tents. "We're glad we could give ye the pleasure."

"Can I sleep with Beatrice?" asked Mary.

"I'll make her a wee bed beside mine," said Beatrice, "if 'tis all right with ye. She's no bother. I enjoy having a child to care for."

"Can I, please?"

"Of course," said Kit, "but ye remember to be a proper lady when ye're in someone else's room."

Mary skipped over to Kit, kissed her on the cheek, and skipped back to Beatrice, who took her by the hand and into the tent she and Damon shared.

Hugh and Kit climbed the ladder into the wagon that had become their bedchamber. They arranged the curtains into two thick piles and covered them with worn but soft quilts to create makeshift beds. A smaller pile in the back corner was Mary's bed.

"Did ye see," said Kit as she smoothed out her quilt, "that all three of them switched their dice before they showed them to ye and changed them again before they rolled?"

"I saw, but a few extra chores are worth the price of their friendship. 'Tis the least I can do after all they've risked for us."

Hugh reached up and opened the two hatches in the roof that let in fresh air and moonlight while Kit snuggled into her quilts. Hugh took off his long robe and boots before flopping down on his own pile. He wanted her desperately, but he had said he would wait until she was ready, and he would, no matter how he suffered from the wanting.

"Do ye think we're making the right choice to ride

with the Players into Stirling tomorrow?" he asked.

She came up on her elbow. " 'Tis a risk, but we promised the Players they could earn enough to get them through the winter before they take us north. Jolene says that if they put on a Feast of Fools play twice a day over the three days that we're at the Stirling Fair, they can earn more than enough. She has quite a good head for figures."

"Aye, we do owe them that. What do ye ken about Stirling? I dinna want any surprises."

"The town is a fair-sized trading town, and it has two fairs a year, both crowded with people. The danger is being recognized, even with these disguises, but Damon promises we will camp as far away from the castle as we can get, and the sheer number of people will hide us.

"As for the castle itself, 'tis quite elegant. James V was crowned there, as was the babe, Mary. I stayed there with our Mary when I first met her, so I ken my way around, but we winna be going inside. Too much of a risk." She chuckled. "Peter is disappointed that he winna be able to steal some of the goblets and silverware. That man is a thief and a liar, but he has a heart of gold."

"We will have to keep our Mary verra close. She may blurt out something without thinking."

"She is verra good at pretending. Quite often we had to disguise her and pass her off as a common lass. She thinks 'tis a game, and she plays it well."

The inside of the wagon grew darker until, despite its small size, Hugh and Kit couldn't see each other anymore.

"Do ye think there is a chance that Arran will be

there?" asked Hugh. "He's told everyone that I am a traitorous spy, and we dinna ken how desperate he is to find our Mary. We're proof he's only out for his own good. Personally, I think he secretly wanted a Scottish defeat to help cover his conniving."

"I dinna ken if he will be there." Kit left her bed, padded across the floor, and knelt beside Hugh. "I have missed having ye close."

He lifted his quilt and motioned for her to lie next to him. "I have missed ye, too," he said. Tugging her into him, he kissed her, and they sank into each other's warmth.

"Do ye want to hear something funny about Stirling?" she asked.

"Always."

"Years ago, a man named John Damien decided he could fly."

"Fly? What a loony doo."

"He jumped off the wall of the castle and…" She broke out laughing. "He landed in a dung pile and broke his leg! It made Stirling the butt of a joke all over Scotland."

When their laughter at the ridiculous idea that a man could fly like a bird died down, Kit said, "It feels good to laugh. I havena laughed in a verra long time, but ye, Hugh Cullane, make me smile on the inside, and I thank ye for that."

Hugh said, "Jolene says ye love me. Is it true? Do ye?"

She didn't answer but instead clung to him and pressed her ear against his chest. "I can hear yer heartbeat. 'Tis comforting. 'Tis the first time since we left Fawside that I can think of something other than my duty. 'Tis being with these people and with ye beside me. For the first time, I feel like a woman instead of a soldier."

With his fingers, Hugh turned her face toward his. "If I could give ye one thing, it would be to see yerself as I see ye. Ye say ye've been made hard by being trained as a soldier. Aye, it has made ye determined and focused, but I see the woman ye are meant to be. I kenned that woman from our first kiss in the forest, the kiss that got me thrown in the dungeon."

"I regret that now."

"Dinna. In the short time I have kenned ye, ye have threatened to have me flogged and beheaded. I sat chained to a tree in the rain a night and part of a day, and I carried an old woman back to the castle thinking it meant certain death. I've been cold, hungry, and scared, but I want ye to ken that, for as long as I live, I will be glad for the experience."

Slowly, and with great gentleness, he let his finger caress her collarbone and shoulders. "I see wonder and beauty in yer eyes. I feel yer strength, and both have changed me when I thought nothing, and no one, could. Whatever happens, I'll be grateful that I kenned ye." He kissed her forehead. "I see in yer eyes the man I should be."

Wrapping her bandaged hands around his neck, she kissed his cheek. "No regrets?"

"The path that brought me to ye...I wouldna change one step of it because it led me here, and I am grateful to be here with ye."

For a long time, they took ease in each other's arms.

"The day we left the circle of rocks," she said in a

191

halting voice, "I told ye my duty would always come first, 'twould come before ye, before everything, but I only said that because no one had ever given me such a gift as ye did that night. I ne'er surrendered myself…or my heart, to anyone afore. I pushed ye away because I didna ken what to say or how to repay ye."

Leaning in closer, he said, "Ye dinna have to repay me, ever. Juliana said that Hell winna take gamblers. I dinna think Heaven will either, but whatever happens, I will spend my eternity looking for ye, Katherine, only ye, with no regrets, ever."

She stopped smiling. "Those are fine words."

He shifted back and stared at her face, his sorrel eyes darkening. "Before I came north, I would have agreed with ye that my words didna always speak true, but no' now. I canna explain it, and I dinna want to. If ye cry, I will be yer shoulder to cry on, and if ye are happy, I will be yer smile. No matter what happens, ye willna be alone, no' ever, and ye canna stop me, no matter how hard ye try."

The cool breeze wafted in from above, and Hugh tugged the quilt closer around her.

Nestling against him, Kit hummed a soothing sound deep in her throat. "After we go into Stirling, we may no' have a chance to be alone. Will ye love me tonight as a man loves a woman? Completely? And let me love ye the same way?"

He didn't answer but kissed her, deeply and abundantly. She responded in kind. They couldn't seem to get close enough to each other. Her hands roamed his back, pulling him tighter. His hands smoothed away the tension she held in her body until she melted into him like wax in the sun.

After slipping off any clothing that separated them, he caressed every part of her with his hands and lips. It was as if he had many hands, many mouths, as he gently covered her body until she quivered under his touch. The curtains and quilts bunched up between their legs and around their arms, but it did not hinder their bodies from moving against each other.

When his hands stroked between her legs, she bucked her hips upward.

He stopped. "Are ye all right?"

Although no louder than a whisper, the raw husky tremor in her voice filled the small space. "I want more of ye." She shuddered. "Give me more."

And he did, plunging his fingers deep inside her while his mouth surrounded her core. She swayed to match his rhythm. When she tugged on his hair, he slid up the length of her, bracing himself on his elbows.

"Let me feel the weight of ye on me," she said. He eased himself down, pressing her into the makeshift bed. "This time I want to give to ye," she breathed in his ear.

"We will give to each other," he answered.

They did, joining their bodies, their lives, their hopes, and dreams. She gave, and he gave, tumbling and grasping each other as if tonight was all they would ever have. She held onto her release until she felt his need to surrender his all inside of her. Together, they plunged into the night.

Chapter Seventeen

As the Countryside Players, now the Grand Company, approached Stirling, crowds of travelers clogged the road. After the defeats at Pinkie Cleugh, the people of this part of Scotland needed something to look forward to, and a lively fair would be just the thing.

Wagons and carts, loaded with goods of all sorts for sale at the marketplace, bounced over the road, along with visitors who had come to buy. Some people could barely pull their ramshackle carts while others rode in opulent luxury in stately carriages drawn by teams of matched stallions. This fair would have something for everyone, rich and poor, to sell or buy.

The marketplace put coin in the merchants' pockets who sold goods from Scottish wool to salt, knives, pots, and pans to vegetables and meat still on the hoof, to wine and oils, to freshly fried pastries and buns. It was all for sale or trade.

The Stirling Fair, franchised by James Hamilton, second Earl of Arran and regent for Queen Mary, was in honor of the upcoming Michaelmas holiday on September 29. Michaelmas celebrated the angel, St. Michael, who fought against all the dark angels and became a symbol for protection from the dark days of winter to come after the harvest.

A highlight at the feast would be a delicious St.

194

Michael's Bannock, or Struan Micheil, a large scone-like cake made from cereals grown during the year that represented the fruits of the fields. Cooking it on a lambskin stood for the fruit of the flocks. As the cake was being made, the eldest daughter of the family offered this blessing, "Progeny and prosperity of family, Mystery of Michael, Protection of the Trinity."

For those not looking to buy or sell, there would be entertainment galore. Jugglers, magicians, dancing bears, minstrels, and the highlight of any festival, the plays. Some troupes performed atop wagons and carts, telling short stories of a religious origin, while other tales were bawdy and vulgar, but none would be like the Grand Company's "Feast of Fools" pageant. Generally, the Feast of Fools, a parody on the traditional Christmas story, was put on around January 1, but winter rarely brought large crowds, so this fall season provided the best stage for such a presentation.

Unbeknownst to any of the visitors pouring through the gates of Stirling, James Hamilton had ordered all his guards and soldiers into the courtyard behind Stirling Castle. Standing on a platform in the center of the yard, he announced that this Michaelmas Fair in Stirling was to be the best that had ever been given and ever would be.

"Nothing, and I mean absolutely nothing, is to tarnish the festivities. I have already ordered that the castle, the grounds, and the gardens are to be spotlessly cleaned and beautified beyond any our visitors have ever seen. Ye guards are to do the same to the town. All beggars, vagrants, outlaws, and anything resembling filth or dirt or rats that might sully our reputation are to be dealt with and removed, starting with that man in the pillory over there." He pointed to the wooden stocks against the wall at the back of the open yard or close.

"No' a single criminal will remain in Stirling. Empty the prison cells if ye have to. And if I smell that open pile of garbage behind the stocks, ye will find yerselves sleeping in it! If ye have to wash the streets yerselves, 'twill be done. I have suffered enough with the defeat at Pinkie Cleugh, and this fair will make all others forget it!"

The company of guards stood at attention with only the bravest daring to move even their eyes.

"And tear down any and all Wanted posters. As far as the visitors and guests who have come at my request are to ken, I have made Stirling the finest example of safe and lawful living. All criminals have been banished."

Spit dribbled out of Arran's mouth as he shrieked out the words. "While our armed troops may have been defeated, I have not! And furthermore, should any crime or difficulty present itself, ye will deal with it immediately, and I dinna want anyone, especially no' me or my noble guests upon whose support I depend, to ken anything about it. Not a whisper of trouble. Not a hint of disruption or even unpleasantness. To them this fair will be without blemish, without disruption, without scandal, or I will ken the reason why!"

Arran started to leave the platform when he turned back to add, "The highlight of the fair will be the presentation of a spectacular Feast of Fools play. I demand that a troupe worthy of such a play be found. At any and all cost! The riffraff may enjoy any play they like outside the walls, but the one within the castle will be the finest ever seen. If I am disappointed…" He swung his arm over the guards assembled there. "I will no' be disappointed, or ye will all pay dearly. Am I understood?"

"Aye, my lord!" came the unison reply.

****

The hairs on the back of Hugh's neck started to tingle as the castle on the hill above the town came into sight. The imposing stone walls and towers surrounded the inner close, a courtyard housing the palace and outbuildings. The main entrance to the castle was across an imposing drawbridge over a ditch. Inside, to the left of the gate stood the Royal Palace, a luxurious structure inside and out, built by King James V, that served as one of the royal residences.

Most merchants and entertainers wanted a place close to the castle in hopes that the nobles and wealthy men and women who stayed there would have easy access to their goods and services. This was not the hope of the Grand Company. Damon directed their wagons down the slope to a flat area some distance away from the hundreds of stalls and carts.

Hugh had just started to unhitch the mules when four guards in the familiar royal black uniforms with gold stitching ran toward him.

"Stop!" shouted one of the guards. "Stop!"

Hugh put his hand on the dirk hidden in his robe as Friar Hubert. His body tensed as he let the guards approach, grateful that the rest of the Players were at the stream behind the wagons washing up and laying out costumes for the play. If the guards tried to arrest him, he would surrender and hope the rest of the troupe had the good sense to ride away, leaving him behind.

He shot a glance down at the Players beside the

stream and caught Gus's eye. Gus gave a quick look toward the guards and, with a nod of his head to Hugh, went back to his work without acknowledging their presence.

"Hail and greetings!" said another of the guards when the four reached the wagon. "We have come to welcome ye to the Stirling Fair franchised by the Earl of Arran. He has been waiting for a troupe of actors to arrive. The earl is looking for special entertainment for his guests."

Another guard smiled. "How did a monk come to be with actors such as these? I do say that they need prayer more than most, but to travel with them? I couldna do it."

Putting his lifelong talent for avoiding the truth to use, Hugh tightened his hand on his dirk and said, "God's work is done in many places. We will prepare a seat worthy of the earl and all his guests at one of our performances."

"He wants ye to put on the Feast of Fools for him. 'Tis one of his favorites."

"We will give him a fine presentation. We await the earl's visit."

"Nay, fool, he willna come to ye. Ye are to come to him. Ye're to come inside the gates and give the play in the Great Hall."

Hugh's eyes widened in alarm. They couldn't go inside the walls. He had to convince them that his objection to coming within the gates was because they were a bunch of actors unacceptable in polite society. Not because they feared for their lives!

"Come inside? We canna. We are but a simple troupe of players. Our name may be grand, but we are no' worthy of coming inside. It wouldna be proper."

"The earl is no' interested in 'proper.' He wants all his invited guests to be entertained without having to go out among the rabble. He will pay ye handsomely."

At that moment, Mary peeked around the wheel of the wagon. "Hello," she said. "Ye have fancy uniforms. Can I touch them?"

"Nay," ordered one man. "Ye are no' to touch anything. Ye are to come to the side gate that the servants use and come through the kitchen to the Great Hall. And do ye hear me, lad? Dinna touch a thing. No' with those dirty hands."

With all the indignation the young child could muster, she held out her hands. "My hands are no' dirty."

In two strides, Hugh was in front of Mary and turning her around. He had to chase her away before the guards became suspicious of such a brazen lad. "Go back to Beatrice," he said. "No more words from ye or I will take a strap to ye. Go back to Beatrice! Now!" He'd explain and beg her forgiveness later.

Frightened by Hugh's anger, Mary darted back between the wagons and into Beatrice's skirts, sobbing.

"Pardon the lad. He is young and has much to learn about respect. How much will the earl pay?" asked Hugh.

"He will pay one hundred pounds Scots."

One hundred pounds Scots was more money than the former Countryside Players would see in five lifetimes. Only a nobleman could expect that much income. That fee would last them, not only through the winter, but through the next several years. Still, if Hugh could perhaps discourage the earl from inviting them inside the walls with a ridiculously larger fee…

Raising one eyebrow in a questioning slant, Hugh said, "We will consider his offer if the earl is willing to pay twice that much in advance. For that price, we can promise the most wonderous Feast of Fools he has ever seen."

The guard took a step closer. "In advance? Nay, ye would run off with it. I ken yer kind, thieves all of ye."

"Then perhaps the earl will agree to this. To be certain that we will perform for twice the fee, now two hundred pounds Scots, his lordship will come up on stage and pay us in person. That way there will be witnesses, and we can guarantee to give him a play he willna ever forget." Hugh counted on the earl refusing to stoop so low as to stand on the same platform as the actors.

The guard pursed his lips. "I dinna ken."

"Think of how generous the earl will appear to everyone in the audience. They will have great appreciation for the man who rules for our young queen when they see what he is doing for them." Again, Hugh was certain that even flattery wouldn't overcome the earl's disdain for a troupe of stage performers.

"I will bring yer proposition to the earl and the earl's exchequer and return with the answer within the hour."

"We will wait with bated breath," said Hugh, turning his back and rolling his eyes.

****

By evening, Hugh's misplaced confidence that the earl's arrogance would keep them safe found both wagons belonging to the Grand Company parked just outside the servants' entrance on the west side of the wall. The door at the gate wasn't wide enough to allow the wagons inside, so each of the Players traipsed from the wagons, through the inner close to the kitchen, through the kitchen and into the back of the Great Hall, carrying props and costumes. They would perform in the King's Presence Chamber, a space more elegant than any they had ever imagined. A platform had already been built, creating a performance area three times larger than any they had ever set foot on.

A series of carved oak portraits, comprised of fifty-six heads of prominent people, including King Henry VIII and Mary of Guise, known as the Stirling Heads, decorated the ceiling. Complementing that elegant ceiling were the polished wooden floors and the beautiful tapestries on the walls.

The first time Gus and Peter came into the room carrying props, they dropped what they had and lay down on their backs to get a better look at the artwork.

"This place is fit for a king," said Peter.

"Really, is that the best ye can do? Fit for a king?" said Gus.

"I'll do better during the performance. Funny looking blokes, dinna ye think?"

"Do ye ken who any of them are?"

Just then, three palace maids came in to polish the floor one last time before the crowds left their dirty footprints all over it. "Out! Out!" shouted one of them.

Jumping to his feet, Gus said, "We're the players. We have to set up for the Feast of Fools tomorrow."

"I dinna care! Off my floor!"

The men hurriedly stowed their props on the corner of the stage and, after taking one more upward glance, left for the kitchens.

Hugh first noticed the overlooked and forgotten poster tacked on the outside door of the wall. Pulling it down, he studied the face drawn on it. Holding it out to Gus, he said, "Does this man look familiar to ye?"

Gus quietly sucked in his breath. "Aye, 'tis ye. Fine likeness, if I do say so."

"I thought as much. What does it say underneath?"

"How would I ken? I canna read. But it looks like trouble to me, Brother Hubert. The Widow Carney should see it." He shoved the paper back at Hugh and darted out the gate.

Hugh's mother, Suannoch, had patiently tried to teach him to read, and he had done his best to make sense of the letters. He was better with numbers. Say the figures aloud, and he could add, subtract, divide, and multiply to get the right answer. Whenever Robin went to market, Hugh stayed right by his side to figure the prices and how much was spent or owed. But words on paper or in a book just looked like changing jumbles.

He struggled to figure out what it said on the poster. He knew a few of the words. "Hugh Cullane, wanted." He thought one might be "enemy." He'd have to show it to Kit to know exactly what it said.

"What are ye looking at?" asked the Widow Carney as she limped past him carrying three robes.

He handed her the poster. "Read it, " he said.

She dropped the robes and studied the poster.

After a minute of silence, he said, "Read it aloud."

Grateful that she didn't add to his humiliation by saying "Canna ye read?" she began to softly read Hugh's poster. "Wanted, Hugh Cullane, dead or alive. Enemy of Scotland. Spy and Traitor. Reward. Is this the only one ye found?"

"Aye."

"The soldiers following us on the road at the cliff must have told the earl I was dead after my fall."

"There may be more posters around. We have to get rid of them."

"Maybe no'," she said. "No one would think Brother Hubert might be the notorious Hugh Cullane."

She picked up the dropped robes and handed them to Hugh, saying, "Help the poor widow woman with her chores." Glancing around and seeing no one, she kissed him on the cheek.

Chapter Eighteen

Since being ordered to the side gate, the Grand Company slept in their wagons, forgoing the tents. Together in the wagons, they locked the doors as protection from the many people visiting the fair who didn't like unsavory actors showing their faces. People threw rotten apples, and even horse dung, at the sides of the wagons, which Peter cleaned off every morning, grumbling the entire time.

"If I ever find the fops doing this, I'll show them a thing or two," he muttered, shaking his fist.

"What will ye show them?" sneered Gus, carrying a bucket of water over to Peter. "How fast ye can run?"

Tossing a smashed apple in Gus's direction and laughing as Gus dodged it, Peter said, "All I have to do is run faster than ye!"

Crouching under the wagon, Mary dug holes in the dirt while Peter cleaned the sides, and she soon grew bored listening to him complain. Looking over her lovely holes, she decided she needed some flowers to fill them up. Perhaps seeing the flowers would make Peter happier. She remembered where just the right blooms grew, and even though she had orders to never leave sight of the wagons, she decided that getting the flowers would only take a minute or two. Then the space under the wagon would look beautiful, and Gus and Peter wouldn't even know she had gone.

Darting through the open gate, she headed right for a large well-tended flower garden in the back corner of the close near the wall. She held her nose as the smell from the castle garbage dump behind the pillory across the close, despite the tarpaulin covering it, wafted over to her, and with relief, she stepped into the sweet smelling garden.

She didn't know the names of any of the flowers growing there, but learning the flowers was next on her list after she learned the names of all the trees, but no matter the names, they were colorful and beautiful. Just what she needed.

Humming a tune she made up, she picked one, two, three bright orange multi-petaled blossoms. Stepping into the center of the garden, she reached for a soft pink bloom. "Ouch!" she said when a thorn pricked her finger. She sucked on it, regretting her decision to pick this particular flower, when she felt herself being lifted off the ground.

"What do ye think ye're doing?" asked the guard dragging her out of the flower bed by the arm. "Those are the queen's flowers."

Piqued, Mary answered, "I am the queen!"

"A thief and a liar to boot." Squatting down, the guard hoisted Mary over his knee and began to spank her. She kicked her legs and screamed at the top of her lungs as the man gave her one vicious swat after another until he suddenly found the child snatched off his knee and himself sprawled on the flowers.

"How dare ye?" cried the gray-haired old woman who had grabbed Mary from him and kicked him to the ground.

The guard pulled himself up to his feet and lifted

his spear, the only weapon ceremonial guards carried within the castle walls. The well-trained soldiers with more deadly weapons patrolling the walls could not be bothered with something so trivial as a child in the flower garden.

He pointed the spear at Widow Carney's throat.

Putting the child on the ground, Kit said, "Run, Mary, run!"

The child did as she had been taught, running as fast as her little legs would carry her back toward the wagons as Kit pushed the spear up and away with her arm. Ducking under the spear, she picked up an abandoned hoe on the edge of the garden and turned to face the guard. The two used their weapons to parry and thrust, forward and retreat, just as Rand had taught her. After one hard hit against the guard's spear, she leaped forward and thrust the wooden handle of the hoe into the guard's face with a quick jab. He instantly fell to the ground and pressed his hand against his bleeding eye.

Stepping beside the fallen guard, she dug the sharp end of the hoe into his throat.

"Dinna ye ever lay a hand on that child again!" she shouted.

Gus and Peter, having heard Mary's cries, came through the gate into the close. Gus scooped up Mary and held her tight while Peter ran toward the garden. Brother Hubert, lifting his robe over his long legs and running in the same direction, soon overtook him. As he did, he withdrew the dirk from the band around his waist. Holding out the weapon, he faced down three more guards who heard the commotion and had come to the aid of their now-moaning comrade lying in the flower bed.

Although clearly at a disadvantage with his shorter dirk against the long reach of the spears, Hugh held them off using techniques learned from his grandfather. He even backed them away toward the center of the yard, taking only a few glancing blows from their weapons.

Two more guards appeared at the flower garden, lunging at Kit, who held them off with her hoe until the man on the ground sat up, swung his spear at Kit's legs, and swept her feet out from under her. She landed hard, and although quickly able to leap back up, her advantage had been lost. The guards swarmed over her, beating her with their spears and fists.

The tide turned against both Kit and Hugh when four soldiers, this time ones trained in actual combat instead of ceremonial parade marching like the first four, entered the fray. They were startled at how ferociously an old woman could fight. Even without her hoe, she landed blows with enough strength to make each of them in turn step back, but even so she was no match for four against one.

Hugh sliced open one man's leg with his dirk, which allowed him to pick up that soldier's fallen sword. Now Hugh had a weapon of equal strength and the skill to match theirs. The clashing of the metal echoed with the grunts of the men as they fought.

Beatrice, hearing the commotion, came through the gate into the close. Grabbing Gus's arm, she said, "Get Mary away from here. Hide her in the wagon. Go!" Gus obeyed. Next, she took Peter by the arm. "Get back to the wagons!"

"I can help!"

"Nay, ye canna. Get the wagons ready to leave. If

Kit and Hugh are victorious, we will have to run. If they lose, 'tis our job to protect wee Mary. Go!"

This time Peter did as she said.

Hugh pressed his advantage by backing one guard against the wall when he heard another one shouting, "Stop or I'll run her through!"

Kit lay on her back on the ground with the man's sword pressed against her chest, both of his hands clutching the hilt ready to thrust. "Surrender or she dies!"

On her back like a helpless turtle, Kit called out to Hugh, "Leave me! Leave me! She is more important."

With no time to think, and really no need to even think about it anyway, Hugh dropped his sword and fell to his knees. "Let her go. Ye have me. I am the one the earl wants. 'Tis my face on the poster, no' the old woman's."

The three uninjured guards straightened their stances but did not take their eyes or their weapons off Hugh. The man hovering over Kit released his grip on his sword and dragged her to her feet while another forced her arms behind her back. The man on the ground with the injured eye stood up, and still clutching his eye, without saying a word, backhanded Kit across the face.

Hugh cried out, "Stop!" and for his trouble received the hilt of a sword to his jaw, knocking his face into the dirt.

"She goes to the dungeon. He goes to the stocks," said the guard closest to Kit.

"Let the old woman go!" shouted Hugh as two guards lifted him by the arms and dragged him toward the pillory at the back of the close. "There is a reward for me, no' her!"

At that Kit yanked off her wig. "I am Katherine Payne. Ye may have told the earl I was dead from the fall off the cliff, but I am no'."

Another slap across her face silenced her and knocked her backwards. "To the dungeon. The earl doesna want anything to disrupt the fair. He'll sort this out after the fair is closed. Take the bitch away!"

The guards dragged Kit away as the others forced Hugh's head and arms into the three cut-out holes on the pillory and slammed the top bar shut over him. It locked on the side, leaving him standing and trapped. He growled and shook the wooden stocks holding him.

"Cover him," said one guard. Two guards dragged off the tarpaulin covering the garbage pile and tossed it over Hugh, leaving him in dark and airless confinement.

"Are we going after the wee girl?" asked one of the older soldiers.

"Nay!" shouted the guard with the injured eye. "The earl demanded that naught disturb him until the fair is over. And naught will. Surround the wagons of the actors for the Feast of Fools, and dinna let them out of yer sight. When they're done with the play, we'll hang the lot of them."

"Even the wee lass?" asked another incredulous guard.

"Do ye want to hang in her place?"

Gulping hard, the guard said, "Nay, sir!"

Within minutes the wagons of the former Countryside Players, now the Grand Company, were surrounded by six castle guards while the Players trembled inside.

Chapter Nineteen

The Grand Company, surrounded by six guards, spent a sleepless night getting ready for the performance of their lives. Gus scripted a plan to return Hugh and Kit to their loving arms, along with a way for all of them to make their escape. It was indeed a brilliant plan, if only it would work. It had to work! This was their only chance.

That morning those same guards, made surly by having to stand on their feet all night, watched the troupe as they made their way through the gate into the close, past the pillory that held Hugh, into the kitchens, and finally on stage.

"This will be a once-in-a-lifetime entertainment," said Peter to the guard walking beside him.

"My entertainment will be when ye are hanged." He motioned with his arm to look like putting a noose around his neck and hanging from it. "I will enjoy seeing yer eyes pop out of yer head."

Peter's stomach turned over, but he didn't let his face show it. "I'd like to see that myself."

The soldier, giving Peter a hard shove, caused him to stumble, but Peter kept on laughing.

Once inside the castle, the guards followed the remaining actors through the pantry and then the kitchen to the backstage area behind the curtains.

"Ye can see the play better out front, once we open

the curtains for the crowd," said Damon to the soldiers.

"We have orders to no' let ye out of our sight," said the captain.

"Open the curtains, and we will be in yer sight on stage the whole time."

After a moment's hesitation, the captain said, "MacDuff, stay back here and make certain none of them go out the way we came in. The rest of ye, follow me." He led them to stand in a row on the floor at the front of the stage.

Damon, peeking around the edge of a curtain on the side of the stage with Jolene standing between his legs doing the same, stared in awe at the lavish decorations covering nearly every space and corner of the great hall. Fresh-smelling pine boughs tied together with bright red ribbons hung on every wall and across the three huge fireplaces. Each step anyone took on the polished floor crunched with thousands of colorful dried autumn leaves that dozens of maids swept out every night and then replaced every morning.

Also, each morning, enormous plates of pastries and breads and trays of sausages, pork, and sweetened porridge lined the long tables against the walls. At midday and again at sunset, cooks brought in plates of ham, roasts, and pies made from fresh game birds, all of it to be washed down with barrels of beer spiced with apples. The whiskey and wine were reserved for high ranking nobles and officials who wandered in randomly throughout the day. The crowds inside that afternoon numbered well into the hundreds.

Damon caught a glimpse of Peter darting in and around the food tables with a cloth bag that got mysteriously heavier and lumpier as he went. When he could barely lift his bag, he stepped back onto the stage, and Damon heard him clank. "Sounds like ye have noisy food in yer bag."

Peter winked. "We'll eat good tonight. The earl also has plenty of goblets to go around, and some to spare for us."

Today's showing of the Feast of Fools would begin on an elevated platform surrounded by red velvet curtains. A second section on wooden uprights, bordered on four sides by curtains, served as a changing area and as a hidden hallway out of the main hall to the kitchen, designed for the actors to enter and leave without a decent person having to look upon them. It would also ensure their escape with no one being the wiser.

To keep MacDuff distracted, Gus and Mary entertained him with their jokes and stories while Mary smothered him with childish hugs and kisses as Damon and Beatrice quietly rearranged the curtains to make two exits into the kitchen. MacDuff guarded only one of them while the other stayed out of his sight. The Company knew that double exits could be easily discovered and could still trap them onstage, so they also put together yet another plan to escape with their lives.

The captain insisted that the front curtains be open at all times, so the Company gathered backstage, but still within sight of the guards, for their final performance. Never again would they be able to perform together. If their rescue plan failed, they would be hanged. If it were successful, they would be outlaws for as long as the Earl of Arran lived.

"MacDuff, will ye join us in prayer?"

MacDuff shook his head and stepped to the edge of the stage.

"Mary," said Damon, "ye're the only one of us who kens how to pray. Will ye say some words to give us courage?"

"Is it all right if I make up the words?" she asked.

"If 'tis all right with the Lord, 'tis all right with us."

Mary began. "We need yer help, Lord. We are afeared, but we ken ye are with us. Give us courage to be strong until we are with ye in Heaven, but, Lord, dinna make that too soon. I canna go to Heaven without everyone I love, everyone. Amen!"

Now the company once known as the Countryside Players was ready.

The comedy premise of the Feast of Fools, being a bawdy spoof on religion, followed the same basic script every year, yet the acting company was expected to provide at least one original aspect to keep the production interesting.

The castle castellan called for everyone in the audience to be seated on chairs or pillows as dozens of actors entered and sat down in front of the stage. The castellan noticed that the acting troupe had grown considerably in size since he hired them, it being common practice to recruit servants from the household staff, a tradition he approved of as long as the extras didn't ask to be paid. These new Players were all clad in an array of colorful costumes, such as priests with deer antlers strapped to their heads, wolves' heads with knights' leggings, bearded men dressed as women, and a bevy of jesters and minstrels.

Damon, dressed as a priest, took the stage and

motioned for the Earl of Arran to come up. Arran strode forward and climbed the steps. Standing beside Damon, he handed over a cloth pouch that jingled with coins.

"Witness that I have paid this troupe, and I give ye permission to laugh at the rituals of the church that we all hold sacred every other day of the year. Ye need no' fear the fires of Hell for the mockery ye will see today. We have been promised the best Feast of Fools ever seen, and if they disappoint, well, for this much coin, they willna disappoint. Will ye?"

Damon opened the pouch and peeked in. With a look of utter glee at the amount, he shook the bag and smiled. "We willna fail ye, my lord. Prepare to be entertained!" He waved one hand for Arran to return to his seat and with the other signaled for the Parade of Fools to begin.

The audience shouted and cheered as the ridiculously costumed servants danced across the floor. They waved at ones they recognized, and sometimes even left their seats to pat their friends in the parade on the back.

After all the extras seated themselves along the outer walls, Damon went into his act by chanting nonsense syllables in front of a makeshift altar. Then turning to the audience, he declared, "A new pope has been ordained by the high Lord Himself, and he is within our walls! Approach, yer Royal Eminence!"

Stepping out of the side curtains, a small version of the pope appeared. His white robes, obviously far too big, dragged on the floor, and he kept tugging at them from behind. His tall, papal hat slipped over his eyes, and he flailed his arms around trying to find his way. Damon dashed over to help the tiny pope, also known as Mary within the Grand Company, to a throne on the rear of the stage. Mary had begged to be part of the production, and with her promise to not vary one bit from the script and to sit very still on the throne, the Players agreed.

The audience again roared in laughter at the thought of a "boy" pope. "I dub ye the Lord of Misrule!" shouted Damon, falling to his knees and struggling in a most humorous way to get back to his feet.

Immediately, he went back to the altar where, between outlandish rituals when he couldn't remember how to cross himself, he raced around a curtain to a spot visible to the audience. There he passionately kissed a woman, really a man in disguise—Peter! Each time Damon kissed "her," he announced loudly, "The bishops says I must reach my parishioners in a way they understand. This is all a stewholder's wench understands. Jesus healed the lepers, and so I must heal her with my lips!"

Later, that same "woman" appeared at the altar, greatly pregnant, saying in a squeaky, high-pitched voice, "My name is Mary, and I found myself in a family way with no man to claim the deed. I wouldna ken which one of the dirty blades to blame anyway. What can I do? I ken! I will say 'tis a gift from God, a virgin birth. Me mum's so daft, she'll believe anything!" The audience could not contain their hoots and hollers.

This provided all the distraction Gus needed to slip out the hidden exit and move through the hallways of the castle unseen.

Before the soldiers had arrested Kit, she had drilled

the Players on an escape plan should things go awry since the troupe had been forced to perform inside the walls. She taught them where every nook, corner, and hiding place was in Stirling Castle. She drew pictures and questioned each of them on what to look for so that, even blindfolded, they could make their way out of the castle to the wagon and escape.

But now that she was locked in the dungeon and Hugh in the pillory, the plan had to change. After much discussion the night before and arguing back and forth about who would take the most risk, it became Gus's role to first free Hugh and then go after Kit. The trio would come back on stage in costume, and the entire troupe could leave together with no one being the wiser—if all went as planned.

Everyone took a role in the performance, even Beatrice and Jolene, although if the audience discovered a woman out front of the curtains it might cause a riot. Beatrice declared it absurd that a woman on stage meant the worst kind of bad luck. "Without the women to make the costumes, the men would go on stage naked."

Mary delighted in working with Beatrice and Jolene organizing the costumes and helping the men make quick changes for the different characters. When she wasn't on stage as the "pope," she wore her own costume of cut down breeches and tunic to fit. Jolene tightly tied a scarf over her now brown hair, making the child look more like a lad than the possible queen of Scotland.

****

After the play began, Gus flung a heavy pack over his shoulder and left through the curtained tunnel leading to the kitchen. From there, he followed Kit's map through the now deserted pantries and laundry and into the dank passageway leading to the dungeon. Just where Kit said it would be was the heavy door that served as the entrance to the prison from the outside, and across from it another door to the interior of the close. The pillory stood about ten yards to the left of that door inside the close.

Gus knelt, opened the door a crack, and peeked out. A pair of black military boots appeared before his eyes.

He went rigid.

Chapter Twenty

Back on stage, Peter, still dressed as Mary, dragged a very reluctant Beatrice, disguised as Joseph, on stage and ordered the priest to marry them. Joseph's confused expressions and outlandish reactions entertained the audience to no end. Damon drew out the ceremony by reading from an upside-down Bible and drinking copious quantities of sacramental wine. He closed the marriage service with a lingering kiss on Mary's mouth. While Joseph waited for the kiss to end, he also got drunk on the wine. Later, Mary rode across the stage on Joseph's back, still kissing the priest, while the extras from the castle made endless jokes about Joseph the ass.

****

Trapped between the entrance to the pit prison on one side and the outside yard on the other, Gus silently closed the door and waited until he thought the guard had moved away on his rounds. Easing the door open again, he scanned the outside yard of the close. Scrambling out, he ran toward the most putrid and foul accumulation of rotting garbage he had ever seen, the castle refuse dump, behind the pillory just where Kit said it would be. The pile consisted of every imaginable form of garbage—animal, vegetable, and mineral—and created a stinking haven for vermin of all sorts. Gus held his breath and dug a hole for himself in the muck.

Hidden, he let three more patrols of guards pass by as he counted how long it took them to make the monotonous circuit through the prison itself, walk outside around the wall, and then back into the yard. Now that he had it calculated, it became time to act.

When the last patrol passed, Gus pushed his way out of the refuse and dashed to the pillory. Lifting the tarpaulin, he crawled into the darkness, dragging his heavy bag behind him.

Hugh felt the whiff of fresh air, followed by the sensation of something crawling over the platform between his legs. "Get away!" he said, stomping his feet.

"Shh!" whispered Gus. "I've come to get ye out, but we canna have anyone peeking in. Be quiet."

"Ye stink," Hugh whispered back.

"I canna help it. Twenty-six, twenty-seven. I canna see a bloody thing in here. Which side is the lock on?"

"My left."

"Thirty-five, thirty-six, thirty-seven," said Gus as he stood and reached for the lock. It clicked against the wood when he fingered it.

"What are ye counting?"

"Footsteps."

****

At the Feast of Fools, another performer, a giant of a man dressed in a flowing black robe, appeared on stage with his face hidden by a grisly mask of white and black painted to represent Death. Fierce eyes glared at the audience. As he strode to center stage, the laughter stopped, and the audience fell into tomblike silence. Even the extra actors of the servants stopped their antics and stared.

In a frighteningly hoarse voice, Death shouted, "I foresee the great day! The day of my coming is near! It will be a bitter day of wrath and fear, a day of darkness and terror, a day that will come for ye!"

Peter, Beatrice, and Damon crouching at Death's feet, shivered and cried in absolute agony. "Who are ye here for today?" pleaded each of them in turn. "No' me! No' me!"

****

Gus tugged a circle of keys out of his sleeve. "These are Peter's personal set of keys. He claims he can open anything with them." Choosing one, Gus pushed it into the lock and turned. After only a few seconds, the lock fell open. "Got it on the first try. Ninety-eight, ninety-nine, one hundred. Hush!"

Both men froze as the trio of guards marched by. One of the soldiers jabbed his spear into the tarpaulin, and Hugh moaned just as he had all the other times the guard had poked at him. Laughing, the guard kept marching.

Gus said, "On my say, get ready to step out of the stocks, but hold on to the post and no falling off the stone base. After a night and day in the stocks, a man's joints seize up. So be ready. I dinna want those long legs sticking out."

The hinge on the board over Hugh's head and arms creaked open.

"Thirty-five, thirty-six. Step out."

Hugh stumbled backwards but was able to grasp the post and stay upright. Gus reached for the large bundle he had carried into the tarpaulin with him.

"Ye have to help me," he said. "Hold up the bar." Gus hefted the bag of cloth, stuffed and sewn into the shape of a man, into position while Hugh forced his stiff muscles to lift the bar. "Sixty-seven, sixty-eight." The bag fell out.

"Try again." This time Hugh grabbed onto one of the stuffed arms and jammed it into an armhole. With the cloth "man" in place, Gus lowered the upper bar and relocked it.

"They'll think it's witchcraft," grinned Gus. "Eighty-seven, eighty-eight. Duck down and dinna move."

Before long, the guards passed by again, and again one of them poked his spear into the tarpaulin. Hugh moaned as the tip of the spear poked the "head" of the stuffed man in the stocks.

"Hold on to me," Gus said, lifting the tarpaulin. "We're going after Mistress Katherine."

****

The figure of Death waved a trembling bony finger in the direction of James Hamilton, the Earl of Arran, seated on a chair high on a platform at the center of the hall. " 'Tis ye who wagers the lives of others in search of a throne!"

The earl gave a nervous laugh, saying, "I hope the bairns are no' too afeared."

"The day I come will be a day of ruin and devastation, of anguish and terror," continued the seven-foot-tall figure of Death, his voice echoing from one end of the room to the other. "One man will cry out for the thousands he led to their deaths, but his tears will be useless. I will take my vengeance, and he will suffer in the burning fires!"

Calling back to the "pope" on stage, Death said, "Father of Misrule, do ye sentence such a man to Hell?"

The "pope" raised her hand and waved it in the air. When all eyes turned again to the giant figure of Death, the "pope" jumped off the throne and slipped behind the curtains.

The lightheartedness of the play vanished as children hid behind their mothers' skirts and the men, suddenly sober, put down their mugs. The earl gripped the arms of his chair and gritted his teeth against the terrifying turn this event had taken.

"Yer flesh shall rot as a carcass in the burning sun. Ye will walk blind among the men ye have sinned against! Their blood will pour over yer skin!"

Death inched its way off the stage, down the steps, and down the aisle toward the earl's chair. People scampered out of the way, their eyes wide with terror.

"Yer gold and silver canna deliver ye from my wrath! I will deliver ye to Satan!"

The figure of Death stood within a few feet of the earl's chair with every eye in the hall fixed on the two of them.

"Are ye a fool?" said Hamilton in a low, rough voice. "Get back on that stage and change the tone of this play, or ye will be the one meeting death."

Death bowed respectfully, the top of his mask nearly touching the top of the earl's head, but Death did not leave his position in the aisle.

A woman seated nearby screeched and fainted.
                          ****
Once in the dim light of the prison hallway, Hugh called out softly, "Katherine, can ye hear me?"

"Over here," she replied.

He darted past two empty cells until he came to hers. Peering through the small barred window in the

222

door, he saw her standing in the center of the cell on the stone floor. One of her eyes was swollen shut, and her lip had split open in the corner of her mouth.

His heart suddenly pounded, and his fists convulsed with rage. In the hours earlier, trapped in the pillory, he'd resolved to get free and get to her. Now he and Gus had a mission with a duty to fulfill, but all he wanted to do was lash out at whoever dared do this to Kit. In her eyes, he saw they had broken her spirit. They had broken her courageous heart, and he had to get to her to bring back the Goddess Athena to the woman who had changed his life.

Gus touched him on the arm, but Hugh shook him off.

"Ninety-two, ninety-three, ninety-four," counted Gus. The rhythmic footsteps of the three guards making their rounds that took them along the cells inside and then outside, over and over again, came closer.

Reluctantly, Hugh whispered, "They're coming. Sit down on the floor. We'll be back." He and Gus ducked into the shadows of a small alcove between the cells and, despite Gus's stench of garbage, the guards walked by without noticing.

"One, two, three," Gus began when once more they stood at Kit's cell door.

"Are ye all right?" Hugh asked. "Are ye in pain?"

"I survived."

Reaching into his tunic, Gus pulled out his ring of keys. One by one he inserted them into the lock, twisting and turning until, on the sixth try, the cell door swung open. "Peter is one clever fellow, if I do say so myself."

Hugh crossed over to Kit and put his arms around

her.

Despite flinching with pain, she leaned her head into his chest.

"I've got ye now," Hugh said.

"Twenty-three, twenty-four," Gus said.

"Follow me," said Hugh. "We'll have more time when we're out of here." Taking her hand, he took a step toward the door.

She didn't move. In a lifeless monotone, she said, "I'm chained to the wall."

A heavy shackle wrapped around her ankle with a five-foot chain buried into the wall. Squatting down beside her, he inserted each one of Peter's skeleton keys in the lock, but the shackle wouldn't open. "Peter was wrong."

"Eighty-seven, eighty-nine. They're coming."

Hugh, tucking himself into as small a ball as he could next to the bench on the back wall, crouched as Kit hurried to stand in front of him. Gus pressed himself against the door below the window. Again, the three guards marched by without breaking their rhythm or looking into the cell.

Hugh knelt again to examine the chain attached to the wall. He tugged at it, and, with a crunching sound, it gave way a little. Standing, he grabbed the chain with both hands and pulled with a loud grunt. It held fast.

"Help me," he said. "Mayhap we can do it together."

"Thirty-three, thirty-four."

Three sets of hands locked onto the chain, and the three gave it their best effort. The chain loosened but didn't pull free.

"Sixty-one, sixty-two."

"Again!"

The bolt wiggled in the ever-widening hole, and when it released, all three landed on their backsides on the floor of the cell with a thud.

"Ye're free," Hugh said. "Now let's get out of here."

"Seventy-six, seventy-seven."

"On their next round."

Hugh scrambled to hide by the bench again while she tossed the chain behind her and stood to cover him. Gus squatted by the door.

On the count of ninety-nine, the trio of guards strode past again, but this time one of them stopped and looked through the bars at Kit.

"Even with a black eye, ye're a fine-looking woman," he said, jingling the keys on his belt. "A tumble with ye might liven up the day. How about it, lads?" He inserted one of his keys into the lock and turned it, not noticing how easily the door swung open, so eager he was to get at Kit.

****

In the main hall, Death stood steady in the aisle beside the Earl of Arran's chair. Arran whispered, "Go back to the stage."

Instead of obeying, Death put a wooden skeletal hand on Arran's shoulder, saying in the same grating voice, "We see how ye have suffered, how ye long for deliverance, how ye hope to be saved from the souls that haunt ye! Put yer hope and trust in what ye canna see. Come with me!"

Death's hand tugged on Arran's shoulder, but the man had no intention of cooperating. "Let me go! Guards!"

Boots clicked against the wooden floor as four guards raced toward the figure of Death, but instead of releasing the earl, Death yanked him even closer. Arran struggled, but Death refused to let go.

"Guards!" the man screamed.

Two soldiers stepped within reach, wrapped their arms around Death, and tackled him to the floor. The seven-foot figure, now entangled by two soldiers in chest armor, spun down the aisle, arms and legs flying. When the tumbling trio finally came to a stop, the audience watched in horror as Death's head left his shoulders and continued up the aisle.

When the head finally stopped rolling just short of the stage, a small boy cried out, "He killed Death!"

But now the secret to Death's imposing size had been revealed. His head was only a black and white mask secured to a wooden form that in turn was attached to a set of wooden shoulders. Two long sticks jutted out above each shoulder, which had been hidden under a flowing black robe that now stretched out limply on the floor. Peering out of a split in the robe held together with a mesh-like piece of fabric was the actor who had so brazenly threatened the earl.

With a sheepish grin, the actor stood up, unveiled and exposed to Arran's fury and to the disgusted looks of the audience. Adults curled their lips in revulsion. Children pointed and covered their faces.

"Well, what have we here?" asked James Hamilton as he left his chair and loomed over the figure on the floor.

"Hello, milord," said Jolene. "I hope I didna offend."

Chapter Twenty-One

The door opened wide while Gus scooted into the corner behind it out of sight. The guard, a burly man with a flat nose and narrow mouth, walked in and crossed over to the prisoner while at the same time untying his breeches. "Come on, lads. A fine time can be had by all."

The words were barely out of his mouth before Kit reached behind her, picked up the chain dangling from her ankle and swung it into his face. His cheek split open, exposing his jaw and his teeth, and he fell against the wall in an unconscious heap.

Hugh greeted the other two guards who had followed their comrade into the cell, by charging at them. He grabbed the closest one by the collar and threw him against the wall near the door, where Gus chopped the side of his hand into the guard's Adam's apple. Choking and coughing, the man collapsed.

The third guard had time to draw his sword and swung it in Hugh's direction, but Hugh avoided the man's wide swing before using his head and neck to ram into the man's stomach, driving him into the wall. The sword clanked to the floor and slid out the open cell door into the hallway out of reach.

When this third guard regained his senses, he stood and reached out for Kit, but he had not anticipated her devastating fighting skills. After ramming the heel of her hand into his nose, she grabbed his wrist with both hands and rolled under his arm twice until she heard the elbow snap. A sharp kick to his groin finished him off. He vomited and fainted.

Gus's victim against the wall wobbled into a sitting position right before Hugh rammed a knee into the man's chin, breaking his jaw and rendering him unconscious.

Hugh gasped for breath. "We have to hurry. The play may already be over."

He took her hand, but she tugged back. "Where is Mary? Ye're to take care of her first."

"Mary is safe."

"Why did ye risk her safety to come for me?" she demanded.

The two creases on each side of his smile covered his cheeks. "Because ye are here."

Grabbing the keys off the first guard's belt, Hugh found the one to release the shackle from Kit's ankle. All of them darted out of the cell, and Hugh locked the door. They started to run until Hugh saw that the usually strong and agile Kit struggled to keep up. Sweeping her up in his arms, they headed toward the main hall.

Nestling her head on Hugh's shoulder, she whispered, "Thank ye."

****

Arran glared down at the female dwarf on the floor at his feet. "Take her away," he snarled, "far away."

Just as the guard closed in on Jolene on the main floor, Hugh, Kit, and Gus reached the back of the stage. Spying their return, Beatrice dashed off stage and ushered them into the newly created second exit, pointing to a pile of curtains to set Kit down.

"What is going on?" asked Hugh. "I want to see."

Beatrice pushed him back, whispering, "There's a guard right there."

MacDuff had moved to the edge of the curtain to see what was going on in the audience, and he couldn't help himself but to cheer on the little dwarf.

Hugh, nodding to acknowledge that he understood they were being watched, said, "We have to get out of here. 'Tis too dangerous."

"Wait," Beatrice said. "We'll soon be gone."

"But how?"

Gus interrupted, "Follow our lead. We got ye this far. We can get ye the rest of the way. Now watch this. It works like a charm, and Jolene is just the woman to do it."

Jolene's high-pitched voice floated over the crowd. "Huzzah! Huzzah! Milord, ye performed splendidly. Huzzah! Huzzah!" Her little hands clapped eagerly as she jumped up and down.

"Is the earl no' the best?" she said to the people seated around her.

The guard reached for her red hair to jerk her into his grasp, but all he got for his trouble was her wig. Her own beautiful tresses fell out in shiny waves of cinnamon.

"What the bloody hell?" cursed the guard as Jolene somersaulted between the guests and away from him. "Get back here, ye wee hobgoblin!"

She answered with a shrill giggle. "Come and get me."

The guard got down on his hands and knees and crawled after her while the audience laughed and cheered her on. "He's close, wee one! Run!" Some of them even moved into the guard's path to slow him down.

All at once, Jolene thrust her head between a standing man's legs and, looking up at him, said, "Did ye think I could truly frighten our brave Earl of Arran?" The man shook his head.

She scrambled away, crawled between another man's legs, and then hopped up on the lap of yet another visitor to the castle.

" 'Twas all the earl's idea, ye ken," she said in a loud voice. "He thought to add spice and class to our miserable Feast of Fools. Didna he do a fine job of it?" Pulling herself up on the man's thighs to standing, she pointed at the earl, shouting, "Huzzah! Huzzah!" With her encouragement, the audience soon joined in the chant. "Huzzah! Huzzah!"

On cue, Peter shouted over the clamor until the noise quieted down so everyone could hear him. "Ye willna be forgetting this Feast of Fools! The earl wanted ye to have something remarkable to talk about through the year to come. What could be more memorable than a dwarf dressed as a giant? What better way to keep yer attention than to threaten the master of the house? 'Twas all the earl's idea to please ye! Are ye pleased?"

The audience responded with cheers and shouts.

The scowl on the face of James Hamilton, however, told Peter exactly what he thought of this production, but that he would never express it in public, not now that the crowd so definitely enjoyed the farce.

The frustrated guard chasing Jolene finally caught up with her and, reaching over the man's head, picked up the little woman and held her under the armpits out in front of him. All the while she kicked her legs and flailed her arms, still shouting about the brilliant creativity of the earl.

As the guard carried her toward the door, Jolene said seductively, but still loud enough for the audience to hear, "Ye can have yer way with me any time ye want, ye brute. I love a man who takes charge." Her sloppy loud kisses between almost every word, and the guard's look of utter horror at the thought of kissing a dwarf, sent the audience into more gales of laughter. Without warning, she reached up and tweaked his nose. It startled him so much he dropped her to the floor where she again somersaulted down the aisle toward the stage.

At the stage's edge, Peter leaned over and lifted her up where she took several long deep bows.

A young boy cried, "Do it again! Do it again!"

A finely dressed man shouted, "Ye had me fooled, earl!"

Others joined in, "More! More!"

Waving his arms for silence, Peter announced, "An encore it is! Give us time to change our costumes. Stay seated, and we'll be right back with more to entertain and amaze before ye can blink!"

The captain of the guard reached up on the stage and grabbed Peter by the leg. "Ye canna get out of our sight." To the rest of the soldiers standing on the floor, he ordered, "Dinna let them out of yer sight!"

They jumped up onto the stage, but Damon spread his arms, saying, "If ye sit here on the edge, ye can still see us changing behind the curtain. MacDuff, come here and sit with yer comrades. Ye have all been on yer feet for too long."

The captain gave him a skeptical look.

"Do ye see the black curtains over there?"

"Aye."

"We'll be behind there changing, but 'twill spoil the surprise if ye see our costumes afore we come out on stage. How about we keep hitting on the curtain the whole time we're back there? Ye'll see the curtain billow every time, so ye'll ken we're still there."

The captain's expression darkened.

Not to be deterred, Damon shouted to the audience, "Do ye want to be surprised by something even greater than our giant dwarf?"

The audience responded with, "Aye! Aye! Surprise us! Surprise us!"

The captain, still uncertain as to his duty to guard these prisoners, turned his head toward the earl. His expression asked, "What do ye want us to do?"

The earl stood up and waved his hands for silence. "As yer host, I have no greater duty than to please my guests. Let these performers change behind the curtain so we may all be enchanted by their next presentation. Captain, keep an eye on that curtain." He sat down to boisterous cheers, stomping of feet, and snapping of fingers.

Behind the curtain, Hugh ordered Peter and Damon to leave with the women and to be in the wagon ready to go, while Gus set up the most ingenious and inventive part of their escape plan.

From under the pile of curtains, Gus pulled out two wooden devices, one about two feet high and the other about three feet in height. A center post held up a wheel made into a circle by exact placement of small spokes of wood, and each wheel had seven wooden arms with thick chunks of wood attached on the ends.

"What are these?" asked Hugh.

"Wait and see," whispered Gus.

He set one device on the floor close to the curtain and the other on a bench a little way away. Tapping on the first one, the arms started to whirl around, hitting the curtain in a regular rhythm. The weight of each arm as it twirled forced the wheel to keep turning by itself. As each arm hit the curtain, it billowed out. Counting the hits in his head, Gus watched until he was satisfied that he could start the second device so that its arms hit with a different rhythm higher up on the curtain.

"Clever," said Hugh. "I'll stay and keep them moving until I'm certain ye're all gone. Then I'll follow."

"No need," said Gus, puffing his chest out with pride. " 'Twill keep moving by itself. I dinna ken how long, but long enough for us to be out of Stirling afore they figure we're gone. Come on."

Following Gus, Hugh said to himself, "Perpetual motion. Clever!"

Passing through the kitchen, Gus and Hugh pushed a large table in front of the door to slow down anyone following them. In the pantry, a set of shelves laden with food did the same for that door. At the outside door, Hugh propped a long piece of lumber against the door and held it in place with a smaller piece in the dirt.

Outside the back gate, while waiting for Hugh and Gus, Damon and Peter dragged the lavender-painted wagon, wedging it into the opening to stop anyone who might follow them while Beatrice, Mary, and Kit tugged all the drapery off the green wagon, cut the cloth off the wheels, and flipped the signs, nailing them in place.

After Hugh and Gus crawled out under the lavender wagon blocking the gate, the newly created ratcatchers clambered into the remaining wagon, and Peter urged the two mules around the back of the castle, along the outskirts of the fair, and up the north road.

Arran and his audience waited and waited, growing more and more restless until, much to the Earl of Arran's fury and to the audience's disappointment, they realized they had been abandoned.

Chapter Twenty-Two

Fear from their dangerously close escape at the castle lingered inside the wagon, and everyone, except Peter who drove the mules, held their loved ones near. Beatrice and Damon sat in the back corner of the wagon close to each other, silently holding hands. Gus and Jolene cuddled in the opposite corner on a jumbled pile of quilts as Gus murmured soothing sounds to his wife, while Hugh and Kit couldn't seem to get close enough to each other in the front corner, nearly hidden in the pile of curtains made from the "robes of dead lepers." Wee Mary scampered between Beatrice and Kit, not seeming to be able to settle anywhere, resting only briefly within each one's arms before jumping up and moving again.

Kit said to Hugh in a low voice, "They beat me. I fought back, but they were four against one. I finally had to curl in a ball and endure." Her arms and back were covered with painful purple bruises and raw scrapes that only added to her injuries from the fall off the cliff, but she needed to get as near to Hugh as she could. His heartbeat restored her resolve, and his body warmth soothed her aches.

Hugh continued to seethe inside, furious that he hadn't been there to stand beside her and fight with her. His only consolation was that he now gave her ease in his arms. He held her close but with a gentle touch.

"I thought I'd ne'er see ye again," she said with a catch in her voice. "When they left me alone, I was desperate for ye."

"What about the others?"

"I kenned I would miss Beatrice and Damon, Jolene and Gus, and even Peter, but I couldna go on without ye."

"And Mary?"

"She'd be safe with Beatrice and the others, and ye would make sure she was protected, so I didna worry for her, but ye…I needed ye."

Again, his chest caught at the thought that she had withstood this without him. "I can hardly bear that I wasna there with ye, but ken that my heart ne'er left ye alone."

Stretching her arm tighter around him, she said, "I felt ye, right here." She tapped between her breasts. "I ne'er let anyone into my heart afore, no' the nuns in the convent who raised me, and no' the man who wed me. I had only me, and I needed no one else. I thought that was how life was meant to be …until ye jumped out of that tree."

Propping herself up on her elbow to look directly at him, she went on. "I fought against letting ye in. When we first met, I ne'er kenned how much ye could mean to me, until I was alone in that cell, when I couldna fight anymore. Hugh Cullane of Makgullane, I love ye with all I am, and without ye the daylight ne'er comes." She dropped her head back to his shoulder.

His waiting for her to love him was over.

"I want to tell ye something," he said. "I still dinna ken the why of it, but all my life I searched for something, for someone, without ever kenning what I was looking for. All the mistakes I made, all the wrong directions I went, were worth it because if I had done one thing differently, I ne'er would have found ye. With ye, with ye, I've found my place in the world."

She lifted her eyes to him. "We found each other when we didna expect it."

"By promise made, I will always find ye," he said. "No matter how long it takes, no matter what I have to do, I will find ye. That is my promise, my vow, my oath. I will find ye. My life depends on it."

He kissed her, and their bond was sealed.

Not wanting her to see the tear of joy forming in the corner of his eye, he softly caressed her head while avoiding her swollen eye and lip, as he hummed a tune he had learned as a child, a lullaby.

She closed her eyes. "That's pretty," she said.

"I dinna ken where I first heard it, but I sang it when I was afraid. It soothed me and made me feel safe. The words go like this."

Baloo baleerie, Babo baleerie,
Baloo baleerie, Babo baleerie,
Gang awa' peerie faeries, Gang awa' peerie faeries,
Gang awa' peerie faeries, Frae oor ben noo.
Doon come the bonny angels, Doon come the bonny angels,
Doon come the bonny angels, Tae oor ben noo.
Sleep saft my baby, Sleep saft my baby.

"Ye have a nice voice."

He went back to humming while stroking his fingers through her hair that had started to grow out from Beatrice's shearing to fit under the wig. Soon her abundant chestnut hair would flow down her back again.

"I like that," she murmured. After a time, her body relaxed, and she slept peacefully for the first time in a very long time.

Peter, having hung lanterns on either side of his seat, kept the wagon moving, however slowly, through the night. The rain started at daybreak.

The patter of rain falling on the roof comforted those inside until the mules, struggling to pull the weight through the muddy ruts and bumps on the road, brayed and balked, tossing the passengers against the walls.

Peter, still tugging the reins, opened the small sliding door behind the driver's seat. "Soldiers," was all he said before closing the little door again.

Immediately, Gus covered Jolene completely with a thick robe before sitting in front of her and leaning back as if the lump were his bed. Hugh and Kit buried themselves in the curtains as Damon pushed one of the costume trunks in front of them while Beatrice gathered Mary in her arms, covered her with a shawl, and whispered, "Stay asleep, wee one. No matter what happens, stay asleep. Do ye understand? No matter what." Mary nodded and closed her eyes.

Outside, Peter tugged his cloak over his head and face and asked the men who rode up to the wagon, "Is there trouble ahead? Is the road washed out?"

"Where ye headed?" asked a hoarse voice that Kit recognized as one of the guards who had beat her in the prison at Stirling Castle.

Peter answered, "To Perthshire."

"Yer business there?"

With a hearty laugh, Peter slapped his knee and

declared, "The Michaelmas Fair in Stirling was a boon for us! Rats all over the place, but we kept the fair clear of the vermin. Burned every wee beast we caught. What a fire, it was! Tell the earl 'twas our privilege to do it." Leaning close to the man on the horse beside the wagon, he smiled and said, "And that Feast of Fools! 'Twas all the talk in the market. Wish we could have seen it, but folks like us are ne'er allowed to set foot inside the walls."

The heavily bearded guard spit. "I asked ye what yer business was in Perthshire."

Peter replied, "We live there. The town has plenty of rats, and we make a good living. We heard there was a dwarf. I would give that mule right there to see that. I ne'er saw one afore. Are ye looking for the dwarf?"

"Nay! We're looking for escaped prisoners, a man, a woman, and a lass." He held up a poster for Peter who took it from him. Whoever the artist was that the Earl of Arran employed drew careful and accurate sketches of Hugh, Kit, and Mary. Peter would have recognized them anywhere, as would anyone else who saw their faces.

But Peter showed no sign of recognition as he continued his banter. "A fine-looking trio if I ever saw one. Have they got all their teeth? That would make them hard to miss around here." Peter, who was missing one tooth in the front and another on the side, opened his mouth wide. "See! I always look at the teeth. Ye should always look at the teeth."

"Ye got a face like a mud puddle, so we ain't looking for ye or yer teeth."

Peter took the insult about being ugly in stride and kept on jabbering. "Ye had a wee girl in prison? And she got away from ye? What did she do? Slip through the bars?" Peter laughed as he mimed pulling apart bars and sticking his head through, making a flabbergasted face.

"Shut yer mouth, bampot!"

"Is there a reward? I could sure use a reward."

With an angry growl, the guard said, "We're going to search yer wagon." He reined his horse to the back of the wagon and tugged on the door. It opened, letting the rain blow in. "Who's in here?" he demanded.

Peter, thrust his face through the small door in the front, saying, " 'Tis my wife, Honey, my uncle, Charles, and my brother, Simon." Each one in turn waved. "We been ratcatchers for three generations."

"What ye got in yer arms, woman?" challenged the soldier.

Beatrice turned on the tears. " 'Tis my grandbairn. He's verra sick, goes from hot to cold, and is covered with spots. Do ye want to see him?" Beatrice held out her bundle without uncovering Mary's face. "Mayhap ye can help him."

"Measles!" shouted the man, slamming the door shut. "Move along and dinna stop!" he shouted at Peter. "If I see this wagon again, I'll burn it with all of ye inside! Be off!"

Peter slapped the reins and urged the mules forward while the three soldiers rode back in the direction of Stirling.

Nearly thirty minutes passed before Peter slid open the small door again and said, "I canna see them, and ahead is clear. No one on the road." He handed back the Wanted poster, which Damon took from him after moving the trunk out of the way so Hugh and Kit could uncover themselves.

Jolene threw off the quilts saying, "Ye're heavier than ye look, Gus, my dear one. Let me stretch my legs."

"Ye did a fine job, Mary," said Beatrice.

Mary pulled her fingers out of her mouth. "Now I really am sleepy." So Beatrice tucked her under a quilt in the corner and kissed her on the forehead. "Ye are loved," she said.

"I ken," said Mary with a yawn.

"I canna believe Arran would put a reward out on a wee lass," said Hugh in a whisper so as not to wake Mary. Kneeling beside the small door in the front, he said to Peter, "We have to get off the main road and stay hidden if we can. Is there anywhere ye can get out of sight?"

A half a mile later, Peter turned off the main road leading toward Perth onto not much more than a cow path. He hadn't gotten very far when it became too hard for the mules to pull the wagon through the thick, wet mud no matter how hard he slapped the reins.

Peter said, "We have to rest the beasts. Hugh and Gus, come out and see if we can coax them behind that abandoned croft I see ahead."

The rain continued to fall in sharp drops blown by the wind into sheets that ran down the faces and backs of the men tugging on the harnesses of the defiant mules. By what seemed like inches, the wagon eventually ended up partially hidden behind the deserted croft. Its thatched roof had disintegrated, leaving large gaps, and the mixture of stone and sod sides barely stood, but at least the wagon was not in the open.

The men unhitched the mules and led them into what little shelter the broken-down croft offered. Despite the continuing heavy rain, the men went back out again to pull up handfuls of grass and carry it in to feed the mules. A bucket from the wagon held enough water for both animals and would be filled up by the rain dripping through the holes in the roof.

Inside the wagon, the three shivering men dried off, and because they'd been forced to leave most of their costumes and props at the castle, they put on the only spare clothing available. Hugh donned the leggings and tunic of a knight. Gus tugged on tights and a shirt that made him look like a spritely elf while Peter could now pass for an elegantly dressed mayor of a burg. They all ate heartily from the food Peter stole at the castle, and when the sun set, the entire cast of the former Countryside Players, now ratcatchers, settled into a restless sleep.

The next morning, over another plentiful meal thanks to the Earl of Arran, the troupe talked about plans for their future while Beatrice scavenged for odd pieces of cloth, turning them around, cutting the edges, and stitching them together into suitable tunics and leggings for all her men.

Damon suggested the troupe head for the coast for a simple life of fishing. "We catch them; they pay us to eat them. Nothing could be easier."

"I'd love to have a place to cook that wasna an open campfire," mused Beatrice, handing Gus a new brown tunic.

"What do ye ken about fishing?" snapped Peter.

"I was raised by the ocean. I ken more than enough to feed ye."

"I think," said Peter, "we should go far enough away from here so we can be the Players again. If we change our names to something like the Masterful Company, then we can perform all over the north. Or maybe sail to Ireland. Nobody kens us there."

Gus tugged Jolene close. "We want to look for a place away from people where we can raise a few sheep and grow vegetables enough to keep us fed. A place where no one will take offense at my Jolene, where we can live in peace. I want to look for a place like that."

Even Mary had her own ideas. "I want a home that has a lot of children to play with. I dinna care if they are lads or lasses, just so they want to play with me. I ne'er had someone to play with." Nestling her face into Beatrice's ample chest, she said, "Please!"

Hugh, however, knew exactly how quickly the winds of fortune could turn.

"These are all fine plans," he said, "but we canna do any of them right now. Arran willna give up looking for us for a verra long time, and together we're easier to find. All it takes is for one person to spot the lot of us and turn us in for the reward. I think we need to split up and go in different directions."

No one spoke.

Peter stuck out his lip. "None of us want to split up. Ye canna make us."

"I dinna want to make ye do anything. I only want us to be safe. Yer best chance is to be as far away from me and Kit as ye can get."

Kit put her hand on Hugh's shoulder. "I believe Hugh is right. Together we're too easy to recognize. Even as ratcatchers we're hard to miss." She paused. "Hugh and I and Mary will go to Makgullane, Hugh's home in the Highlands. We'll be safe there. The rest of ye can choose where ye want to go, and we'll do our best to make it happen."

The Players spent the rest of the day making plans, sharing their memories, and putting into words the love they had for each other. Tears flowed as they grieved for the end of their years together.

Chapter Twenty-Three

Hugh, Gus, and Peter set out the next morning on foot in different directions to see what they might find that could help them. Hugh made it clear that with Arran still in power, they couldn't spend any of the silver coins from their fee at the Feast of Fools, at least not yet, so to get what they needed, they had to be creative. Fortunately, being creative was something the Players did well.

Hugh walked up to a small cluster of six houses at a curve in the road that included a cartwright with, among other things, one wagon and three carts in various stages of construction behind his shed.

"Hail, my friend," said Hugh. "I see ye have a fine business here. Are any of these carts for sale?"

"They all are," replied the man whose broad shoulders and callused hands came from a life of hard work. "The problem is that the chain on my saw snapped and broke in three pieces a sennight ago. By hand the work takes three times longer, and I'll starve before I can get them done, but ye're welcome to wait. I willna have coin for the blacksmith to repair the chain until I sell a cart, so ye can see my problem." The man held up the thick chain that turned the saw blade when he pumped the pedal. Two links were worn through and in pieces.

Scratching his head, Hugh said, "I have no use for

a cart that willna carry me or my goods, but we might be able to strike a bargain."

"I'm listening."

"If I can get the chain on yer saw repaired, will ye finish the three carts for me in exchange? I will help ye so the work will go faster. 'Twill be an even trade, a chain and my labor for three carts."

The cartwright studied the proposition for a moment before saying, "A chain, yer labor, and two carts. I can promise ye two sturdy carts."

Hugh walked over to the wagon beside the carts in the yard. "It looks like this wagon needs a new hitch. I will make one and a tongue for three carts. The wagon will get ye more coin than the three carts together, but without a hitch and tongue, ye willna get any coin at all. So, my labor, a hitch and tongue for the wagon, and three carts in trade for a new chain."

The man studied Hugh and gave the proposition considerable thought before saying, "Ye drive a hard bargain, but 'tis the best I can do. Ye have my word, and I have yers. A hitch and tongue and a chain for three carts, and ye do the work." The men shook hands. Hugh picked up the broken chain and left to find a blacksmith.

As he headed back to the wagon, he saw Peter coming toward him. "Any luck?" asked Hugh.

"I found a sailmaker who broke all his stitching needles. He had only unfinished sails and no one to buy them. He needs needles, and a mule kicked his cart to pieces. Without a cart, even if he did have finished sails, he couldna haul them to the ships. I told him I'd see what I could do, but I dinna ken how that will help us." Peter shrugged, and Hugh agreed.

Once they came within sight of the broken-down croft, panic set in for both men. "Where's the wagon?" cried Peter. "I canna see it! They didna leave without us!"

Hugh started running. He dashed around the building to where they'd left the wagon and nearly tripped over a pile of green boards.

"Careful!" called out Jolene. "There are still nails in them."

"What have ye done?" demanded Hugh. "What have ye done?"

Mary ran into Hugh's arms and, after he picked her up, she kissed him on the cheek. "We took it apart," she said.

"I can see that, but why?"

"To build a new house." She pointed toward the cottage with green boards nailed together across the top, making a nearly complete roof. On two sides of the cottage additional green boards covered the worst of the gaps in the walls.

"While ye were gone," explained Damon, "we got to thinking. We need to get rid of the wagon, and if we did that, we needed a place to stay while ye, Gus, and Peter got us new carts. So we did both. Like it?"

Hugh grinned. "If I didna see it myself, I wouldna believe it. Right clever! The earl is no' looking for a green cottage."

Taking Mary from Hugh's arms, Kit said, "We kept the floor of the wagon in one piece, so if ye will help us haul it inside, we'll have a small but dry place to lay our heads tonight. By tomorrow we'll finish the job, and we'll have a right cozy home."

"We might be here for a while. Peter and I didna

have much luck with new carts," said Hugh.

Just then Gus darted around to the back of the repaired cottage. "The wagon is gone!"

"Aye!" replied everyone in unison.

Once Gus inspected the work done that day, he said, "I'm sorry, but I have naught that will help us. There is a blacksmith about three miles to the east, but his roof blew away in the storm. He canna work in the rain, it puts out the fire in his forge. I couldna help him, and he couldna help us."

Over a rich stew that Beatrice made from what they had left of the stolen castle food, Hugh said, "Surely we can make something out of this. We have a wagonmaker with carts but no chain. We have a sailmaker with no needles and no cart, and we have a blacksmith with no roof. There must be a way to bring all of them together and get us the carts."

"This reminds me of how we moved with Mary," said Kit. "We need to organize what we have and what we want. Many things have to happen at once, and many promises have to be kept. Who do ye think might take our word for promise of delivery? Gus, do ye think the blacksmith will make the needles in exchange for a roof from the sailmaker? Needles are no' a big job, one that can be done quickly with verra little fire from the forge."

"He seemed verra eager to get his forge back in business. We joked a bit, so mayhap he might."

Jolene, catching on to the chain of events, said, "Next, we go to the sailmaker. We will provide the needles and a cart to carry a sail large enough to make the roof for the blacksmith. We give up a cart in exchange for the roof, a fair bargain, I think."

"That will leave us with two carts," said Damon. "We can make that work."

"Finally, the blacksmith repairs the chain. We take it to the cartwright, who will repair three carts, two for us and one for the sailmaker. I think it will work if everyone keeps their word."

Peter groaned. "I kenned this would be a lot of work."

"And we all kenned ye'd be so lazy," answered Gus. "Tonight, we eat well and sleep soundly, for on the morrow we have work to do."

For the next seven days, everyone worked diligently. Damon and the women finished repairing the cottage, creating a warm, dry place with enough room for everyone. Gus worked alongside the blacksmith to make a dozen large sturdy needles, which he handed to Peter, who took them to the sailmaker along with the measurements for the new roof covering. Peter helped drag the heavy tent cloth into position so the sailmaker could stitch it, all the while promising the cart would be here soon.

Hugh followed the cartwright's instructions and completed a tongue and hitch, cutting and smoothing it by hand. The cartwright, although pleased with Hugh's work, did not lift a finger to help. He sat on a stool and watched, making certain that it was done to his satisfaction. Hugh didn't complain. A bargain was a bargain, and he would keep his end of it no matter how much the man on the stool irritated him.

On the third day, the cartwright surprised Hugh by having already completed one of the carts by hand, which Hugh, Peter, and Gus pulled six miles to the sailmaker, and then, loaded with the new roof, pulled it four miles back to the blacksmith.

On the fourth day, the former Countryside Players worked from dawn until dusk setting the roof in place over the blacksmith's forge and tying it securely to the posts. The blacksmith, being well pleased, fired up his forge to repair the cartwright's chain.

The next day, Hugh carried the chain back to the cartwright, who set to work finishing up the other two carts with Hugh's help, and finally two days after that the men showed up at the green cottage with two carts.

All that remained to do now was to get two horses for Hugh and Kit. Neither of them had much in the way of possessions, so a saddle with saddlebags and two sturdy mounts would easily get them home to Makgullane.

The discussion that night about how to accomplish this part of their escape plan often got heated.

"Ye canna spend the coins. We already decided that we couldna do that until we were away from here," said Peter. "Ye put us all at terrible risk."

"He's right," said Gus. "Our luck has held so far, and we got the carts, but to spend the coins could land us all in prison or worse. 'Tis too much money for the likes of us to carry."

Jolene spoke up. "Ye're no' thinking about it right. What have we done for years to make a living?"

The others looked at her in confusion.

"Disguising ourselves and play acting, ye silly oafs. If I can be a seven-foot giant, then ye, Damon, can be a wealthy merchant with coins to trade in the marketplace in Perth. Ye exchange our large coins for lesser ones. And ye, Peter, can be a nobleman whose horse went lame, and who needs to buy a fresh one with the lesser coins ye get from Damon. Ye go to one stable, and Hugh goes to another with the same story. Bing, bang, we have ourselves two horses complete with saddles, and we've spent our coin with no one being the wiser."

"And the best part is," added Beatrice, "none of ye will look like who ye are. So, who wants a black mole on their nose? Hugh, 'twill have to be ye. We've got to hide that pretty face."

Chapter Twenty-Four

Peter paced in front of the cottage, waiting for his turn to go into the busy city of Perth. He wore a fine robe and cap that Beatrice fashioned from one of the "robes of the dead lepers." Jolene increased the size of his already large nose with makeup and gave him black chin whiskers.

"They itch!" he said.

"So now ye ken what the rest of the men go through every day," snapped Jolene. "Ye should consider yerself lucky that ye canna grow the hairy things."

"Do ye ken what to do?" asked Beatrice for the third time. "Kit and Hugh gave ye the lay of the town after they went in yesterday to look things over, didna they?"

"Aye," he said in disgust. "If I can learn lines, I can learn how a town looks. I go to the stable closest to South Street. I tell a tale of a runaway horse and how I need to get back to Stirling right away. I have business with the high court. Once I have the beast, I get back here as quick as I can."

"Gus and I will have a cart and mule packed up and ready for ye to go with Jolene and him."

Mary spoke up. "I can help!"

"Aye, ye can," said Beatrice. "Put these apples in Jolene's wagon for them to eat on the way. Damon and

252

I will leave as soon as Hugh is back with his horse."

"I see Damon!" said Mary, pointing to the lumbering merchant on the road heading toward the green house.

Beatrice gave a heavy sigh of relief at seeing her beloved man. "He will have changed the earl's coin for smaller ones that we can spend on our way. We'll save the rest of the silver ones for later when we need them."

Again, Peter grumbled. "I ken what to do." Pacing away from the women, he stomped his feet.

"Ye're nervous, Peter," said Kit. "Dinna take it out on Beatrice."

Peter's shoulders relaxed, and he hung his head. "I am sorry, Beatrice. I will miss all of ye so much, and it tears at me on the inside. I can barely think of leaving."

" 'Tis the same with us," said Kit.

Damon struggled to catch his breath after he jogged the last few yards to the house. "The town is full of soldiers," he said. "And the news is that Arran has secretly sent Queen Mary to France to marry the prince there."

Just last night Kit had explained to Mary about the true queen and Mary's role in keeping the true queen protected.

"So he doesna look for me anymore?" asked Mary, tugging on Damon's robe. "I am no' the queen, but I did a good job of helping to keep the real one safe."

"Ye are a queen to us," said Damon. Going on in a soft voice, he added, "I wish that no one still looked for ye, but the soldiers are searching harder than ever. I am sorry, wee one, but if the King of France isna absolutely sure that the wee lass sent to him is the true queen…" Taking her into his arms, he said, "We will keep ye safe. Ye dinna have to be afeared. We love ye."

"I ken," she said with assurance. "I am no' afeared."

"Time for ye to go, Peter," said Kit. "Bring me back a strong animal."

"Aye, mistress!" Peter took off running toward the busy town of Perth along the Tay River.

****

Hugh strutted in front of the Players for their approval before leaving to cross the Perth Bridge into town dressed as a merchant from Spain. Would he pass as a Spaniard? His colorful snug-fitting doublet tucked into a skirt-like piece, and he wore tights on his legs. All were in bright blues and greens and garnished with polished stones Beatrice cut off other costumes. He brushed back the feather on his matching cap to keep it from blowing into his face, and he threatened to rub off the mole now on his nose.

"Ye look right proper for a Spaniard," Gus said. "I ne'er seen one, so ye'd fool me."

"I feel like a real coxcomb," said Hugh. "People will laugh."

"Let them," said Kit. "They'll be laughing at a Spanish nobleman, no' an escaped prisoner with a price on his head. Ye dinna have the experience at acting that these people do, but ye must play the part, and ye canna forget. Do ye have yer accent yet?"

"I am from Spain," Hugh said in what Damon had taught him was a Spanish dialect.

Hugh had also learned a few words in Spanish. "*Caballo* is horse. *Comprar* is buy, and *adios* is goodbye. *Bueno* is good. I hope that's enough, especially when I buy a horse with silver coin. Do I

254

look like a verra wealthy man from Spain?"

All the Players nodded.

Later in town, true to the way his luck had run lately, the stable Hugh picked to get his horse just happened to be the only one with a Spanish-speaking stable hand.

Hugh stumbled through, "I want to buy a horse," in a mixture of English and Spanish until the owner waved Pablo over to them.

"*¿Puedo traducir para vosotros?*"

Hugh quickly turned his confused expression into one of complete disdain. "Nay!" he said as rudely as possible, turning away from Pablo to face the owner. With his chin in the air, he repeated in broken English and Spanish, "I want to buy a horse."

Fortunately, the owner, used to dealing with the arrogance of foreign aristocracy, dismissed Pablo with a flick of his hand and let Hugh choose the horse and saddle he wanted. Hugh waited patiently with his chin still in the air as Pablo saddled his choice. Hugh handed the owner the wrong amount of coin in pounds Scots, wanting the owner to think that, as a Spaniard, Hugh didn't understand Scottish money.

"Dinna ye have that Spanish money? *Pesos*?" said the man.

Hugh quickly shook his head and mounted the horse he had just purchased. Kicking the horse in the ribs, he started out the stable door.

"Ye paid too much. Dinna ye want what I owe ye back?" called the owner after him.

"Nay!" said Hugh as he pushed the horse into a fast trot.

Chapter Twenty-Five

Saying goodbye was by far the hardest thing Kit ever had to do. She couldn't bring herself to let go of Beatrice's neck. "I canna bear to ne'er see ye again," she said as she choked out her words. For the first time in her life, she had let other people into her heart and letting them go nearly broke her.

" 'Tis no' forever," said Beatrice. " 'Tis only until we meet again. The day will come when ye will walk down my path, or I will walk down yers, and it will be as if we had ne'er left."

Releasing Kit, Beatrice tugged Mary close. "Ye, wee one, are the joy of my life, and ye always will be."

"I ken," answered Mary in her usual way, not with a rude attitude, but with complete confidence that she was loved and would be well taken care of. "When Kit teaches me to write, I'll get a messenger to take my letter to ye."

"And I promise to learn to read so I can read all yer news. Ye will listen to Kit and Hugh, will ye? I dinna want to hear that ye didna behave or that ye grew up to be a selfish lass."

"I will do the best I can."

Mary, Kit, and Jolene said their goodbyes with hugs and tears while Peter, Gus, Damon, and Hugh did it in that manly way with claps on the back and much clearing of their throats that in truth swallowed their tears.

Damon and Beatrice left first, intending to lead their mule and cart north past Perth and then east toward the sea. Jolene and Gus took their cart to the west to look for a private spot to spend their lives, and Peter traveled with them until he decided exactly what he wanted to do. He talked a lot about Ireland.

Hugh on his horse and Kit on hers with Mary sitting in front of her headed northwest toward Makgullane. Knowing it was bad luck to watch someone leave, none of them looked back as each rode out of sight. Their tears would have blurred the view anyway.

The sun had moved downward in the sky when Hugh saw a little stone building with a cross on top up ahead. Untamed grass and weeds grew up around it, giving it a forlorn look, but the chapel itself stood strong as a sign of the people it once served in faith.

Hugh reined his horse to a stop and dismounted.

"What are ye doing?" asked Kit. "There's still enough light to see by. We need to get as far away as we can."

"Come down here with me," he said, "and Mary, too."

"Why are we stopping?"

"Please, here in front of this chapel." He reached out his hand to her. With a shrug, she shifted in the saddle to lift Mary down to the ground, and then took his hand and climbed off the horse.

"Mary," said Hugh, "I have something to say to ye, but I want to talk to Kit first. Then I will talk to ye. Can ye wait quietly?"

Cocking her head to look up at him, she said, "I

can, but I need to use the privy."

"Soon."

Taking both of Kit's hands in his, he released a deep calming breath before saying, "I ne'er believed in fate or destiny. My life was my own, and every choice was mine...until ye said ye would cut off my head and send it back to England in a jar."

Mary gasped. "Kit, ye canna do that to my man! I winna let ye!" Stomping her foot, she clutched onto Hugh's leg. "I winna let ye!"

Kit squatted in front of Mary. "I winna ever do that. By promise made with all my heart."

Wiping her eyes, Mary said, "Was it an empty threat?"

Kit nodded.

Releasing Hugh's leg, she pulled herself up to her full height and said, "I ken that. Dinna worry, my man. Ye may keep yer head."

"Thank ye, my queen," he said with a deep bow.

Hugh, pulling Kit to her feet, said, "I ne'er had a purpose in my life that lasted longer than the next roll of the dice, but now I do." He inhaled deeply and slowly again. "I make ye a pledge that ye are my purpose. I vow to share our challenges, and whate'er we face, we will face it together. I swear with all that I am to be yer partner, no' to own ye, no' to be yer master, but to work beside ye and with ye for all time to come."

"Hugh..." Kit breathed.

"Eternity is beyond my understanding, but by promise made, I will love ye with all I am in this world and with all I hope for in the next. Will ye marry me? Right here, right now, for today and always? Will ye,

Katherine Payne, take me as yer husband?"

Staring into his eyes, her own sky-lit eyes brightened as her lips curled into a smile meant just for him. "I didna ken it then, but I have been yers since I first kissed ye in the forest. For all my life afore I met ye, I didna think there was anything beyond my duty, but with ye, I have found my love and my life. Aye, Hugh Cullane, I will take ye as my husband with all my wonder and joy, for now and always."

Their kiss was long and deep.

Mary rocked back and forth on her feet until she could wait no longer. "Now me!" she cried. "Now me!"

"All right," said Hugh as he reluctantly took his lips away from Kit's. Kneeling down in front of the child, he said, "I canna be with Kit without being with ye. Ye and Kit have been two for a long time, and from now on, I want ye, Kit, and me to be three. Will ye be three with me and Kit?"

"Aye! Aye! I have to use the privy!"

Laughing, both Hugh and Kit pointed to the small wooden outhouse about thirty feet away from the chapel. "Ye use the privy, and then come inside with us."

Mary darted toward the outhouse and opened the door. Holding her nose, she closed it behind her.

The heavy wooden door on the chapel creaked loudly as Hugh pushed it open and peered through the gap. "This place looks deserted." He took a step inside with Kit right behind him.

"I was hoping to find a priest to make it official," he said. "It doesna look like anyone has used this place for a long time."

"That's all right. There's an altar, and we can say

our vows to God. The nuns in the convent taught me that we say marriage vows to God. 'Tis the law that needs the rest of it, but since we are outlaws, all we need is God. Without a priest, 'tis called handfasting. 'Tis as legal as a marriage. Come on!"

Hugh laughed and followed her into the church. At one time, it must have been a simple but lovely chapel, but it had fallen into disrepair with no one to care for it.

They made their way across the broken stone floor, stepping around and over the weeds that grew in the spaces between the stones, and knelt at the rock altar.

"Dear Lord," Kit began, "Ye ken our hearts, so if our words are no' exactly right, I ken Ye will understand." She turned to face him until their knees touched. "I, Katherine Payne, invite ye, Hugh Cullane, into my life. I give ye my hand and my life, in the good times and the hard times. I pledge ye my faithfulness and my love. Now ye."

Hugh kissed her hand. "I, Hugh Cullane, give ye, Katherine Payne, my heart, my love, and my protection. I vow to walk with ye through whatever the future holds. I pledge ye my honor, my faithfulness, and my gratitude for whatever we will share. I thee wed."

"And I thee wed. Ye may kiss the bride," said Kit.

And he did. The kiss began like a gentle breeze that warms a body on a cool night, but it soon exploded into a heated gale of passion and devotion, confirming their spoken vows. For both of them, the world passed away. They only had each other, and it was all they needed.

Reluctantly, Hugh pulled his mouth from hers. "I dinna have a ring, but I do have this." He tugged his leather pouch out of his breeches, opened it, and laid his three wooden dice on the altar. All three of the cubes had thin chains drilled through the center of them.

He turned the dice so that the first die had one pip showing. "This one is mine. I was one, but no more. This one, with the two pips, is for the two of us. Now we are two, and this is for ye. I had the blacksmith put a chain through each so the right number of pips will always show. Ye wear it as a necklace. I polished it and everything. 'Tis no' fancy, but 'tis all I have."

" 'Tis lovely," said Kit, "and 'tis all I need. Truly 'tis all I want." Taking the chain, Hugh put it around her neck and, sliding the ball end into the circle on the other end, let it dangle just below her collarbone. Picking up Hugh's chain, Kit secured it around his neck.

"This one with three pips is for Mary because now we are three."

"She will love it."

"Where is Mary?" asked Hugh. "I want to say some vows for her. Mary, come in here!"

When the girl didn't answer, Kit stood up and went to the door. Looking around the corner, she saw the privy door swinging open in the wind and Mary nowhere in sight.

Chapter Twenty-Six

Mary did her business in the smelly privy as quickly as she could. Once outside in the fresh air, she took in a deep breath and looked around. Just behind a nearby tree, she spotted a patch of tall purple flowers. "Kit needs flowers to get married to Hugh. I'll pick some for her."

Mary stepped into the center of the bluebell patch and began gathering the blooms. She had four in her hand when, as she bent down to get another, a pair of muddy boots stepped in front of her. Just as she righted herself, the man in the boots dragged a heavy brown cloth sack over her head. Hoisting her up, he turned her upside down, and she fell completely into the sack. Shoving her kicking feet deep into the bag, he tied it shut, and flung it over his shoulder.

"Got her!"

With his prize in hand, he started back the way he had come.

****

Hugh and Kit circled the chapel calling Mary's name.

"Mary!"

"Mary!"

Then Hugh found the footprints left in the muddy ground.

"It looks like two men took her here," he said,

pointing to the bluebell patch. "One of them carried her away. See how the footprints are deeper from the extra weight?"

"The footprints stop at the road," said Kit. "They took our horses!" She started running with Hugh right behind her.

Two miles later, Hugh called out to her, "Wait, I have to rest." He bent over his knees and sucked in deep breaths. "How can ye keep this up for so long?"

Kit stopped running and walked back to him. "I trained with Rand so I could go long distances with Mary on my back, but we should change up our rhythm and alternate running and walking. That'll be easier on both of us and give us longer endurance until we catch up. Ready to go again?"

Hugh's heart rate hadn't gone completely back to normal, but he said, "Walk first?" She agreed but still kept up a quick pace.

The sun set behind the hills, but Hugh and Kit kept moving, thankful for a full moon so they could avoid ruts in the road while scanning the land beside it.

It had been dark for two hours when they heard the voices. Crouching down, they crawled as close as they dared to a small group of two civilian men and three soldiers in the Earl of Arran's colors sitting around a low campfire surrounded by a small cluster of trees.

"Ye have yer reward," said one of the soldiers. "Be on yer way."

"We'll sleep here," said one of the men. "There are wolves about."

"We'd expect ye to be more friendly since we brought ye the lass," said the other man. "Ye'll earn an even bigger reward when ye bring her back to the earl.

Or do ye intend to kill her first? She'd be less trouble then."

At the threat to kill Mary, Hugh had to shove Kit flat to the ground to stop her from charging into the group of men. He put his finger to his lips but said nothing. Kit slowly nodded.

"I want out!" came Mary's voice. Kit and Hugh spotted her, still in the sack, hanging from a branch on a tree. "Let me out!"

One of the soldiers sitting nearby lifted his sword, and with the flat side, swatted the sack, sending it spinning. "Ye'll be quiet, or ye'll be sorry!"

Kit and Hugh heard Mary whimper and then gag from the swinging motion. Again, Hugh pushed Kit to the ground.

Hugh tapped the side of his head as if he had an idea. He made a motion like he was grabbing his necklace and then held out his hand. She understood, took her necklace off, and handed it to him. He slid the die off the chain. Taking the other two dice, one on his chain and the other still in his pouch, he jiggled the three in his hand and stood up.

"Gentlemen," he said loudly as he walked toward the group. " 'Tis my luck to have stumbled upon ye in the dark."

All five men immediately jumped to their feet. "Who goes there?" called out the first soldier.

Hugh stepped within the light cast by the fire and replied, "A traveler with an itchy palm for a game of chance that might fill his stomach. I smelled yer fire from way back. Are ye interested in a simple wager in exchange for some of yer beans?"

"We might," said the soldier. "What do ye have to

wager?"

"I have five silver pounds Scots. I'll take ye all on, one at a time. Interested?"

" 'Tis a hefty lot of coin for a man on foot."

"I was lucky at the game, but ye canna eat coin. Will ye wager?"

Each man nodded.

He glanced back to where he had left Kit, but she was gone, and her figure moved in the shadows circling behind the men. She would be ready when he gave the signal.

He pointed to the first soldier. "With ye, I will wager a bowl of those beans. High number wins. Yer beans against my coin." Hugh and the soldier shook hands, and after they both rolled, the soldier passed over a steaming bowl of beans to Hugh, who set it aside on the ground.

Pointing to each of the civilian men, he said, "I will wager ye my coin against whatever ye have in yer pockets."

The men looked at each other. "I dinna have anything," said one of them.

"Aye, ye do," said the second. "Ye got yer reward money for the lass."

"Ye fool! He didna ken that."

"Is that yer wager?" asked Hugh, fighting to keep his face calm as if he didn't care a whit about any lass. The men nodded, and Hugh shook hands with each of them in turn. Each man rolled the dice and then reluctantly handed over one silver coin to Hugh.

"Nay," said Hugh. "I saw the poster same as ye. The reward was four pounds Scots, so I'll be taking one more from each of ye."

The men hesitated until Hugh reached for a soldier's sword left carelessly leaning against a nearby tree and aimed it at them. Reaching across the campfire, he jabbed it into the chest of the first man, knocking him over a boulder as he retreated, and then swung it in the direction of the leg of the second man who jumped aside and sat down with a thud. Within a few seconds, two more silver coins landed at Hugh's feet.

Resting the sword back against the tree, Hugh said, "Thank ye for the use of yer weapon," to the soldier who was on his feet and scowling at his own carelessness.

One of the remaining two soldiers said, "I dinna want to wager. Ye got yer beans and their coins, so be off with ye."

"But, my good man, I am raising the stakes for yer benefit. I will wager my roll of the dice against both of ye proud fighting men together. Ye will each get a roll, and I have to beat ye both with my one roll."

"And what will the stake be?" asked a squint-eyed soldier in a dirty uniform.

"Hmm," said Hugh. He looked over the campsite. "I can see ye two have naught of value so...I will take whatever is in that sack against what I have in my hand. All the wagers so far, even the beans. All of it against what is in the sack, sight unseen."

He said a silent prayer that Mary had not recognized his voice and that she would stay quiet.

"We willna give up that sack," said the first soldier, clearly the leader of the patrol. "The game is over. The sack stays here." He drew his weapon and took a fighting stance. "And so will ye, Hugh Cullane. I recognize yer face from the poster with the lass. I will claim the reward for ye. Dinna move."

But Hugh did move ever so slowly back toward the tree and the sword leaning against it. Brushing close enough to the tree, he grabbed the sword, and held it out toward the careless soldier who owned it. Moving in a wide circle toward the sack swinging from the branch, Hugh said, "What could be in there that means so much to ye? The Queen of Scotland?"

With that, he swung the blade at the soldier closest to him, slicing his jacket and wounding him deeply across the chest. The man collapsed.

At the same time, Kit raced out of the darkness, cut the rope holding the sack, and caught the bag just before it hit the ground. She slashed open the tie and lifted Mary out. Setting the frightened girl on her feet, Kit said, "Run! Run! We'll find ye! Go!" Mary obeyed and ran as fast as she could away from the fire and toward the road.

The second soldier jumped to his feet, drew his weapon, and stepped up to engage Hugh. At the same time, the two men who had stolen Mary started running in the direction of the child, but before they got more than a few steps, Kit swung a nearby fallen branch at the first one's head, leaving a bloody gash, knocking him out cold. Charging after the second man as he ran, she caught up to him, seized the edge of his jacket, and flung him to the ground. Before he could recover, she stomped on his face, and he, too, was no longer a threat.

The first soldier, the leader of the group, took off after Mary, but Mary proved to be a quick and clever runner, just as Kit had practiced with her since the time she could walk. She ducked under branches and bushes that the soldier had to run around. She never looked back, trusting completely that Kit and Hugh would find her.

Kit took off after that soldier. Her well-honed strength and quickness served her once again. Soon she drew close enough to throw her knife. Even while moving, her aim was true. The knife landed in the center of the man's back. He collapsed and didn't move. Kit headed back to the campsite to see how she could help Hugh.

Hugh's grandfather, Bretane, had taught him to wield a sword and to fight like a real warrior. The soldier, on the other hand, had grown fat and lazy, and when Kit arrived back at the fire, the soldier lay on the ground with Hugh's sword buried in his gut.

Kit and Hugh dashed into each other's arms.

"Are ye hurt?" she asked anxiously, patting him all over, looking for injuries.

"Nay, are ye?"

She shook her head. "We have to get Mary. The horses ran off in the commotion, so ye'll have to run with me."

Hugh nodded, pulled the sword from the man, and carrying it, followed her into the darkness, calling Mary's name.

After a couple of furlongs, they found one of the horses grazing quietly by the side of the road. Climbing aboard, they kept calling Mary's name.

"Mary! Mary! Where are ye?"

" 'Tis Kit and Hugh! Ye're safe! Where are ye?"

A few minutes later, if Hugh hadn't tugged up on the reins when he did, the horse would have trampled over the little girl when she stepped out of the brush.

"Here I am," she said.

Kit jumped down and hugged her charge, kissing her head, and saying her name over and over. "Are ye all right? Did they hurt ye?"

"I'm hungry. 'Twas dark in the sack, and I...needed the privy again." Hanging her head, she said sadly, "I went inside the sack. I'm sorry."

"It doesna matter. Ye are the bravest lass I ken. We have to go now. Ye can sit on the horse in front of me."

The three of them moved cautiously along the road away from the campsite in the direction of Perth. The horse seemed to know the way and didn't balk at the extra weight on his back or the uneven road.

After a time, Hugh broke the silence. "We canna keep her with us. We left a bloody mess of bodies back there, and the guard recognized me. We are a threat to our Mary's safety and will be until Arran is dead or safely in power in France."

Kit sucked in a sob. " 'Twas my prayer that the three of us would be safe at yer Makgullane, but getting there is more dangerous than I thought. I ken ye're right, but what can we do?"

Mary took her fingers out of her mouth. "I can live with Beatrice and Damon. No one kens them. When the mean man forgets what ye look like, I will come back to ye and Hugh."

Kit hugged her close, and Hugh reached around to stroke Mary's arm. "Ye are a verra smart lass," he said.

"I ken," answered Mary, putting her fingers back in her mouth and leaning her head onto Kit.

It took another full day for Hugh and Kit to catch up with Beatrice and Damon as they headed east for the coast.

"I have this for ye," said Hugh as he held Mary for

the last time. "The dice has three pips on it because ye, me, and Kit are three. I have one pip, and Kit has two, and ye are three. No matter where we are, the three of us are family. I love ye."

Mary tugged on the necklace around her neck and pointed to each of them in turn. "One, two, three, ye and me."

Knowing it was bad luck to watch someone leave, Beatrice, Damon, and Mary moved toward the coast while Hugh and Kit again turned northwest to the southern Highlands. Neither family looked back.

Kit held in her grief until she and Hugh were out of sight.

"We did what was best for her," she sobbed, "but I ne'er felt such terrible pain." Tears racked her. "I ken that Beatrice and Damon will take good care of her and raise her to be a fine woman. I only wish it could be me and ye." She broke down in his arms and cried her heart out.

Hugh could only hold her against his chest. He had no words to comfort her as his own grief at leaving Mary was as strong as hers.

Chapter Twenty-Seven

Six days later, Hugh and Kit spent their last night on the road at an inn in Kirkcaldy, only a few hours' ride from Makgullane. Both were exhausted from their days on the road and from their grief at knowing that even though it was for the best, they would never again see the wee lass or the friends they loved. They ate the meal the innkeeper's wife set before them, but they hardly tasted it.

On the stairs leading up to their room, Hugh said, "We're almost home, and I ordered a special surprise for ye." At their door, he said, "Now close yer eyes."

Picking her up, he carried her across the room and over to a large copper tub filled with water beside the hearth, dropping her in, clothes and all. "Neither of us have had a bath in a verra long time."

She sputtered when her head dipped beneath the surface, but she found the water wonderfully warm. Standing up, she quickly stripped off the filthy, torn overdress and kirtle and tossed them on the floor.

"Ye're so lovely," he said, staring at her naked body. Putting his hands around her waist, he gently massaged her stomach with his thumbs. "The tub is only big enough for one, so may I wash ye first? Then ye wash me."

Although they had made love along the way, the hard ground had been uncomfortable and they couldn't linger in each other's arms, but this time they would, and enjoy every touch, every kiss, every pleasure.

"Please, wash me and hurry."

A burning log popped, sending a spray of sparks up the chimney, and Kit felt a similar rush of passion spark through her. She didn't know if she could wait to be washed, but she found he had no intention of making her wait.

Sitting back down in the tub, she let his hands wander over her. His long fingers and wide palms began soaping and then rinsing her hair. Starting at her face, he treated her body to the same glorious massage, first rubbing her temples, moving to her cheeks, and finally to her lips. His hands and fingers drifted down her neck to her breasts with the easy, flowing movements she'd grown to adore. She squealed with delight as he finished his sensual journey under the water. Moaning with ecstasy, she climaxed at his touch.

When none of the dirt remained on her creamy white skin, he put his hands on either side of her head and kissed her lips again and again.

"I'm no' perfect, and ye may find that out soon enough, but ye'll ne'er find anyone who loves ye more. May I dry ye off?"

She could only nod, forgetting how to speak as the tingling through her legs and hips remained so powerful it dulled her other senses. He had become part of her like the air she couldn't live without.

After lifting her out of the tub, he pressed a rough towel over her damp skin. Using the thick warm cloth, he absorbed the moisture from under her breasts, from her bottom, and between her legs. His hands glided over her, rubbing and massaging, and she sighed. When his hand slipped under and the towel fell away, his fingers tickled and stroked her flesh until her desire rose to a frenzied peak again.

She wove her fingers into his hair with the auburn tinges, crying, "Hugh, I canna wait. I want ye now."

His fingers slid inside her and eased her suffering in another thrilling climax.

Stripping off his own dirty clothes, he fell into the tub with a mighty splash. The water barely covered him as most of it overflowed and soaked the wooden floor. Kit laughed and, cupping her hands, threw some of the fallen water up over him, letting it flow down his chest and back in rippling streams.

Dipping a washcloth that hung over the edge of the tub into the water, she washed him from head to foot.

"Tomorrow I'll trim yer beard, but dinna shave it off. My husband should wear a beard, especially a beautiful auburn one like this one."

He'd always been clean-shaven until he became Brother Hubert, but now it would please him to keep the beard that pleased her. "All right, I'll keep it for ye."

When she finished washing him, she asked, "Are all men as beautiful as ye?"

"Nary a one," said Hugh, "so there is no need for ye to look at any of them."

"I only have eyes for ye. How does it feel if I touch ye here?" She palpated her fingers over his nipple. "Or here?" She moved to the other nipple, giving it the same erotic treatment.

He groaned softly.

"Or how about here?" Her hand and the cloth slid down his chest and stomach to what made him a man.

Grasping it firmly, she massaged and moved the cloth over and around it.

"Oh!" he exclaimed.

"I have a few more questions," she said, laying the washcloth over his face, completely covering it. "Do ye like this?" Her fingers danced along his inner thighs, fluttering close to his stiff manhood and then bolting away. Finally, she stroked him slowly from the tip to the base and back again.

A muffled voice came from under the cloth. "Kit!"

"Or do ye prefer this?" She stepped over the edge of the tub into the water, placing a foot on either side of his hips and lowered herself over him, sheathing him. His hand went up to snatch away the cloth, but she stopped him, pressing his hands back behind his head.

"Nay, ye canna watch. This time ye can only feel my loving."

Up and down she moved over him. Leaning closer, she nipped and kissed his chest, but still moving her hips in a luxurious rhythm.

"Ye are mine, completely," she murmured.

"Kit!" he cried as he surrendered his passion to her in a turbulent burst of energy and longing.

Several minutes later, he sat up, and the washcloth fell into the water, his sorrel eyes flickering like fire. "Katherine, I'll never have enough of ye. I ken yer heart."

"Ye do?" she asked, arching her eyebrows.

"Aye, I'll prove it. If I canna guess what ye're thinking, I'll leave this tub and ne'er return."

The corners of her mouth turned up. "I'll take that wager. What am I thinking?"

Hugh put his finger to his forehead and scratched.

"I believe ye're wondering when I'm going to make love to ye again."

Pushing him back against the side of the tub, she said, "Ye're wrong. I was thinking that this bath has made me verra hungry."

"Then I was right," said Hugh, pulling her head to his and kissing her. "I win." His hand reached for her breast.

"Aye, ye win!"

Chapter Twenty-Eight

The next day Hugh and Kit stood on the rise at the end of the road leading into the main yard of the Makgullane estate. He tugged her close.

"This is the best place I've ever known," he said. He slowly added, "The hardest part of coming home will be having to tell Robin what happened to my dagger."

"That can wait," she said. "Ye being home is what will matter the most. This is a beautiful place."

The yard in front of the manor house bustled with activity as it did every day. Hugh's grandfather, Bretane, hoed the flower bed under one of the front windows. All the blooms had gone dormant in anticipation of the coming colder weather, but Bretane always made certain the bed was free of weeds and primed for when spring came again.

Two of the house maids hung damp clothing on a rope strung between the house and a nearby tree while Clive, the longtime cook's assistant, dropped his fishing line into the pond in search of perch for today's midday meal.

Hugh's father, Robin, his black hair now sprinkled with white, stood just outside the stable talking to three other men. Hugh recognized Darby, the assistant reeve, but the two others had to be new to Makgullane. He wondered what else had changed in the five years he had been gone. He was a different man, but he hoped his home hadn't changed so much.

"Over there is room for a house just for us." He pointed to a cleared space on the west side of the manor house.

"For us?"

"I am the oldest son," he said. "Robin told me since I was a lad that I would have that plot of land for a house all my own. He even showed me the plans he drew. Wait until ye see."

Kit stretched her head up to kiss him. "Let's wait until I learn everyone's name before we start building a house."

"He always said that I was theirs first and I'd be theirs forever." He paused. "I think I want that on my tombstone."

"Yer tombstone!"

"Aye, we're going to be here for the rest of our lives. 'Tis ne'er too soon to start planning ahead."

He pointed to the woman and two girls standing in the doorway of the main house. " 'Tis my mum, Suannoch, and my little sisters, Kathleen and Meara. They were just babes when I left. Kathleen had only started to walk, and Meara was still in nappies."

"Yer mum looks like she is about to have another bairn. Ye came home just in time to meet him or her," said Kit with a wink.

"I dinna see the twins, Taran and Dillon, or the older one, Bran. Mayhap they're out in the fields."

"What about Fergus, yer first friend at Makgullane?"

"If he is no' at university by now, he is in the library getting another book to read while he works.

277

Once Mum taught him to read, I ne'er saw him without a book."

A lanky young man with ginger hair came out of the house to stand by Suannoch and the girls. All at once, he pointed across the yard to Hugh and Kit, calling out, "Look, Da!"

" 'Tis Fergus," said Hugh.

A cacophony of voices filled the air. "Hugh! Hugh!"

Robin and Fergus came running across the yard toward them with the lasses right behind. Suannoch, heavy with child, walked much slower up the slope to the road, but the grin on her face was as broad as everyone else's.

"Ye're home!" shouted Robin as he raced into Hugh's arms, nearly knocking him over.

"Ye're home!" cried Fergus, taking Hugh's hand and tugging him out of Robin's arms and into his own. "I almost dinna recognize ye with yer beard!"

Suannoch patted Hugh's arm before stepping around her men to greet Kit. "Welcome to Makgullane, lovely lady."

"I'm home," said Hugh, still in his father's and his brother's grasp. "And this is Kit."

Chapter Twenty-Nine

Twenty years later, Makgullane in the southern Scottish Highlands, July 1567

Hugh pulled closed the heavy barn door on his way to wash up for the evening meal. At the edge of the Makgullane yard stood five people. He didn't recognize them, and neither did they call out to introduce themselves as was the custom when strangers arrived anywhere in this part of the Highlands.

Hugh started in their direction, calling to the visitors, "Are ye lost? Do ye need shelter for the night?" as was also the custom in the Highlands.

A young woman took a step out of the group. "My man, dinna ye ken me?" She hooked her finger under a thin chain around her neck and held it up.

Hugh cocked his head and brushed his gray-streaked hair off his forehead. She had a vaguely familiar look about her, but ginger hair and blue eyes were common throughout Scotland. Then she smiled, and he knew at once who she was.

"Mary! Our Mary!" he shouted as he rushed toward her. Grabbing her up in his arms, he swung her around. "Mary!" Putting her down on her feet, he held her out to get a good look at her, saying, "Ye've grown!"

"Aye, my man, 'tis what sometimes happens in

twenty years. Where is Kit?"

"She's inside the house. She'll be so excited to see ye." He reached for her chain, laying the die hanging off it across his palm. "Ye still have yer necklace with three pips on the die. Kit and I have ours as well." He opened his shirt to show her that he still carried his own die around his neck, the one turned to show only one pip.

With his arm still around her waist, he started leading her toward the manor house across the yard. "Tell me what ye've been doing, where ye've been. I want to hear all about it."

She frowned. "Dinna ye want to meet my family first? They're standing right back there."

Hugh turned abruptly, swinging Mary nearly off her feet again. "Of course! Of course! I am so happy to see ye I forgot my manners." He reached out his hand in greeting to the man.

"This is my husband, Tavish," she said, pointing to a tall, slender man, most likely in his late twenties, with blond hair tied in a queue down his back. He had one blue eye and one green eye, giving an almost cherubic look about him.

Tavish grinned broadly. "Glad to meet ye, sir. Mary speaks of ye often."

"These are my children, my son, Duncan, and my daughter, Lauri," Mary continued.

The girl, in a carrying sack on her father's back, squirmed, and her father leaned over to let her down, helping her to climb out of the sack and to stand on her own. The boy bowed and the girl curtsied.

"We are glad to meet the man who saved our mother," said Duncan, a lad about five years old with the same ginger hair as his mother. The girl, Lauri, younger still, was blond and favored her father.

"I couldna be more pleased to meet ye," said Hugh with a grin so broad his cheeks hurt. "I dinna think I would ever see yer mother again, but God has shone on me today. Ye're beautiful bairns."

The small girl took a cautious step toward Hugh, curtseying again. "I am happy to meet my grandfather. I thought I ne'er would."

An overwhelming feeling of joy blazed through Hugh. "Grandfather?"

Mary nodded. "No other name suits ye."

"I am honored."

Mary tugged on the arm of a young woman with bright cinnamon-colored hair and green eyes, pulling her forward. "Lastly, I want ye to meet Sheena," she said. "She is Jolene and Gus's daughter." The girl, nearly as tall as Mary, smiled and curtsied.

"Jolene and Gus came to the coast to be near Beatrice and Damon when it was Jolene's time to deliver the babe," said Mary.

"I, too, am pleased to finally meet ye," said Sheena. She had a high-pitched voice just like her mother. "Mary took me as her own when my mother died on the day I was born. Mary was only nine years old at the time, but a better mother I couldna have." Wrapping her arms around Mary from the side, Sheena hugged her.

"I am sorry to hear that Jolene is gone, but, Sheena, ye are as beautiful as she ever was," said Hugh. "What about Gus?"

"He went to join Jolene in Heaven last month. His dying wish was for us to find ye at Makgullane, and so we have come."

"It grieves me to hear about the loss of such great friends. What of Beatrice and Damon?" asked Hugh.

"They are still on the coast near Aberdeen, where Damon makes and sells fishing nets, and Beatrice rocks in her chair when she isna cooking fine meals for all their friends. Before ye ask, we havena seen Peter in many years. He couldna abide staying in one place."

"We have so much to talk about," said Hugh. "Please, everyone come into the house for something to eat, and ye can tell me about the last twenty years. I canna believe twenty years have gone by."

Mary put her hand on Hugh's arm. "Before ye take us into yer home, ye should ken that we have nowhere else to go."

"Then this will be yer home."

"There is more ye should ken. Have ye heard that Lord Darnley, husband of our Queen Mary, was murdered, strangled to death?"

Hugh shook his head. "News travels slowly here."

"Tavish is a goldsmith who often did work for Darnley, who spent too much of the queen's money too fast, and anyone with any connection to Darnley, especially if money was exchanged, is being arrested and imprisoned. Even the queen herself is a suspect. Tavish is completely innocent, but we couldna take the chance, so we fled. Unless the true killer is found, ye may be hiding fugitives. 'Tis a risk."

"Makgullane will keep ye safe, just as it has kept me and Kit safe all these years. Come and meet my family."

Inside the kitchen of the manor house, Kit nearly collapsed when she recognized Mary standing in the doorway. She had to grab a chair to steady herself.

"Mary, I think my heart will stop," she said, once she was able to stand upright and throw her arms around her beloved former charge. "Peter, Gus," she said to two teenage boys sitting at the table, "get up and give yer seats to our guests. These are our sons, and we have taught them better manners."

The lads jumped up and pulled out their chairs, indicating to Mary and Tavish to sit in their places.

"I'll get clean dishes," said Peter, the younger, auburn-haired one.

Gus, the older son who like his mother had thick chestnut hair and blue eyes, brought three additional chairs to the table for the children and Sheena. With a flourish and a broad grin, Gus assisted Sheena into her seat.

Hugh walked to the head of the table to stand behind an older man with bright white hair and bright blue eyes. "This is my da. This is Robin," said Hugh, and then, pointing to a small woman sitting next to him whose green eyes flashed despite her years, said, "This is my mum, Suannoch."

Mary gave each of them a hug. "My man talked about ye all the time, but I was so wee, I dinna remember much." Taking Peter's seat, she added, "If we may stay for a few days, I will so enjoy hearing all about ye."

Robin said, "Hugh and Kit nearly talked our ears off about ye, and I feel I already ken ye. Ye will stay a lot longer than a few days. Ye can stay as long as ye want."

Seeing the hesitation on Mary's face, he added, "Makgullane welcomes ye, no matter what reason ye are here. Suann, do ye think we could enlarge yer mother's cottage for this family? 'Tis only about a mile down the path, and Thalassa has been gone six years now."

"I think that would be a wonderful idea," said Suann. "That cottage needs life and laughter in it again. Sit down, please. Tonight, we feast. Tomorrow we will make plans for this new chapter of our family."

The chatter continued around the table long into the night.

Scottish/Gaelic Translations

amadan—a fool
athair/da—father
bairn—child
couldna—couldn't
coxcomb—fancy dandy
didna—did not
dinna—do not
ell—a measurement of cloth
fashious—troublesome, bothersome, annoying
ken—to know
kenned—knew
loony doo—loony bird
màthair/mum—mother
nappies—diapers
naught—nothing
ne'er—never
no'—not
Sassenach—a slur for an Englishman
shandy berk—foolish, a fool
shouldna—shouldn't
skamelar—a parasite
verra—very
werena—weren't
ye—you
yer—your

Historical Information

Mary Stuart, known as Mary, Queen of Scots, was crowned queen in December of 1542 when she was just six days old, after her father, James V, died at age thirty of unknown causes. He left behind at least nine illegitimate children, but only one rightful heir to the throne, Mary.

The original spelling of the royal family's name is "Stewart," but Mary, after spending most of her childhood in France, changed the spelling to "Stuart" because there is no "w" in the French language.

The order of succession to the Scottish throne was complicated, not least because so many people shared the same name.

James II became king at age seven in 1437. His children included a son, James, and a daughter, Mary.

James III became king at age eight until he died in 1488. He had four children, including James who became James IV.

James IV, crowned at age fifteen, died in 1513 fighting at the battle of Flodden. He had a son, James, and five illegitimate children.

James V became king at seventeen months old and lived as a prisoner of his stepfather until he escaped and regained the throne at age sixteen.

The 1st Earl of Arran, James Hamilton, was the son of James II's oldest daughter, Mary Stewart. His son,

James Hamilton, became the 2nd Earl of Arran, and was the great-grandson of James II. Through the lines of royal births and deaths, the 2nd Earl of Arran was considered the future heir to the throne until Mary's birth. Instead he was appointed Mary's regent until 1556, making him a "not-quite-king," something that must have influenced many of his decisions.

He wanted Mary to marry his son, James Hamilton, the 3rd Earl of Arran, but Mary's mother, Mary of Guise, was opposed. When Queen Mary was four years old in 1547, she traveled to France with the sixteen-year-old 3rd Earl of Arran, and, again, his marriage to her was proffered, but they did not wed.

While the 2nd Earl of Arran was Mary's regent, she was betrothed as an infant to English King Henry VIII's son, Edward, as part of Henry's plan to unite the two countries, but the Scottish government refused to ratify the treaty endorsing the marriage. In retaliation, King Henry waged war on Scotland in what became known years later as "rough wooing." The so-called "wooing" ended after the disastrous defeat of the Scots at the Battle of Pinkie Cleugh, and soon after, four-year-old Mary was betrothed to the Dauphin, France's five-year-old prince. It was said that Mary's marriage to the Dauphin was a happy one, more like playmates than husband and wife, but he died of an ear infection while still in his teens, and Mary was sent home in 1561.

Scotland's treaty with France for her betrothal not only prevented her marriage to the English king, but also stopped England from imposing its Protestant religion on Scotland to replace the country's prevailing Catholic beliefs at the time. The Protestant Reformation, however, continued to be a source of contention within Scotland, and for Mary, for many years.

Mary remained a staunch Catholic all her life, but her official policy was one of non-discrimination based on religion. Still, her nobles opposed her all during her reign, often using her Catholic faith against her, and she was forced to concede much of her power to her enemies. Her cousin, Mary I of England, however, whose reign overlapped Mary of Scotland's, became known as "Bloody Mary" for her persecution of Protestants.

Mary of Scotland married Henry, Lord Darnley, in 1565, and while it was said that she was very much in love with him, the marriage became a disaster. Henry was weak and jealous and ended up murdering Mary's secretary and close friend, David Riccio, in front of Mary when she was six months pregnant. Two years later, Lord Darnley's house was mysteriously blown up and burned, but when he was found dead in the garden, he had been strangled.

Because of her affair with James Hepburn, Earl of Bothwell, the man charged with killing Lord Darnley, Mary was accused of being complicit in the murder. After Bothwell was acquitted, the nobles demanded that she marry him to stabilize the country. Although he and Mary did marry, he deserted her after Protestant leaders imprisoned her in Leven Castle to once again protest her Catholic leanings. She gave birth to still-born twins there. Later, she escaped, but she soon fell into the hands of English Queen Elizabeth I, her cousin, who imprisoned her in England for nineteen years.

Mary, still hoping to regain her throne, wrote a series of letters that appeared to plot Elizabeth's assassination, which later became known as the Casket Letters. In 1587, Elizabeth had Mary beheaded. It is said that when the executioner held up Mary's head for everyone to see, her head fell, leaving him holding only her wig. This was yet another humiliation for a woman who, through no fault of her own, had been forced to be queen.

Mary lived for a time at Fawside Castle as an adult, but as a child before the treaty between Scotland and France could be finalized, she spent time at Inchmahome Priory on an island in the middle of the Lake of Menteith, northwest of Stirling, and later at Dumbarton Castle, west of Edinburgh.

The Battle of Pinkie Cleugh is considered the first modern battle fought on British soil because of the English use of artillery over the hand-to-hand combat of the Scots. It proved to be a ruinous defeat for Scotland known as Black Saturday. When it became clear that the battle would be lost, Arran of Scotland offered the English Duke of Somerset two options to settle the dispute. One was for twenty men to battle it out, and the second was for Arran and Somerset to duel. Somerset resoundingly rejected both scenarios.

After the crowning of Mary's son, James I, as monarch for both England and Scotland in 1603, the Battle of Pinkie Cleugh became the last major battle fought between the two countries until the first Jacobite uprising of 1715.

****

Perpetual motion machines such as Gus's have been created over the centuries, but since their continuous operation defies the laws of physics, none have been successful.

****

The Findern Manuscript is a collection of stories and poems written for the gentry living around Derbyshire in the fifteenth century. They were first transcribed as separate booklets and later bound into a single manuscript, in what is thought to be an attempt to express and improve the quality of the literature in the area. Several of the poems are thought to be written by women because the names of five women are included in the manuscript, along with the names of several courtly royal poets of the time, such as Geoffrey Chaucer, John Gower, Thomas Hoccleve, and John Lydgate.

The poem which inspired the titles of my first two books is translated from Middle English into modern vernacular and printed below.

> Where I have chosen, steadfast will I be,
> Ne'er to repent in will, thought nor deed,
> You to serve, whatever ye command me,
> Ne'er to withdraw for any manner of dread.
> Thus am I bound by your godlyhead,
> Which hath me caused, and that in every wise
> While I in life endure, to do you my service.
> Your desert can none other deserve,
> Which is in my remembrance both day and night.
> Before all creatures I you love and serve
> While in this world I have strength and might,
> Which is in duty, of very due right,
> By promise made with faithful assurance,
> Ever you to serve without variance.

A word about the author...

Susan Leigh Furlong has always been a storyteller, but writing took a back seat to being a wife, mother, teacher, writing coach, director of a music and drama ministry, and generally living a busy life. Now retired from all the above, she writes full-time. She loves to drop her hero and heroine into a true historical event and force them, and their love, to survive.

Steadfast Will I Be was her first historical romance novel, and her second book, *By Promise Made*, again focuses on the history and adventure found in her Scottish ancestry. She also authored two nonfiction books about her hometown.

She thanks her cat, Hobbes, for demanding to sit on her lap and help her write—fur-covered keyboard aside.

Enjoy her books, sold on Amazon.com and other online sellers in ebook format or paperback.

Find her website at:

www.SusanLFurlong.com

and her Facebook page at:

SusanLeighFurlong

Lightning Source UK Ltd.
Milton Keynes UK
UKHW020632250920
370514UK00014B/1558

9 781509 232284